O TONGUE, GIVE SOUND TO JOY AND SING OF HOPE AND PROMISE ON DRAGONWING!

My nightly craft is winged in white;
A dragon of night-dark sea.
Swiftborn, dreambound and rudderless;
Her captain and crew are me.
I sail a hundred sleeping tides
Where no seaman's ever been
And only my white-winged craft and I
Know the marvels we have seen.

Bantam Books by Anne McCaffrey

DRAGONSONG
DRAGONSINGER

DRAGONSINGER

ANNE McCAFFREY

*This low-priced Bantam Book
has been completely reset in a type face
designed for easy reading, and was printed
from new plates. It contains the complete
text of the original hard-cover edition.*
NOT ONE WORD HAS BEEN OMITTED.

RL 7, IL 8-up

DRAGONSINGER

*A Bantam Book / published by arrangement with
Atheneum Publishers*

PRINTING HISTORY

*Atheneum edition published February 1977
2nd printing ———October 1977
3rd printing ————May 1978
A selection of the Junior Literary Guild September 1977
Bantam edition / October 1978*

ISBN 0-553-11835-8

Published simultaneously in the United States and Canada

*Bantam Books are published by Bantam Books, Inc. Its trade-
mark, consisting of the words "Bantam Books" and the por-
trayal of a bantam, is registered in the United States Patent
Office and in other countries. Marca Registrada. Bantam
Books, Inc., 666 Fifth Avenue, New York, New York 10019.*

PRINTED IN THE UNITED STATES OF AMERICA

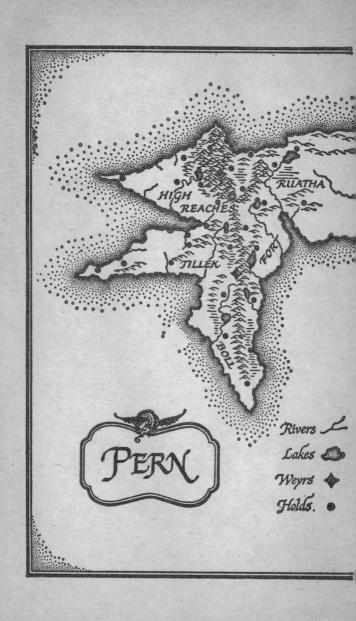

RUATHA

HIGH
REACHES

TILLEK

FORT

BOLL

PERN

Rivers
Lakes
Weyrs
Holds

BITRA

LEMOS

TELGAR

BENDEN

IGEN

KEROON

Half-
Circle
Sea Hold

NERAT

N.

≋ Hill Lands
≋ Mountains
▦ Plateau and Tablelands
▢ Plains

At the Harper Craft Hall

Robinton—Masterharper; bronze fire lizard, Zair

Masters Jerint—Instrument maker
         Domick—Composition
         Morshal—Musical Theory
         Shonagar—Voice
         Arnor—Archivist
         Oldive—Healer

Journeymen Sebell; gold fire lizard, Kimi
         Brudegan
         Talmor
         Dermently

Apprentices Piemur
         Ranly
         Timiny
         Brolly
         Bonz

Menolly; 9 fire lizards
         gold,   Beauty
         bronze, Rocky
                  Diver
         brown, Lazybones
                  Mimic
                  Brownie
         blue,   Uncle
         green, Auntie One
                  Auntie Two

Students Amania
          Audiva
          Pona
          Briala

Silvina—headwoman
Abuna—kitchen worker
Camo—half-witted kitchen drudge
Dunca—cotholder of girl's cottage

At Fort Hold

Lord Holder Groghe; gold fire lizard, Merga
Benis—son of Groghe
Viderian—fosterling
Ligand—journeyman tanner
Palim—baker
T'ledon—dragonrider

At Half-Circle Sea Hold

Yanus—Sea Holder
Mavi—Sea Holder's Lady
Alemi—son of Yanus
Petiron—old Harper
Elgion—new Harper

At Benden Weyr

F'lar—Weyrleader
Lessa—Weyrwoman
T'gellen—bronze dragonrider
F'nor—brown dragonrider; gold fire lizard Grall
Brekke—queenrider; bronze fire lizard Berd
Manora—Headwoman
Felena—second in charge
Merrim—fosterling of Brekke; 3 fire lizards

Dragonsinger

Chapter 1

The little queen all golden
Flew hissing at the sea.
To stop each wave
Her clutch to save
She ventured bravely.

As she attacked the sea in rage
A holderman came nigh
Along the sand
Fishnet in hand
And saw the queen midsky.

He stared at her in wonder
For often he'd been told
That such as she
Could never be
Who hovered there, bright gold.

He saw her plight and quickly
He looked up the cliff he faced
And saw a cave
Above the wave
In which her eggs he placed.

The little queen all golden
Upon his shoulder stood
Her eyes all blue
Glowed of her true
Undying gratitude.

When Menolly, daughter of Yanus Sea Holder, arrived at the Harper Craft Hall, she came in style, aboard a bronze dragon. She was seated on Monarth's neck between his rider, T'gellan, and the Masterharper of Pern, Robinton. For one who had been told that girls could not become harpers, who had run away and actually lived holdless because she could not continue life without music, this was something of a triumphal success.

Yet it was also frightening. To be sure, music would not be denied her at the Harper Hall. True, she had written some songs that the Masterharper had heard and liked. But they were just tunings, not anything important. And what could a girl, even one who had taught her Hold's youngsters their Teaching Songs and Ballads, do at a Harper Hall from which all teaching songs originated? Especially a girl who had inadvertently Impressed nine fire lizards when everyone else on Pern would give a left arm to own just one? What *had* Master Robinton in mind for her to do here in the Harper Hall?

She couldn't think, she was so tired. She'd had a busy, exciting day at Benden Weyr on the opposite side of the continent where night now was well advanced. Here in Fort Hold, the sky was just darkening.

"Just a few minutes more," said Robinton in her ear. She heard him laugh because just then bronze Monarth trumpeted a greeting to the Fort Hold watch dragon. "Hang on, Menolly. I know you must be exhausted. I'll put you in Silvina's care the moment we land. See, there," and she followed the line of his pointing finger and saw the lighted quadrangle of buildings at the foot of the Fort Hold cliff. "That's the Harper Hall."

She shivered then, with fatigue, the cold of their passage *between* and apprehension. Monarth was circling now, and figures were pouring out of the Harper Hall into the courtyard, waving wildly to cheer the Masterharper's return. Somehow, Menolly hadn't expected that there'd be so many people in the Harper Craft Hall.

They kept well back, though their shouts of welcome didn't abate, while the big bronze dragon settled in the courtyard, giving him plenty of wingroom.

"I've got two fire lizard eggs!" shouted Master Robinton. Hugging the earthen pots tightly against his body, he slid from bronze Monarth's shoulder with the ease of considerable practice in dismounting dragons. "Two fire lizard eggs!" he repeated joyfully, holding the precious egg pots above his head and striding quickly to show off his prizes.

"My fire lizards!" Anxiously Menolly glanced up and about her. "Did they follow us, T'gellan? They're not lost *between*."

"No chance of that, Menolly," T'gellan replied, pointing to the slated roof behind them. "I asked Monarth to tell them to perch there for the time being."

With infinite relief, Menolly saw the unmistakable outlines of her fire lizards on the rooftop against the darkening sky.

"If only they don't misbehave as they did at Benden . . ."

"They won't," T'gellan assured her easily. "You'll see to that. You've done more with your fair of fire lizards than F'nor has with his one little queen. And F'nor's a trained dragonrider." He swung his right leg over Monarth's neckridge and dropped to the ground raising his arms to her. "Bring your leg over. I'll steady you so you won't jar those sore feet of yours," and his hands braced her as she slid down Monarth's shoulder. "That's the girl, and here you are, safe and sound in the Harper Hall." He gestured broadly as if only he could have accomplished this mission.

Menolly looked across the courtyard, where the Masterharper's tall figure and presence dominated those surrounding him. Was Silvina one of them? Wearily Menolly hoped that the Harper would find her quickly. The girl could put no reliance on T'gellan's glib assumption that her fire lizards would behave. They'd only just got used to being at Benden Weyr, among people who had some experience with winged antics.

"Don't worry so, Menolly. Just remember," said T'gellan, gripping her shoulder in awkward reassurance, "every harper on Pern has been trying to find Petiron's lost apprentice . . ."

"Because they thought that apprentice was a boy . . ."

"That made no difference to Master Robinton when he asked you to come here. Times are changing, Menolly, and it'll make no difference to the others. You'll see. In a sevenday you'll have forgotten you've ever lived anywhere else." The bronze dragonrider chuckled. "Great shells, girl, you've lived holdless, outrun Thread, and Impressed nine fire lizards. What's to fear from harpers?"

"Where *is* Silvina?" The Masterharper's voice rose above the others. There was a momentary lull and someone was sent to the Hall to find the woman. "And no more answers now. You've the bones of the news, I'll flesh it out for you later. Now, don't drop these egg pots, Sebell. Right now, I've more good news! I've found Petiron's lost apprentice!"

Amid exclamations of surprise, Robinton broke free of the crowd and beckoned T'gellan to bring Menolly forward. For a brief second, Menolly fought the urge to turn and run, impossible as it was with her feet barely healed from trying to outrun Thread and with T'gellan's arm about her. His fingers squeezed on her shoulder as if he sensed her nervousness.

"There's nothing for you to fear from harpers," he repeated in her ear as he escorted her across the court.

Robinton met them halfway, beaming with pleasure as he took her right hand. He flung up his other arm to command silence.

"This is Menolly, daughter of Yanus Sea Holder, late of Half-Circle Sea Hold, and Petiron's lost apprentice!"

Whatever response the harpers made was covered by an explosion of fire lizard cries from the rooftop. Fearful that the fair might wing down on the harpers, Menolly turned, saw that their wings were indeed spread and sternly commanded them to stay where they were. Then she had no excuse for not confronting the sea of faces: some smiling, some with mouths ajar in surprise at her fire lizards, but too many, many people.

"Yes, and those fire lizards are Menolly's," Robinton went on, his voice easily projecting above the murmurs. "Just as that lovely song about the fire lizard queen is

Menolly's. Only it wasn't a *man* who saved the clutch from the sea, it was Menolly. And when no one would let her play or sing in Half-Circle Sea Hold after Petiron died, she ran away to the fire lizard queen's cave and Impressed nine of the eggs before she realized what she was doing. Furthermore," and he raised his volume above the ragged cheers of approval, "furthermore, she found another clutch, which provided *me* with two eggs!"

The second cheer was more wholehearted, reverberating in the courtyard and answered by shrill whistles from the fire lizards. Under cover of good-natured laughter at that response, T'gellan muttered, "I told you so" in her ear.

"And where is Silvina?" asked the Harper again, a note of impatience audible.

"Here I am and you ought to be ashamed of yourself, Robinton," said a woman, pushing through the ring of harpers. Menolly had an impression of very white skin and large expressive eyes set in a broad-cheeked face framed by dark hair. Then strong but gentle hands took her from Robinton's grasp. "Subjecting the child to such an ordeal. No, no, you lot calm down. All this noise. And those poor creatures up there too scared out of their wits to come down. Haven't you any sense, Robinton? Away! The lot of you. Into the Hall. Carry on all night if you've the energy but I'm putting this child to bed. T'gellan, if you'd help me . . ."

As she upbraided everyone impartially, the woman was also making her way, with Menolly and T'gellan, through the crowd which parted respectfully but humorously before her.

"It's too late to put her with the other girls at Dunca's," said Silvina to T'gellan. "We'll just bed her in one of the guest rooms for the night."

Unable to see clearly in the shadows of the Hall, Menolly barked her toes on the stone steps, cried out involuntarily at the pain and grabbed at the supporting hands.

"What happened, child?" asked Silvina, her voice kind and anxious.

"My toes . . . my feet!" Menolly choked back tears that the unexpected pain had brought to her eyes. Silvina mustn't think her a coward.

"Here! I'll carry her," said T'gellan and swung Menolly up into his arms before she could protest. "Just lead the way, Silvina."

"That dratted Robinton," Silvina said, "*he* can go on all day and night without sleep but forgets that others—"

"No, it's not his fault. He's done so much for me . . ." Menolly began.

"Ha! He's deeply in *your* debt, Menolly," said the dragonrider with a cryptic laugh. "You'll have to have your healer see to her feet, Silvina," T'gellan continued as he carried Menolly up the broad flight of stairs that led from the main entrance of the Hall. "That's how we found her. She was trying to outrun the leading edge of Threadfall."

"She was?" Silvina stared over her shoulder at Menolly, her green eyes wide with respectful astonishment.

"She nearly did, too. Ran her feet raw. One of my wingmen saw her and brought her back to Benden Weyr."

"In this room, T'gellan. The bed's on the left-hand side. I'll just open the glow baskets . . ."

"I see it," and T'gellan deposited her gently in the bed. "I'll get the shutters, Silvina, and let those fire lizards of hers in here before they do get into trouble."

Menolly had let herself sink into the thick mattress of sweet rushes. Now she loosened the thong holding the small bundle of belongings to her back but she hadn't the energy to reach for the sleeping fur folded at the foot of the bedstead. As soon as T'gellan had the second shutter open, she called her friends in.

"I've heard so much about the fire lizards," Silvina was saying, "and had only the glimpse of Lord Groghe's little queen that. . . . Gracious goodness!"

At Silvina's startled remark, Menolly struggled out of the thick mattress to see the fire lizards dipping and wheeling about the woman.

"How many did you say you have, Menolly?"

"There are only nine," replied T'gellan, laughing at

Silvina's confusion. She was twisting about, trying to get a good look at one or another of the gyrating creatures.

Menolly told them to settle down quickly and behave. Rocky and Diver landed on the table near the wall while the more daring Beauty took up her accustomed perch on Menolly's shoulder. The others came to rest on the window ledges, their jeweled eyes whirling with the orange of uncertainty and suspicion.

"Why, they're the loveliest creatures I've ever seen," said Silvina, peering intently at the two bronzes on the table. Rocky chirped back, recognizing that remarks were being made about him. He flipped his wings neatly to his back and cocked his head at Silvina. "And a good evening to you, young bronze fire lizard."

"That bold fellow is Rocky," said T'gellan, "if I remember correctly, and the other bronze is Diver. Right, Menolly?" She nodded, relieved in her weariness that T'gellan was ready to speak for her. "The greens are Aunties One and Two," and the pair began to chatter so like old women that Silvina laughed. "The little blue is Uncle but I haven't got the three browns sorted out . . ." and now he turned inquiringly to Menolly.

"They're Lazybones, Mimic and Brownie," Menolly said pointing at each in turn, "and this . . . is Beauty, Silvina," Menolly spoke the woman's name shyly because she didn't know her title or rank in the Harper Hall.

"And a Beauty she is, too. Just like a miniature queen dragon. And just as proud, I see." Then Silvina gave Menolly a hopeful look. "By any chance, will one of Robinton's eggs hatch a queen?"

"I hope so, I really do," said Menolly fervently. "But it's not easy with fire lizard eggs to tell which is the queen."

"I'm sure he'll be just as thrilled no matter what the color. And speaking of queens, T'gellan," and Silvina turned to the dragonrider, "do please tell me, did Brekke re-Impress the new queen dragon at your Hatching today? We've been so worried about her here, since her queen was killed."

"No, Brekke didn't re-Impress," and T'gellan smiled

quickly to reassure Silvina. "Her fire lizard wouldn't let her."

"No?"

"Yes. You should have seen it, Silvina. That little bronze midget flew at the queen dragon, scolding like a wherry hen. Wouldn't let Brekke near the new queen. But she snapped out of that depression, and she'll be all right now, F'nor says. And it was little Berd who pulled the trick."

"Well, that really is interesting." Silvina regarded the two bronzes with thoughtful respect. "So they've a full set of wits . . ."

"They seem to," T'gellan went on. "F'nor uses his little queen, Grall, to send messages to the other Dragon Weyrs. Of course," and T'gellan chuckled disparagingly, "she doesn't always return as promptly as she goes . . . Menolly's trained hers better. You'll see." The dragon-rider had been edging toward the door and now gave a huge yawn. "Sorry . . ."

"I'm the one who should apologize," replied Silvina, "indulging my curiosity when you two are all but asleep. Get along with you now, T'gellan, and my thanks for your help with Menolly."

"Good luck, now, Menolly. I know you'll sleep well," said T'gellan with a jaunty wink of farewell. He was out of the door, his boot heels clicking on the stone floor before she could thank him.

"Now, let's just have a quick look at these feet you ran ragged . . ." Silvina gently tugged off Menolly's slippers. "Hmmm. They're all but healed, Manora's clever with her nursing, but we'll have Master Oldive look at you tomorrow. Now, what's this?"

"My things, I don't have much . . ."

"Here, you two watch that and keep out of mischief," Silvina said, putting the bundle on the table between Rocky and Diver. "Now, slip off your skirt, Menolly, and settle down. A good long sleep, that's what you need. Your eyes are burned holes in your head."

"I'm all right, really."

"To be sure you are, now you're here. Living in a cave, did T'gellan say? With every harper on Pern looking for you in holds and crafthalls." Silvina deftly tugged at skirt tapes. "Just like old Petiron to forget to mention you being a girl."

"I don't think he forgot," Menolly said slowly, thinking of her father and mother and their opposition to her playing. "He told me girls can't be harpers."

Silvina gave her a long hard look. "Maybe under another Masterharper. Or in the old days, but surely old Petiron knew his own son well enough to—"

"Petiron was Master Robinton's father?"

"Did he never tell you that?" Silvina paused as she was spreading the sleeping fur over Menolly. "The old stubborn fool! Determined not to advance himself because his son was elected Masterharper . . . and then picking a place halfway to nowhere. . . . I beg your pardon, Menolly . . ."

"Half-Circle Sea Hold *is* halfway to nowhere."

"Not if Petiron found *you* there," said Silvina, recovering her brisk tone, "and sponsored you to this Craft. Now that's enough talking," she added, closing the glow basket. "I'll leave the shutters open . . . but you sleep yourself out, you hear me?"

Menolly mumbled a reply, her eyelids closing despite her effort to remain politely awake while Silvina was in the room. She let out a soft sigh as the door banged softly shut. Beauty immediately curled up by Menolly's ear, and the girl felt other small hard bodies making themselves comfortable against her. She composed herself for sleep, aware now of the dull throbbing of her feet and the aching of her banged toes.

She was warm, she was comfortable; she was so tired. The bag that enclosed the thick rushes was stout enough to keep stray edges from digging into her flesh, but she couldn't sleep. She also couldn't move because, while her mind turned over all the day's incredible events, her body wasn't hers to command but in some nether region of unresponsiveness.

She was conscious of the spicy odor of Beauty, of the dry sweet scent of the rushes, the earthy smell of wet fields borne in by the night wind, accented occasionally by the touch of acrid blackstone smoke. Spring was not advanced enough to dispense with evening fires.

Strange not to have the smell of sea in her nostrils, Menolly thought, for sea and fish odors had dominated all but the last sevenday of her fifteen Turns. How pleasant to realize that she had done with the sea, and fish, forever. She'd never have to gut another packtail in her life, or risk another infected cut. She couldn't use her injured hand as much as she wanted to yet, but she would. Nothing was impossible, not if she could get to the Harper Hall in spite of all the odds against it. And she'd play gitar again and harp. Manora had assured her she'd use the fingers properly in time. And her feet were healing. It amused Menolly, now, to think that she'd had the temerity to try to outrun the leading edge of Threadfall. Running had done more than save her skin from Threadscoring: it had brought her to Benden Weyr, to the attention of the Masterharper of Pern and to the start of a completely new life.

And her dear old friend, Petiron, had been Master Robinton's father? She'd known the old Harper had been a good musician, but it had never occurred to her before to wonder why he had been sent to Half-Circle Sea Hold where only she had profited from his ability as a teacher. If only her father, Yanus, had let her play gitar when the new Harper first arrived . . . but they'd been so afraid that she'd disgrace the Sea Hold. Well, she hadn't, and she wouldn't! One day her father, and yes, her mother, too, would realize that Menolly was no disgrace to the Hold of her birth.

Menolly drifted on thoughts of triumph until sound invaded her reflections. Male voices, laughing and rumbling in conversation, carried on the clear night air. The voices of harpers; tenor, bass and baritone, in amused, argumentative, cajoling tones, and one querulous, sort of quavery, older, whiny voice. She didn't like that one.

Another, a velvet-soft, light baritone, rose above the cranky tenor, soothing. Then the Masterharper's deeper baritone dominated and silenced the others. Though she couldn't understand what he was saying, his voice lulled her to sleep.

Chapter 2

Harper, tell me of the road
That leads beyond this Hold,
That wends its way beyond the hill ...
Does it go further on until
It ends in sunset's gold?

Menolly roused briefly, reacting to an inner call that had
nothing to do with the sun's rising on this side of Pern.
She saw dark night and stars through the window, felt
the sleeping fire lizards tucked about her, and gratefully
went back to sleep again. She was so tired.

Once the sun had cleared the roof of the outer side of
the rectangle of buildings that comprised the main Harper
Craft Hall, it shone directly at her windows, set in the
eastern side of the Hall. Gradually the light penetrated
the room, and the unusual combination of light and
warmth on her face woke Menolly.

She lay, her body not yet responsive, wondering where
she was. Remembering, she was uncertain what to do
next. Had she missed some general waking call? No,
Silvina had said that she was to sleep herself out. As she
pushed back the sleeping furs, she heard the sound of
voices chanting. The rhythm was familiar. She smiled,
identifying one of the long Sagas. Apprentices were being
taught the complicated timing by rote, just as she had
taught the youngsters in Half-Circle Sea Hold when

Petiron was sick, and later after he died. The similarity reassured her.

As she slid from the bed, she clenched her teeth in anticipation of touching the cool hard stones of the floor, but to her surprise, her feet only felt stiff, not painful, this morning. She glanced out the window at the sun. It was well into morning by the cast of shadow: she'd really slept. Then she laughed at herself, for, to be sure she had: she was halfway round Pern from Benden Weyr and Half-Circle Hold, and she had had at least six hours more rest than usual. Fortunately the fire lizards had been as tired as she or they'd have wakened her with their hunger.

She stretched and shook out her hair, then hobbled carefully to the jar and basin. After washing with soap-sand, she dressed and brushed her hair, feeling able to face new experiences.

Beauty gave an impatient chirp. She was awake. And very hungry. Rocky and Diver echoed the complaint.

Menolly would have to find them food and right soon. Having nine fire lizards would prejudice enough people against her, without having unmanageably hungry ones who would irritate even the most tolerant of people.

Resolutely, Menolly opened the door to a silent hall-way. The aromatic odors of *klah*, baking breads and meats filled the air. Menolly decided she need only follow the smells to their source to satisfy her friends.

On either side of the wide corridor were doors; those on the outside of the Hall were open to let sun and air flood the inside. She descended from the uppermost level into the large entranceway. Directly in front of the stair-case were dragon-high metal doors with the most curious closings she'd ever seen: on the back of the doors were wheels, which evidently turned the heavy bars into floor and ceiling. At Half-Circle Sea Hold there had been the heavy horizontal bars, but this arrangement would be easier to lock and looked much more secure.

To the left was a double-doored entrance into a Great Hall, probably the room where the Harper had been talking last night. To the right, she looked into the dining hall, almost as large as the Great Hall, with three long tables parallel to the windows. Also to her right, by the stairwell, was an open doorway, leading to shallow steps and the kitchen, judging by the appetizing odors and familiar sounds.

The fire lizards creeled in hunger, but Menolly couldn't have the whole fair invading the kitchen and upsetting the drudges. She ordered them to perch on the cornices in the shadows above the door. She'd bring them food, she promised them, but they had to behave. Beauty scolded until the others settled meekly into place, only their glowing, jewel-faceted eyes giving evidence of their positions.

Then Beauty assumed her favorite perch on Menolly's shoulder, her head half-buried in Menolly's thick hair, and her tail wrapped securely about Menolly's throat like a golden necklace.

As Menolly reached the kitchen, the scene with the drudges and cooks scurrying about preparing the midday meal fleetingly revived memories of happier days at Half-Circle. But here, it was Silvina who noticed her and smiled, as Menolly's mother would not have done.

"You're awake? Are you rested?" Silvina gestured imperatively at a slack-featured, clumsy-looking man by the hearth. "Klah, Camo, pour a mug of klah, for Menolly. You must be famished, child. How are your feet?"

"Fine, thank you. And I don't want to bother anyone . . ."

"Bother? What bother? Camo, pour the klah into the mug."

"It's not for myself I'm here . . ."

"Well, you need to eat, and you must be famished."

"Please, it's my fire lizards. Have you any scraps . . ."

Silvina's hands flew to her mouth. She glanced about her head as if expecting a swarm of fire lizards.

"No, I've told them to wait," Menolly said quickly. "They won't come in here."

"Now, you are a thoughtful child," Silvina said in so firm a tone that Menolly wondered why and then realized that she was the object of a good deal of furtive curiosity.

"Camo, here. Give me that!" Silvina took the cup from the man, who was walking with exaggerated care not to slop an overfull container. "And get the big blue bowl from the cold room. The big blue bowl, Camo, from the cold room. Bring it to me." Silvina deftly handed the cup to Menolly without spilling a drop. "The cold room, Camo, and the blue bowl." She turned the man by the shoulders and gave him a gentle shove in the proper direction. "Abuna, you're nearest the hearth. Do dish up some of the cereal. Plenty of sweetening on it, too, the child's nothing but skin and bones." Silvina smiled at Menolly. "No use feeding the fowl and starving the servant, as it were. I saved meat for your friends when we trussed up the roast," and Silvina nodded toward the biggest hearth where great joints of meat were turning on heavy spits, "since meat's what the Harper said fire lizards need. Now, where would the best place . . ." Silvina glanced about her undecidedly, but Menolly had noticed a low door that led up a short flight of steps to the corner of the courtyard.

"Would I disturb anyone out there?"

"Not at all, you are a considerate child. That's right, Camo. And thank you." Silvina patted the half-wit's arm kindly, while he beamed with the pleasure of a job properly done and rewarded. Silvina tipped the edge of the bowl toward Menolly. "Is this enough? There's more . . ."

"Oh, that's a gracious plenty, Silvina."

"Camo, this is Menolly. Follow Menolly with the bowl. She can't carry it *and* her own breakfast. This is Menolly, Camo, follow Menolly. Go right out, dear. Camo's good at carrying things . . . at least what doesn't spill."

Silvina turned from her then, speaking sharply to two women chopping roots, bidding them to slice, not stare. Very much aware of scrutiny, Menolly moved awkwardly to the steps, cup in one hand, bowl of warm cereal in the other, and Camo shuffling behind her. Beauty, who had remained discreetly covered by Menolly's hair, now craned her neck about, smelling the raw meat in the bowl Camo carried.

"Pretty, pretty," the man mumbled as he noticed the

fire lizard. "Pretty small dragon?" He tapped Menolly on the shoulder. "Pretty small dragon?" He was so anxious for her answer that he almost tripped on the shallow steps.

"Yes, she is like a small dragon, and she is pretty," Menolly agreed, smiling. "Her name is Beauty."

"Her name is Beauty." Camo was entranced. "Her name is Beauty. She pretty small dagon." He beamed as he loudly declared this information.

Menolly shushed him, not wanting either to alarm or distract Silvina's helpers. She put down her mug and bowl and reached for the meat.

"Prettty small dragon Beauty," Camo said, ignoring her as she pulled the bowl so firmly clutched in his huge, thick-fingered hands.

"You go to Silvina, Camo. You go to Silvina."

Camo stood where he was, bobbing his head up and down, his mouth set in a wet, wide grimace of childish delight, too entranced by Beauty to be distracted.

Beauty now creeled imperiously, and Menolly grabbed a handful of meat to quiet her. But her cries had alerted the others. They came, some of them from the open windows of the dining hall above Menolly's head, others, judging by the shrieks of dismay, through the kitchen and out the door by the steps.

"Pretty, pretty. All pretty!" Camo exclaimed, turning his head from side to side, trying to see all the flitting fire lizards at once.

He didn't move a muscle as Auntie One and Two perched on his forearms, snatching gobblets of meat directly from the bowl. Uncle secured his talons to the fabric of Camo's tunic, his right wingtip jabbing the man in the neck and chin as the littlest fire lizard fought for his fair share of the meat. Brownie, Mimic, and Lazybones ranged from Camo's shoulders to Menolly's as she tried to distribute the meat evenly.

Alternating between embarrassment at her friends' bad manners and gratitude for Camo's stolid assistance, Menolly was acutely aware that all activity had ceased in the kitchen to watch the spectacle. Momentarily, she expected to hear an irate Silvina order Camo back to his ordinary duties, but all she heard was the buzz of whispered gossiping.

"How many does she have?" she heard one clear whisper out of the general mumble.

"Nine," Silvina answered, imperturbable. "When the two the Harper was given have hatched, the Harper Hall will have eleven." Silvina sounded smugly superior. The buzz increased in volume. "That bread's risen enough now Abuna. You and Kayla shape it."

The fire lizards had cleared the bowl of meat, and Camo stared into its hollow, his face contorted by an expression of dismay.

"All gone? Pretties hungry?"

"No, Camo. They've had more than enough. They're not hungry anymore." In fact, their bellies were distended, they'd gorged so. "You go to Silvina. Silvina wants you, Camo," and Menolly followed Silvina's example: she took him by the shoulders, turned him down the steps, and gave him a gentle shove.

Menolly sipped the good hot klah, beginning to think that Silvina's marked attentions and kindness were deliberate. Or was that foolish? Silvina was just a kind, thoughtful person: look how she treated dull-witted Camo. She was patience itself with his inadequacy. Nonetheless, Silvina was obviously the headwoman at the Harper Craft Hall and, like serene Manora at Benden Weyr, undoubtedly wielded a good deal of authority. If Silvina was friendly, others would follow her lead.

Menolly began to relax in the warm sun. Her dreams last night had been troubled though she couldn't remember details now in the bright morning, only a sense of uneasiness and helplessness. Silvina had done much to dissipate the lingering misgivings. *Nothing to fear from harpers.* T'gellan had repeatedly told her.

Across the courtyard, young voices broke into a lusty rendition of the Saga previously chanted. The fire lizards rose at the eruption of sound, settling again as Menolly laughingly reassured them.

Then a pure sweet trill from Beauty soared in delicate descant above the apprentices' male voices. Rocky and

Diver joined her, wings half-spread as they expanded their lungs for breath. Mimic and Brownie dropped from the window ledge to add their voices. Lazy would not put himself to any such effort, and the two Aunties and blue Uncle were at best indifferent singers, but they listened, heads cocked, jeweled eyes whirling. The five singers rose to their haunches now, their throats thickening, their cheeks swelling as their jaws relaxed to emit the sweet pure notes. Their eyes were half-lidded as they concentrated, as good singers will, to produce the fluting descant.

They were happy then, Menolly thought with relief, and picked up the melody of the Saga, not that the fire lizards needed her voice with the apprentices supplying the tune and harmony.

They were on the last two measures of the chorus when Menolly suddenly realized that it was only herself and the fire lizards singing, that the male voices had ceased. Startled, she looked up and saw that almost every window about the courtyard was filled with faces. The exceptions were the windows of the hall from which the voices had come.

"Who has been singing?" demanded an irate tenor, and a man's head appeared at one of the empty windows.

"Why, that's a grand way to wake up, Brudegan," said the clear baritone of the Masterharper from some point above Menolly and to her left. Craning her head up, she saw him leaning out of his window on the upper story.

"Good morning to you, Masterharper," said Brudegan courteously, but his tone indicated that he was disgruntled by the intervention.

Menolly tried to sit small, heartily wishing herself *between*: she was certainly frozen motionless.

"I didn't know your fire lizards could sing," Silvina said, appearing on Menolly's right and absently retrieving mug and bowl from the steps. "A nice compliment to your chorus, eh, Brudegan," she added, raising her voice to carry across the courtyard. "You'd be wanting your klah now, Robinton?"

"It would be welcome, Silvina." He stretched, leaned further out to peer down at Menolly. "Enter a fair of fire lizards singing! A lovely way to be wakened, Menolly; and a good morning to you, too." Before Menolly could respond, a look of dismay crossed his face. "*My* fire lizard. My egg!" and he disappeared from sight.

Silvina chuckled and she regarded Menolly. "He'll be of no use to anyone until it's hatched and he's got one of his own."

At that point, Brudegan's singers renewed their song. Beauty chirruped questioningly at Menolly.

"No, no, Beauty. No more singing, not now."

"*They* need the practice," and Silvina gestured at the hall. "Now I've the Harper's meal to see to and you to settle . . ." She paused, glancing about at the fire lizards. "But what to do with them?"

"They usually sleep when they're as full as they are right now."

"All to the good . . . but where? Mercy!"

Menolly tried not to laugh at Silvina's astonishment, because all but Beauty, who took her usual perch on Menolly's shoulder, had disappeared. Menolly pointed to the roof opposite and the small bodies landing there, apparently out of thin air.

"They do go *between*, don't they?" Silvina said more than asked. "Harper says they're much like dragons?" That was a question.

"I don't know that much about dragons, but fire lizards can go *between*. They followed me last night from Benden Weyr."

"And they're obedient. I could wish the apprentices were half so willing." Then Silvina motioned Menolly to follow her back into the kitchen. "Camo, turn the spit. Camo, now turn the spit. I suppose the rest of you have been watching the yard instead of the food," she said, scowling indiscriminately about the kitchen. The cooks and drudges alike pretended industry, clanging, banging, splashing or bending with assiduous care over quieter tasks of paring and scraping. "Better yet, Menolly, *you* take the Harper his klah, and check that egg of his. He'll be roaring for you soon enough, so we might as well anticipate. Then I shall want Master Oldive to see your feet, not that Manora hasn't all but healed them anyway. And . . ." Silvina caught Menolly's left hand and scowled at the red mark. "Wherever did you get such a fierce wound? And who bungled the healing of it? There now, can you grip with that hand?" Silvina had been assembling on a small tray the various items of the Harper's breakfast, the last of which was a heavy pot of klah. Now she gave the tray to Menolly. "There now. His room is the second door on the right from yours, Menolly. Turn the spit, Camo, don't just hold on to it. Menolly's fire lizards are fed and sleeping. You'll have another gawk at them later. Turn the spit now!"

As briskly as Menolly could move on her stiff feet, she made her way out of the kitchen and up the broad steps to the second level. Beauty hummed softly in her ear, a gently disobedient descant to the Saga that Brudegan's pupils were singing lustily.

Master Robinton hadn't sounded annoyed about the fire lizards' singing, Menolly thought. She'd apologize to Journeyman Brudegan when she got the chance. She simply hadn't realized she'd cause a distraction. She'd been so pleased that her friends were relaxed enough to want to sing.

Second door on her right. Menolly tapped. Then rapped, then knocked, hard enough to make her knuckles sting.

"Come. Come. And, Silvina . . . oh, Menolly, you're just the person I wanted to see," the Harper said, throwing open the door. "And good morning to you, proud Beauty," he added, grinning at the little queen who chirped an acknowledgement as he took the tray from Menolly. "Silvina's forever anticipating me. . . . Would you please check my egg? It's in the other room, by the hearth. It feels harder to me . . ." He sounded anxious as he pointed to the farther door.

Menolly obediently entered the room, and he walked with her, setting the tray down as he passed the sandtable by the window and pouring himself a mug of klah before he joined her by the hearth in the next room where a small fire burned gently. The earthen pot had been set at the edge of the hearth apron.

Menolly opened it, carefully brushing aside the warm sand that covered the precious fire lizard egg. It was harder, but not much more so than when she had given it to the Masterharper at Benden Weyr the previous evening.

"It's fine, Master Robinson, just fine. And the pot is warm enough, too," she said, running her hands down the sides. She replaced the sand and the top and rose. "When we brought the clutch back to Benden Weyr two days ago, Weyrwoman Lessa said it would take a seven-day for them to hatch, so we've five days more."

The Harper sighed with exaggerated relief. "You slept well, Menolly? You're rested? Awake long?"

"Long enough."

The Harper burst out laughing as she realized how much chagrin she'd put into her tone.

"Long enough to set a few people by the ears, huh? My dear child, did you not notice the difference in the chorus the second time? Your fire lizards have challenged them. Brudegan was only gruff with surprise. Tell me, can your fire lizards improvise descants to any tune?"

"I don't really know, Master Robinson."

"Still not sure, are you, young Menolly?" He didn't mean the fire lizards' abilities. There was such kindness in his voice and eyes that Menolly felt unexpected tears behind her eyes.

"I don't want to be a nuisance . . ."

"Allow me to differ both to statement and content, Menolly . . ." Then he sighed. "You're overyoung to appreciate the value of nuisance, although the improvement in that chorus is a point in my argument. However, it's much too early in the morning for me to expound philosophy." He guided her back into the other room, quite the most cluttered place she had ever seen and in direct contrast to the neatness of his bedchamber. While musical instruments were carefully stored on hook and shelf in cases, piles of record skins, drawings, slates—wax and stone—littered every surface and were heaped in corners and against the walls of the room. On one wall was a finely drawn map of the Pern continent, with smaller detailed drawings of all the major Holds and Crafthalls pinned here and there on the borders. The long sandtable by the window was covered with musical notations, some of them carefully shielded by glass to prevent erasure. The Harper had set the tray on the center island, which separated the sandtable into two halves. Now he pulled a square of wood to protect the sand and positioned the tray so he could eat comfortably. He smeared a thick slice of bread with soft cheese and picked up his spoon to eat his cereal, motioning with the spoon for Menolly to seat herself on a stool.

"We're in a period of change and readjustment, Menolly," he said, managing to speak and eat simultaneously without choking on food or garbling his words. "And you are likely to be a vital part of that change. Yesterday I exerted an unfair pressure on you to join the Harper Hall. . . . Oh yes, I did, but you belong here!" His forefinger stabbed downward at the floor and then waggled out at the courtyard. "First," and he paused to swallow klah, washing down bread and cereal, "we must discover just how well Petiron taught you the fundamentals of our craft and what you need to further your gifts. And . . ." he pointed now to her left hand, ". . . what can be done to correct that scar damage. I'd still like to hear you *play* the songs you wrote." His eyes fell to her hands in her lap so that she was aware of her absentminded kneading of her left palm. "Master Oldive will set that right if anyone can."

"Silvina said I was to see him today."

"We'll have you playing again, more than just those pipes. We need you, when you can craft songs like those Petiron sent me and the ones Elgion found stuck away at the back of the harper's shelves in Half-Circle. Yes, and that's a matter I'd better explain . . ." he went on, smoothing the hair at the back of his neck and, to Menolly's amazement, appearing to be embarrassed.

"Explain?"

"Yes, well, you obviously hadn't finished *writing* that song about the fire lizard queen . . ."

"No, I hadn't actually . . ." Menolly felt that she was not hearing his words properly. For one thing, why did the Masterharper have to explain anything to *her*? And she'd only jotted down the little tune about the fire lizard queen, yet last night. . . . Now she remembered that he'd mentioned the song, as if all the harpers knew about it. "You mean, Harper Elgion sent it to you?"

"How else would I have got it? We couldn't find you!" Robinton sounded annoyed. "When I think of you, living in a cave, with a damaged hand, and you hadn't been *allowed* to finish that charming song. . . . So I did."

He got up, rummaged among the piles of waxed slates under the window, extracted one and handed it to her. She looked at the notations obediently but, although they were familiar, she couldn't make her mind read the melody.

"I had to have something about fire lizards, since I believe they're going to be far more important than anyone has yet realized. And this tune . . ." his finger tapped the hard wax surface approvingly, ". . . was so exactly what I needed, that I just brushed up the harmonics, and compressed the lyric story. Probably what you'd've done yourself if you'd had the chance to work on it again. I couldn't really improve on the melodic line without destroying the integral charm of . . . . What's the matter, Menolly?"

Menolly realized that she'd been staring at him, unable to believe that he was praising a silly tune she'd only scrawled down. Guiltily, she examined the slate again.

"I never did get a chance to *play* it. . . . I wasn't supposed to play my own tunes in the Sea Hold. I promised my father I wouldn't . . . so you see—"

"Menolly!"

Startled, she looked up at his stern tone.

"I want you to promise me—and you're now my apprentice—I want you to promise me to write down any tune that comes into your mind: I want you to play it as often as necessary to get it right . . . do you understand me? That's why I brought you here." He tapped the slate again. "That was a good song even before I tampered with it. I need good songs badly.

"What I said about change affects the Harper Hall more than any other craft, Menolly, because we are the ones who effect change. Just as we teach with our songs, so we also help people accept new ideas and necessary changes. And for that we need a special kind of harpering.

"Now, I still have to consider Craft principles and standards. Especially in your unusual situation, the conventional procedure must be observed. Once we've dispensed with the formalities, we can proceed with your training as fast as you want to go. But this is where you belong, Menolly, you and your singing fire lizards. Bless me but that was lovely to hear this morning. Ah, Silvina, good morning and to you, as well, Master Oldive . . ."

Menolly knew it was impolite to stare at anyone and looked away as soon as she realized that she was staring, but Master Oldive required a long look. He was shorter than herself but only because his head was awry on his neck. His great lean face tilted up from its permanent slant, and she had the impression of enormous dark eyes under very shaggy brows taking in every detail of herself.

"I'm sorry, Master Robinton, have we interrupted you?" Silvina paused on the threshold indecisively.

"Yes, and no. I don't think I've convinced Menolly but that will take time. Meanwhile, we'll get on with the basics. We'll speak again, Menolly," said the Harper. "Go along with Master Oldive now. Let him do his best, or his worst, for you. She must play again, Oldive." The Harper's smile as he gestured to Menolly to follow the man implied complete faith in his ability. "And Silvina, Menolly says the egg's safe enough for four or five days, but you'll please arrange to have someone—"

"Why not Sebell? He's got his egg to check, too, doesn't he? And with Menolly here in the Hall . . ." Silvina was saying as Master Oldive, ushering Menolly out of the room before him, closed the door.

"I'm to see to your feet as well, Silvina tells me," was

the man's comment as he indicated Menolly should lead the way to her room. The Master's voice was unexpectedly deep. And while he might be shorter than herself in the torso, he'd as long a leg and arm and matched her stride down the corridor. As he pushed wider her door, she realized that his stature was due to a terrible malformation of his spine.

"By my life!" Oldive exclaimed, stopping abruptly as Menolly preceded him into the room. "I thought for a moment you were as blighted as myself. It is a fire lizard on your shoulder, isn't it?" He chuckled. "Now, there's one on me, so it is. Is the creature friendly?" He peered up at Beauty, who chirruped pleasantly back, since Oldive was patently addressing her. "As long as I'm friendly to your Menolly, I take it? You'll have to write another verse to your fire lizard song, proving the rewards of kindness," he added, gesturing her to sit on the window side of the bed as he pulled up the stool.

"Oh, that's not my song . . ." she said, removing her slippers.

Master Oldive frowned. "Not your song? But Master Robinton assigns it to you—constantly."

"He rewrote it . . . he told me so."

"That's not unusual," and Master Oldive dismissed her protest. "Proper mess you made of your feet," he said, his voice taking on a distant, thoughtful quality as he looked at first one, then the other foot. "Running, I believe . . ."

Menolly felt reproved. "I was caught out during Threadfall, you see, far from my cave and had to run . . . oooh!"

"Sorry, did I hurt? The flesh is very tender. And will remain that way awhile longer."

He began to smooth on a pungent-smelling substance, and she couldn't keep her foot still. He grabbed her ankle firmly to complete the medication, countering her embarrassed apology by remarking that her twitching proved that she'd done the nerves no harm with the pounding she'd given her feet.

"You're to keep off them as much as possible. I'll tell

Silvina so. And use this salve morning and night. Aids healing and keeps the skin from itching." He replaced Menolly's slippers. "Now, this hand of yours."

She hesitated, knowing that his opinion of the bungled wound was likely to echo Manora's and Silvina's. Perversely she was afflicted by an obscure loyalty to her mother.

Oldive regarded her steadily, as if divining some measure of her reluctance, and extended his own hand. Compelled by the very neutrality of his gaze, she gave him her injured hand. To her surprise, there was no change of expression on his face, no condemnation or pity, merely interest in the problem the thick-scarred palm posed for a man of his skill. He prodded the scar tissue, murmuring thoughtfully in his throat.

"Make a fist."

She could just about do that but, when he asked her to extend her fingers, the scar pulled as she tried to stretch the palm.

"Not as bad as I was led to believe. An infection, I suppose . . ."

"Packtail slime . . ."

"Hmm, yes. Insidious stuff." He gave her hand another twist. "But the scar is not long healed, and the tissue can still be stretched. A few more months and we might not have been able to do anything to flex the hand. Now, you will do exercises, tightening your fingers about a small hard ball, which I will provide you, and extending the hand." He demonstrated, forcing her fingers upward and apart so that she cried out involuntarily. "If you can discipline yourself to the point of actual discomfort, you are doing the exercise properly. We must stretch the tightened skin, the webbing between your fingers, and the stiffened tendons. I shall also provide a salve, which you are to rub well into the scar tissue to make it softer and more pliable. Conscientious effort on your part will determine the rate of progress. I suspect that you will be sufficiently motivated."

Before Menolly could stammer her thanks, the astonishing man was out of the room and closing the door behind him. Beauty made a sound—half quizzical chirp, half approving burble. She'd come loose from Menolly's neck during the examination, watching the proceedings from a depression in the sleeping furs. Now she walked over to Menolly and stroked her head against Menolly's arm.

From the apprentices' hall across the courtyard, the singing was renewed, with vigor and volume. Beauty cocked her head, humming with delight and then, when Menolly shushed her, looked wistfully up at the girl.

"I don't think we should sing again just now, but they do sound grand, don't they?"

She sat there, caressing Beauty, delighting in the music. Very close harmony, she realized approvingly, the sort only trained voices and well-rehearsed singers can achieve.

"Well," said Silvina, entering the room briskly, "you have stirred them up. It's good to hear that old rooter sung with some spirit."

Menolly had no time to register astonishment at Silvina's comment, for the headwoman poked at Menolly's bundle of things on the table, and twitched the sleeping rug into neat folds.

"We might just as well get you settled in Dunca's cottage now," Silvina continued. "Fortunately, there's an outside room unoccupied . . ." The headwoman wrinkled her nose in a slightly disparaging grimace. "Those holder girls are impossible about being outside, but it oughtn't to worry you." She smiled at Menolly. "Oldive says you're to keep off your feet, but some walking's got to be done. Still, you won't be in a chore section . . . another good reason to keep you at Dunca's, I suppose . . ." Silvina frowned and then looked back at Menolly's small bundle. "This is all you brought with you?"

"And nine fire lizards."

Silvina laughed. "An embarrassment of riches." She glanced out the window, peering across the courtyard to the far roof where the fire lizards were still sunning themselves. "They *do* stay where they're told, don't they?"

"Generally. But I'm not sure how good they are with too many people about or unusual noise."

"Or fascinating diversions . . ." Silvina smiled again at Menolly as she nodded toward the windows and the music issuing from the apprentices' hall.

"They always sang along with me . . . I didn't realize we shouldn't—"

"How should you? Not to worry, Menolly. You'll fit in here just fine. Now, let's wrap up your bundle and show you the way to Dunca's. Then Robinton wants you to borrow a gitar. Master Jerint is sure to have a spare usable one in the workshop. You'll have to make your own, you know. Unless you made one for Petiron at the Sea Hold?"

"I had none of my own." Menolly was relieved that she could keep her voice steady.

"But Petiron took his with him. Surely you . . ."

"I had the use of it, yes." Menolly managed to keep her tone even as she rigidly suppressed the memory of how she had lost the use, of the beating her father had given her for forbidden tuning, playing her own songs. "I made myself pipes . . ." she added, diverting Silvina from further questions. Rummaging in her bundle, she brought out the multiple pipes she had made in her cave by the sea.

"Reeds? And done with a belt knife by the look of them," said Silvina, walking to the window for more light as she turned the pipes in a critical examination. "Well done for just a belt knife." She returned the pipes to Menolly with an approving expression. "Petiron was a good teacher."

"Did you know him well?" Menolly felt a wave of grief at her loss of the only person in her home hold who had been interested in her.

"Indeed I did." Silvina gave Menolly a frown. "Did he not talk of the Harper Hall at all to you?"

"No. Why should he?"

"Why shouldn't he? He taught you, didn't he? He encouraged you to write. . . . Sent Robinton those songs . . ." Silvina stared at Menolly in real surprise for a long moment, then she shrugged with a little laugh. "Well, Petiron always had his own reasons for everything he did, and no one the wiser. But he was a good man!"

Menolly nodded, unable for a moment to speak, berating herself for ever once doubting, during those lonely miserable days at Half-Circle after Petiron's death, that he'd done what he said he'd do. Though the old Harper's mind had taken to wandering. . . .

"Before I forget it," Silvina said, "how often do your fire lizards need to be fed?"

"They're hungriest in the morning, though they eat any time, but maybe that was because I had to hunt and catch food for them, and it took hours. The wild ones seemed to have no trouble . . ."

"Fed 'em once and they're always looking to you, is that it?" Silvina smiled, to soften any implied criticism. "The cooks throw all scraps into a big earthen jar in the cold room . . . most of it goes to the watchwhers, but I'll give orders that you're to have whatever you require."

"I don't mean to be a bother . . ."

Silvina gave her such a look that Menolly broke off her atttempt to apologize.

"Be sure that when you *do* bother me, I'll inform you." Silvina grinned. "Just ask any of the apprentices if I won't."

Silvina had been leading Menolly down the steps and out of the cliffhold of the Harper Hall as she talked. Now they passed under an arch that gave onto a broad road of paving stones, never a blade of grass or spot of moss to be seen anywhere.

For the first time Menolly had a chance to appreciate the size of Fort Hold. Knowing that it was the oldest and largest Hold was quite different from seeing it, being outside the towering cliff.

Thousands of people must live in the cliffholds and cottages that hugged the rock palisade. Awed, Menolly's steps slowed as she stared at the wide ramp leading to the courtyard and main entrance of Fort Hold, higher in the cliff face than the Harper Craft Hall, and with rows of windows extending upward in sheer stone, almost to the fire heights themselves. In Half-Circle Sea Hold, everyone had been in the cliff, but at Fort Hold, stone buildings had been built out in wings from the cliff, forming a quadrangle similar to the Harper Craft Hall. Smaller cottages had been added onto the original wings, on either side of the ramp. There were dwellings bordering the sides of the broad paved road that led in several well-traveled directions; south to the fields and pastures, east down the valley toward the low foothills and west around to the pass in the cliff that would lead to the higher mountains of the Central Fort Range.

Silvina guided Menolly now toward a cottage, a good-sized one with five windows, all of them shuttered tight, on the upper floor. The cottage nestled against the slope of the ramp. As they got close enough, Menolly realized that the little cot was also quite old. And the cottage door was metal, too! Incredible! Silvina opened it, calling out for Dunca. Menolly had just time to notice that the metal door closed as the one at the Harper Hall did, with a small wheel throwing the thick rods into grooves in ceiling and floor.

"Menolly, come and meet Dunca who holds the cottage for the girls who study at the Harper Hall."

Menolly dutifully greeted the short, dumpy little woman with bright black eyes and cheeks like a puff-belly's sides. Dunca gave Menolly a raking look, at odds with her jolly appearance, as if measuring up Menolly to the gossip she'd already heard. Then Dunca saw Beauty peeking around Menolly's ear. She gave a shriek, jumping back.

"What's that?"

Menolly reached up to calm Beauty, who was hissing and raising her wings, getting one entangled in Menolly's hair.

"But, Dunca, surely you knew—" Silvina's voice chided the woman, "—that Menolly had Impressed fire lizards."

Menolly's sharp ear caught the edge to Silvina's voice, and so did the little queen, for Beauty thrummed softly and warningly in her throat as her eyes whirled at Dunca. Menolly silently called her to order.

"I'd *heard*, but I don't always credit things I'm *told*," said Dunca, standing as far away from Menolly and Beauty as the hall permitted.

"Very wise of you," replied Silvina. The set of the head-woman's lips and the wary amusement in her glance told Menolly that Silvina was not overly fond of the little cotholder. "Now you've a windowed room vacant, have you not? I think it's best if we settled her there."

"I don't want another hysterical girl who'll panic during Threadfall and scare us all with imagining that Thread is actually *in* the cottage!"

Silvina's eyes danced with suppressed laughter as she glanced Menolly's way. "No, Menolly won't panic. She is, by the way, the youngest daughter of Yanus Sea Holder of Half-Circle Sea Hold, beholden to Benden Weyr. The sea breeds stern souls, you know."

Dunca's bright little eyes were almost lost in the folds of her eye flesh as she peered up at Menolly.

"So you knew Petiron, did you?"

"Yes, I did, Dunca."

The cotholder gave a disgusted snort and turned so quickly her full skirt followed in hasty swirls as she made for the stone steps carved into the wall at the back of the hallway. She kept twitching her skirt, grunting at the steepness of the risers as she heaved her small fat person upward.

Two narrow corridors, lit at either end by dimming glows, went left and right from the stairwell. Dunca turned right, led them to the far end and threw open the last door on the outside.

"Lazy sluts," she said truculently, fumbling at the catch of the glowbasket. "They've cleared the glows."

"Where are they kept?" asked Menolly, wishing to ingratiate herself with the cotkeeper. Fleetingly she wondered if she'd always be trotting up and down narrow steps after glows.

"Where's your drudge, Dunca? It's her task to bring

glows, not Menolly's," said Silvina as she walked past Dunca and flipped open first one, then a second set of shutters, flooding the room with sunlight.

"Silvina! What are you doing?"

"Threadfall's not for two more days, Dunca. Be sensible. The room's fusty."

Dunca's answer was a shriek as the other fire lizards swooped in through the opened window, diving about the room, chittering excitedly. There was nothing for them to cling to, since the walls were bare of hangings and the bed a frame, empty of rushes, the sleeping fur rolled up on the small press. The two green Aunties and blue Uncle fought for landing space on the stool and then zoomed out the window again as Dunca's screams startled them. The little cotholder cowered in the corner, skirts about her head, shrieking.

Menolly ordered the browns to stop diving, told Auntie One and Two and Uncle to stay on the window ledge, got Rocky and Diver to settle on the bedstead while Silvina calmed Dunca and led her from the corner. By the time the cotholder had been cajoled into watching Silvina handle Lazybones, who'd let anyone caress him so long as it involved no effort on his part, Menolly realized that Dunca would never be comfortable in their presence and that the woman disliked Menolly intensely for witnessing her fearfulness. For a long, sad moment, Menolly wished that she could have stayed at the Weyr where everyone could accept fire lizards equably.

She sighed softly to herself as she stroked Beauty, absently listening to Silvina's reassurances to Dunca that the fire lizards wouldn't harm anyone, not her, not her charges; that Dunca'd be the envy of every other cotholder in Fort to have nine fire lizards . . .

"Nine?" Dunca's protest came out in a terrified squeak, and she reached for her skirts to throw over her head. "Nine of those beastly things flitting and diving about *my* home—"

"They don't like to stay inside, except at night," said Menolly, hoping to reassure Dunca. "They're rarely all with me at one time."

From the horrified and malicious look Dunca gave her, Menolly realized that she herself would be rarely with Dunca if the cotholder had anything to say in the matter.

"We can stop here no longer now, Menolly. You've to pick a gitar from the workshop," said Silvina. "If you need more rushes, Dunca, you've only to send your woman to the Hall," she added as she motioned Menolly to precede her from the room. "Menolly will be more closely involved with the Hall than the other girls . . ."

"She's to be back here at shutter time, same as the others, or stay at the Hall," said Dunca as Silvina and Menolly went down the steps.

"She's strict with the girls," Silvina remarked as they emerged into the bright midday sun and started across the broad paved square, "but that's to the good with all those lads vying for their attention. And take no heed to her grumbles over Petiron. She'd hoped to wed him after Merelan died. *I'd* say Petiron resigned as Fort Hold Harper as much to get free of Dunca as to clear the way for Robinton. He was so very proud that his son was elected Masterharper."

"Half-Circle Sea Hold is a long way from Fort Hold."

Silvina chuckled. "And one of the few places isolated enough to prevent Dunca from following him, child. As if Petiron would ever have taken another woman after Merelan. She was the loveliest person, a voice of unusual beauty and range. Ah, I miss her still."

More people were about: field workers coming in for their midday meal; a party of men on leggy runners, slowing to an amble through the crowd. An apprentice, intent on his errand, ran right into Menolly. He was mouthing an apology when Beauty, peering through Menolly's hair, hissed at him. He yelped, ducked with an apprentice's well-developed instinct, and went pelting back the way he'd come.

Silvina laughed. "I'd like to hear his tale when he gets back to his hall."

"Silvina, I'm—"

"Not a word, Menolly! I will not have you apologizing

for your fire lizards. Nor will Master Robinton. There will always be fools in the world like Dunca, fearful of anything new or strange." They had entered the archway of the Harper Hall. "Through that door, across the stair-hall, and you'll find the workshop. Master Jerint is in charge. He'll find you an instrument so you can play for Master Domick. He'll meet you there." With an encouraging pat and a smile, Silvina left her.

Chapter 3

Speak softly to my lizard fair
Nor raise your hand to me.
For they are quick to take offense
And quicker to champion me.

Menolly wished that Silvina had stayed long enough to introduce her to Master Jerint, but she guiltily realized how much of the headwoman's valuable time she had already had. So, squaring her shoulders against her ridiculous surge of nervousness, Menolly entered the square stairhall and saw the door that must lead to the workshop of Master Jerint.

She could hear the sounds of workshop industry: hammering, the scrape of saw on wood, toots and thumps; but the instant she opened the door, she and Beauty got the full impact of various noises of tuning, sanding, sawing, pounding, the twanging of tough wherhide being stretched over drum frames and snapping back. Beauty let out a penetrating shriek of complaint and took off, straight for the bracing beams of the high-ceilinged workshop. Her raucous call and her flight suspended all activity in the room. The sudden silence, and then the whisperings of the younger workers, all staring at Menolly, attracted the attention of the older man who was bent almost double, glueing a crucial piece of inlay on the gitar in his lap. He looked up and around at the staring apprentices.

"What? Well?"

Beauty gave another cry, launching herself from the rafter beam back to Menolly's shoulder now that the distressing sounds had ceased.

"Who made that appealing noise? It was animal, not instrumental."

Menolly didn't see anyone pointing at her, but suddenly Master Jerint was made aware of her presence by the door.

"Yes? What are you doing her? And what's that thing on your shoulder? You oughtn't be carting pets about, whatever it is. It isn't allowed. Well, lad, speak up!"

Titters in various parts of the workroom indicated to the man that he was in some error.

"Please, sir, if you're Master Jerint, I'm Menolly . . ."

"If you're Menolly, then you're no lad."

"No, sir."

"And I've been expecting you. At least, I think so." He peered down at the inlay he'd been glueing as if accusing the inanimate object of his absentmindedness. "What is that thing on your shoulder? Did it make that noise?"

"Yes, because she was startled, sir."

"Yes, the noise in here would startle anyone with hearing and wit." Jerint sounded approving and now craned his head forward, withdrawing the instant Beauty gave one of her little chirps and frowning in surprise that she reacted to his curiosity. "So she is one of those mythical fire lizards?" He acted skeptical.

"I named her Beauty, Master Jerint," Menolly said, determined to win other friends for her fire lizards that day. She firmly unwound Beauty's tail from her neck and coaxed her to her forearm. "She likes to have her head-knob stroked. . . ."

"Does she?" Jerint caressed the glowing golden creature. Beauty closed the inner lid of her brilliant eyes and submitted completely to the Master's touch. "She does."

"She's really very friendly, it's just all that noise and so many people."

"Well, I find her quite friendly," Jerint replied, one long calloused and glue-covered finger stroking the little

36

queen with growing confidence as Beauty began to hum with pleasure. "Very friendly indeed. Are dragons' skins as soft as hers?"

"Yes, sir."

"Charming creature. Quite charming. Much more practical than dragons."

"She sings, too," said a stocky man sauntering from the back of the hall, wiping his hands on a towel as he came.

As if this newcomer released a hidden spring, a murmurous wave of half giggle, half excited whisperings rippled through the apprentices. The man nodded at Menolly.

"Sings?" asked Jerint, pausing in mid-caress so that Beauty butted her nose at his hand. He continued to stroke the now coyly curved neck. "She sings, Domick?"

"Surely you heard this morning's glorious descant, Jerint?"

This stocky man was Master Domick for whom she must play? True, he wore an old tunic with a faded journeyman's markings, but no journeyman would have addressed a master by his bare name nor would be so self-assured.

"This morning's descant?" Jerint blinked with surprise, and some of the bolder apprentices chortled at his confusion. "Yes, I remember thinking the pitch was a bit unusual for pipes, and besides that Saga is traditionally sung without accompaniment, but then Brudegan is always improvising . . ." He gave an irritable wave of his hand.

Beauty reared up on Menolly's arm, startled into fanning her wings for balance and digging her talons painfully through Menolly's thin sleeve.

"Didn't mean you, you pretty thing," Jerint said by way of apology and caressed Beauty's headknob until she'd subsided to her former position. "But all that sound from this little creature?"

"How many were actually singing, Menolly?" asked Master Domick.

"Only five," she replied reservedly, thinking of Dunca's reaction to the figure nine.

"Only five of them?"

The droll tone made her glance apprehensively at the stocky Master, wondering if he were taunting her, since the half-smile on his face gave her no real hint.

"Five!" Master Jerint rocked back on his heels with amazement. "*You* . . . have five fire lizards?"

"Actually, sir, to be truthful . . ."

"It is wiser to be truthful, Menolly," agreed Master Domick, and he was teasing her, not too kindly either.

"I Impressed nine fire lizards," said Menolly in a rush, "because, you see, Thread was falling outside the cave, and the only way I could keep the hatchlings from leaving and getting killed by Thread was to feed them and that . . ."

"Impressed them, of course," Domick finished for her, when she faltered because Master Jerint was wide-eyed with astonishment and incredulity. "You will really have to add another verse to your song, Menolly, or possibly two."

"The Masterharper has edited that song as he feels necessary, Master Domick," she said with what she hoped was quiet dignity.

A slow smile spread across the man's face.

"It is wiser to be truthful, Menolly. Didn't you train all your fire lizards to sing?"

"I didn't actually train them, sir. I played my pipes, and they'd sing along . . ."

"Speaking of pipes, Jerint, this girl has to have an instrument until she can make one herself. Or didn't Petiron have enough wood to teach you, girl?"

"He *explained* how . . ." Menolly replied. Did Master Domick think Yanus Sea Holder would have wasted precious timber for a *girl* to make a harper's instrument?

"We'll see in due time how well you absorbed that explanation. In the meantime, Menolly needs a gitar to play for me and to practice on . . ." He drawled the last two words, his stern glance sweeping around the room at all the watchers.

Everyone was suddenly exceedingly occupied in their interrupted tasks, and the resultant energetic blows, twangs and whistles made Beauty spread her wings and screech in protest.

"I can hardly fault her," said Domick as Menolly soothed the fire lizard.

"What an extrordinary range of sounds she can make," remarked Master Jerint.

"A gitar for Menolly? So we can judge the range of sounds *she* can make?" Domick reminded the man in a bored tone.

"Yes, yes, there's any number of instruments to choose from," said Jerint, walking with jerky steps toward the courtyard side of the L-shaped room.

And indeed there were, Menolly realized as they approached the corner clutter of drums, pipes, harps of several sizes and designs, and gitars. The instruments depended from hooks set in the stone and cords attached to the ceiling beams, or sat dustily on shelves, the layers of dust increasing as the instruments went beyond easy range.

"A gitar, you said?" Jerint squinted at the assortment and reached for a gitar, its wood bright with new varnish.

"Not that one." The words were out before Menolly realized how brash she must sound.

"Not this one?" Jerint, arm still upraised, looked at her. "Why not?" He sounded huffy, but his eyes narrowed slightly as he regarded her; there was nothing of the slightly absent-minded craftsman about Master Jerint now.

"Its too green to have any tone."

"How would you know by looking?"

So, thought Menolly, this is a sort of test for me.

"I wouldn't choose any instrument on looks, Master Jerint, I'd choose by the sound, but I can see from here that the wood of that gitar is badly joined on the case. The neck is not straight for all it's been veneered prettily."

The answer evidently pleased him, for he stepped aside and gestured to her to make her own selection. She picked the strings of one gitar resting against the shelves and absently shook her head, looking further. She saw a case, its wherhide worn but well-oiled. Glancing back at the

39

two men for permission, she opened it and lifted out the gitar; her hands caressed the thin smooth wood, her fingers curling appreciatively about the neck. She placed it before her, running her fingers down the strings, across the opening. Almost reverently she struck a chord, smiling at the mellow sound. Beauty warbled in harmony to the chord she struck and then chirruped happily. Menolly carefully replaced the gitar.

"Why do you put it back? Wouldn't you choose it?" asked Jerint sharply.

"Gladly, sir, but that gitar must belong to a master. It's too good to practice on."

Domick let out a burst of laughter and clapped Jerint on the shoulder.

"No one could have told her that one's yours, Jerint. Go on, girl, find one just bad enough to practice on but good enough for you to use."

She tried several others, more conscious than ever that she had to choose well. One sounded sweet to her, but the tuning knobs were so worn that the strings would not keep their pitch through a song. She was beginning to wonder if there was a playable instrument in the lot when she spotted one depending from a hook almost lost in the shadows of the wall. One string was broken, but when she chorded around the missing note, the tone was silky and sweet. She ran her hands around the sound box and was pleased with the feel of the thin wood. The careful hand of its creator had put an intricate pattern of lighter shades of wood around the opening. The tuning knobs were of newer wood than the rest of the gitar but, except for the missing string, it was the best of all but Master Jerint's.

"I'd like to use this one, if I may?" She held it toward Jerint.

The Master nodded slowly, approvingly, ignoring Domick, who gave him a clout on the shoulder. "I'll get you a new E string . . ." And Jerint turned to a set of drawers at one end of the shelves, rummaged a moment and brought out a carefully coiled length of gut.

As the string was already looped, she slipped it over

the hook, lined it over the bridge and up the neck into the hole of the tuning knob. She was very conscious of intent scrutiny and tried to keep her hands from trembling. She tuned the new string first to the next one, then to the others and struck a true chord; the mellowness of the sound reassured her that she had chosen well.

"Now that you have demonstrated that you can choose well, string and tune, let's see if you can *play* the gitar of your choice," said Domick, and taking her by the elbow, steered her from the workroom.

She had only time to nod her thanks to Master Jerint as the door slammed behind her. Still gripping her arm and unperturbed by Beauty's hissing, Domick propelled her up the stairs and into a rectangular room built over the entrance archway. It must serve a dual purpose as an office and an additional schoolroom, to judge by the sand-table, the record bins, the wall writing board and the shelves of stored instruments. There were stools pulled back against the walls, but there were also three leathered couches, the first that Menolly had ever seen, with time-darkened armrests and backs, some patched where the original hide had been replaced. Two wide windows, with folding metal shutters, overlooked the broad road to the Hold on one side, the courtyard on the other.

"Play for me," Domick said, gesturing for her to take a stool as he collapsed into the couch facing the hearth.

His tone was expressionless, his manner so noncommittal that Menolly felt he didn't expect her to be able to play at all. What little confidence she had gained when she had apparently chosen unexpectedly well ebbed from her. Unnecessarily she struck a tuning chord, fiddled with the knob on the new string, trying to decide what to play to prove her competence. For she was determined to surprise this Master Domick who teased and taunted and didn't like her having nine fire lizards.

"Don't sing," Domick added. "And I want no distraction from her." He pointed to Beauty still on Menolly's shoulder. "Just that." He jabbed his finger at the gitar and then folded his hands across his lap, waiting.

His tone stung Menolly's pride awake. With no further thought, she struck the opening chords of the "Ballad of Moreta's Ride" and had the satisfaction of seeing his eyebrows lift in surprise. The chording was tricky enough when voices carried the melody, but to pluck the tune as well as the accompaniment increased the difficulty. She did strike several sour chords because her left hand could not quite make the extensions or respond to the rapid shifts of harmony required, but she kept the rhythm keen and the fingers of her right hand flicked out the melody loud and true through the strumming.

She half-expected him to stop her after the first verse and chorus, but, as he made no sign, she continued, varying the harmony and substituting an alternative fingering where her left hand had faltered. She had launched into the third repetition when he leaned forward and caught her right wrist.

"Enough gitar," he said, his expression inscrutable. Then he snapped his fingers at her left hand, which she extended in slow obedience. It ached. He turned it palm up, tracing the thick scar so lightly that the tickling sensation made her spine twitch in reaction though she forced herself to keep still. He grunted, noticing where her exertion had split the edge of the wound. "Oldive seen that hand yet?"

"Yes, sir."

"And recommended some of his sticky smelly salves, no doubt. If they work, you'll be able to stretch for the fingerings you missed in the first verse."

"I hope so."

"So do I. You're not supposed to take liberties with the Teaching Ballads and Sagas—"

"So Petiron taught me," she replied with an equally expressionless voice, "but the minor seventh in the second measure is an alternative chording in the Record at Half-Circle Sea Hold."

"An old variation."

Menolly said nothing, but she knew from his very sourness that she had played very well indeed, despite her hand, and that Domick didn't want to be complimentary.

"Now, what other instruments did Petiron teach you to play?"

"Drum, of course."

"Yes, of course. There's a small tambour behind you."

She demonstrated the basic drum rolls, and at his request did a more complex drum dance beat, popular with and peculiar to seaholders. Though his expression remained bland, she saw his fingers twitch in time with the beat and was inwardly pleased by that reaction. Next, she played a simple lullaby on the lap harp, well suited to the light sweet tone of the instrument. He told her he would assume that she could play the great harp but the octave reaches would place too great a strain on her left hand. He handed her an alto pipe, took a tenor one and had her play harmony to his melody line. That was fun, and she could have continued indefinitely because it was so stimulating to play duet.

"Did you have brass at the Sea Hold?"

"Only the straight horn, but Petiron explained the theory of valves, and he said that I could develop a good lip with more practice."

"I'm glad to hear he didn't neglect brass." Domick rose. "Well, I can place your instrumental standard. Thank you, Menolly. You may be dismissed for the midday meal."

With some regret, Menolly reached for the gitar. "Should I return this to Master Jerint now?"

"Of course not." His expression was still cool, almost rude. "You got it to practice on, remember. And, despite all you know, you will need to practice."

"Master Domick, whose was this?" She asked the question in a rush, because she had a sudden notion it might be his, which could account for some of his curious antagonism.

"That one? That was Robinton's journeyman's gitar." Then, with a broad grin at her astonishment, Master Domick quit the room.

Menolly remained, still caught by surprise and dismay at her temerity, holding the now doubly precious gitar against her. Would Master Robinton be annoyed, as

Master Domick seemed to be, that she had chosen his gitar? Common sense reasserted itself. Master Robinton had much finer instruments now, of course, or why else would his journeyman's effort be hidden among Jerint's spares? Then the humor of her choice struck her: of all the gitars there, she had picked the discarded instrument of the Masterharper. Small wonder he was Harper here if this fine gitar had been made when he was still young. She strummed lightly, head bent to catch the sweet mellow quality, smiling as she listened to the soft notes die away. Beauty chirped approvingly from her perch on the shelf. Chirpy echoes about the room apprised her that the other fire lizards had sneaked in.

They all roused and took wing, squeaking, as a loud bell, seemingly right overhead, began to toll. The sharp notes punctuated a pandemonium that erupted from the rooms below and into the courtyard. Apprentices and journeymen, released from their morning classes, spilled into the courtyard, all making the best possible speed to the dining hall, jostling, pushing and shouting in such an excess of spirits that Menolly gasped in surprise. Why some of them must be over twenty Turns old. No seaholder would act that way! Boys of fifteen Turns, her age, were already serving on boats at the Sea Hold. Of course, an exhausting day at sail lines and nets left little energy to expend on running or laughing. Perhaps that was why her parents couldn't appreciate her music—it wouldn't appear to be hard work to them. Menolly shook her hands, letting them flap from her wrists. They ached and trembled from the constricted movements and tension of an hour of intensive playing. No, her parents would never understand that playing musical instruments could be as hard work as sailing or fishing.

And she was just as hungry as if she'd been trawling. She hesitated, gitar in hand. She wouldn't have time to take it back to her room in the cottage. No one in the yard seemed to be carrying instruments. So she put the gitar carefully in a vacant spot on a high shelf, told Beauty and the others to remain where they were. She could just imagine what would happen if she brought her fire lizards to that dining hall. As bad as the noise was now. . . .

Suddenly the courtyard was empty of hurrying folk. She took the stairs as fast as her feet could go and crossed the courtyard with a fair approximation of her normal swinging stride, hoping to enter the dining room unobtrusively. She reached the wide doorway and halted. The hall seemed overly full of bodies, standing in rigid attention at the long tables. Those facing the windows stood taut with expectation while those facing the inner wall seemed to be staring hard at the corner on her right. She was about to look when a hissing to her left attracted her. There was Camo, gesturing and grimacing at her to take one of the three vacant seats at the window table. As quickly as possible, she slid into place.

"Hey," said the small boy next to her, without moving his head in her direction, "you shouldn't be here. You should be over there. With them!" He jerked his finger at the long table nearest the hearth.

Craning her head to peer past the screening bodies, Menolly saw the sedate row of girls, backs to the hearth. There was an empty seat at one end.

"No!" The boy grabbed at her hand. "Not now!"

Obeying some signal Menolly couldn't see, everyone was seated at that precise moment.

"Pretty Beauty? Where's pretty Beauty?" asked a worried voice at her elbow. "Beauty not hungry?" It was Camo, in each hand a heavy platter piled with roast meat slices.

"Take it quick," said the boy beside her, giving her a dig in the ribs.

Menolly did so.

"Well, get yours and pass it," the boy went on.

"Don't just sit there like a dummy," added the black-haired lad opposite her, frowning fiercely and shifting his buttocks on the hard wood of the bench.

"Hey, grab; don't gab," ordered another lad, further up the table with considerable irritation at the delay.

Menolly mumbled something, and rather than waste

time fumbling for her belt knife, she tweaked the topmost slice from the platter to her plate. The boy across from her deftly snagged four slices on his knife point and transferred them, dripping juices, to his plate. The boy beside her struggled with the heavy platter, taking four slices, too, as he passed it on.

"Should you take so much?" she asked, her surprise at such greed overcoming reticence.

"You don't starve in the Harper Hall," he said, grinning broadly. He sliced the first piece into halves, folded one half over neatly with his blade and then shoved it into his mouth, catching the juices with his finger, which he managed to lick despite the mouthful he was busy chewing.

His assurance was borne out by the deep bowl of tubers and roots, and the basket of sliced breads, which Camo deposited beside her. From these Menolly helped herself more liberally, passing the dishes along as quickly as she could.

"You're Menolly, aren't you?" asked the boy beside her, his mouth still full.

She nodded.

"Was it really your fire lizards singing this morning?"

"Yes."

Whatever lingering embarrassment for that incident Menolly retained was dispersed in the giggle from her table companion and the sly grins of those near enough to overhear the conversation.

"You should've seen Bruddie's face!"

"Bruddie?"

"Journeyman Brudegan to us apprentices, of course. He's choir leader this season. First he thought it was me pulling a stunt, 'cause I sing high treble. So he stood right beside me. I didn't know what was up, a'course. Then he went on to Feldon and Bonz, and that's when I could hear what was happening." The boy had so engaging a grin that Menolly found herself smiling back. "Shells, but Bruddie jumped about. He couldn't trace the sound. Then one of the basses pointed out the window!" The boy chortled, suppressing the sound when it rose above the general level of table noise. "How'd you train 'em to do that, huh? I didn't know you could get fire lizards to sing. Dragon'll hum, but only when it's Hatching time. Can *anyone* teach a fire lizard to sing? And do you really have eleven all your own?"

"I've only got nine—"

"Only nine, she says," and the boy rolled his eyes, encouraging his tablemates to second his envious response. "I'm Piemur," he added as an afterthought of courtesy.

"She shouldn't be here," complained the lad immediately opposite Menolly. He spoke directly to Piemur, as if by ignoring Menolly he could be rude. He was bigger and older looking than Piemur. "She belongs over there with them." And he jerked his head backward, toward the girls at the hearth table.

"Well, she's here now, and fine where she is, Ranly," said Piemur with unexpected aggressiveness. "She couldn't very well change once we were seated, could she? And besides, I heard that she's to be an apprentice, same as us. *Not* one of them."

"Aren't they apprentices?" asked Menolly, inclining her head in the girls' general direction.

"Them?" Piemur's astounded query was as scornful as the look on Ranly's face. "No!" The drawl in his negative put the girls in an inferior category. "They're in the special class with the journeymen, but they're not apprentices. No road!"

"They're a right nuisance," said Ranly with rich contempt.

"Yeah, they are," said Piemur with a reflective sigh, "but if they weren't here, I'd have to sing treble in the plays, and that'd be dire! Hey, Bonz, pass the meat back." Suddenly he let out a startled yip. "Feldon! I asked first. You've no right . . ." A boy had taken the last slice as he handed down the platter.

The other boys shushed Piemur vigorously, darting apprehensive glances toward the right corner.

"But it's not fair. *I* asked," Piemur said, lowering his voice slightly but not his insistence. "And Menolly only had one slice. She should get more than *that!*"

Menolly wasn't certain if Piemur was more outraged on her behalf or his own, but someone nudged her right arm. It was Camo.

"Camo feed pretty Beauty?"

"Not now, Camo. They're not hungry now," Menolly assured him because his thick features registered such anxiety.

"They're not hungry, but she is, Camo," Piemur said, shoving the meat platter at Camo. "More meat, Camo. More meat, please, Camo?"

"More meat please," Camo repeated, jerking his head to his chest; and before Menolly could say anything, he had shuffled off to the corner of the dining hall where sliding shelves brought food directly up from the kitchen.

The boys were sniggering with the success of Piemur's strategem, but they wiped their faces clear of amusement when Camo shuffled back with a well-laden platter.

"Thank you very much, Camo," Menolly said, taking another thick slice. She couldn't fault the boys for their greed. The meat was tasty and tender, quite different from the tough or salted stuff she was used to at Half-Circle Sea Hold.

Another slab was dumped onto her plate.

"You don't eat enough," Piemur said, scowling at her. "Too bad she'll have to sit with the others," he told his tablemates as he passed the platter. "Camo likes her. And her fire lizards."

"Did he really feed them with you?" asked Ranly. He sounded doubtful and envious.

"They don't frighten him," Menolly said, amazed at how fast news of everything spread in this place.

"They wouldn't frighten me," Piemur and Ranly assured her on the same breath.

"Say, you were at Impression at Benden Weyr, weren't you?" asked Piemur, nudging Ranly to be silent. "Did you *see* Lord Jaxom Impress the white dragon? How big is he really? Is he going to live?"

"I was at the Impression . . ."

"Well, don't go off in a trance," said Ranly. "Tell us! All we get is secondhand information. That is, if the masters and journeymen *think* we apprentices ought to know." He sounded sour and disgusted.

"Oh, shell it, Ranly," Piemur suggested. "So what happened, Menolly?"

"I was in the tiers, and Lord Jaxom was sitting below me with an older man and another boy . . ."

"That'd be Lord Warder Lytol, who's raised him, and the boy was probably Felessan. He's the son of the Weyrleader and Lessa."

"I know that, Piemur. Go on, Menolly."

"Well, all the other dragon eggs had hatched, and there was just the little one left. Jaxom suddenly got up and ran along the edge of the tier, shouting for help. Then he jumped onto the Hatching Ground and started kicking the egg and slashing at the thick membrane inside. The next thing, the little white dragon had fallen out and . . ."

"Impression!" Piemur finished for her, bringing his hands together. "Just like I told you, Ranly, you simply have to be in the right place at the right time. Luck, that's all it is. Luck!" Piemur seemed to be pressing an old argument with his friend. "Some people got a lot of luck; some don't." He turned back to Menolly. "I heard you were daughter of the Sea Holder at Half-Circle."

"I'm in the Harper Hall now, aren't I?"

Piemur stretched out his hands as if that should end the discussion.

Menolly turned back to her dinner. Just as she finished mopping the last of the juices on her plate with bread, the shimmering sound of a gong brought instant silence to the hall. A single bench scraped across the stone floor as a journeyman rose from the top oval table at the far end of the hall.

"Afternoon assignments are: by the sections; apprentice hall, 10; yard, 9; Hold, 8; and no sweeping behind the doors this time or you'll do an extra half-day. Section 7, barns; 6, 5 and 4, fields; 3 is assigned to the Hold and 2 and 1 to the cothalls. Those who reported sick this morning are to attend Master Oldive. Players are not to be late this evening, and the call is for the twentieth hour."

The man sat down to the accompaniment of exaggerated sighs of relief, groans of complaint and mumbles.

Piemur was not pleased. "The yard again!" Then he turned to Menolly. "Anyone mention a section number to you?"

"No," Menolly replied, although Silvina had mentioned the term. "Not yet," she added as she caught Ranly's black stare.

"You have all the luck."

The gong broke through the rumble of reaction, and the bench under Menolly began to move out from under her. Everyone was rising, so Menolly had to rise, too. But she stood in place as the others swarmed by, milling to pass through the main entrance, laughing, shoving, complaining. Two boys started gathering plates and mugs, and Menolly, at a loss, reached for a plate to have it snatched out of her hand by an indignant lad.

"Hey, you're not in my section, " he said in an accusing tone, tinged with surprise, and went about his task.

Menolly jumped at a light touch on her shoulder, stared and then apologized to the man who had come up beside her.

"You are Menolly?" he asked, a hint of displeasure in his tone. He had such a high-bridged nose that he seemed to have difficulty focusing beyond it. His face was lined with dissatisfaction, and a sallow complexion set off by graying locks tinged with yellow did nothing to alter the general impression he gave of supercilious discontent.

"Yes, sir, I'm Menolly."

"I am Master Morshal, Craftmaster in Musical Theory and Composition. Come, girl, one can't hear oneself think in this uproar," and he took her by the arm and began to lead her from the hall, the throng of boys parting before him, as if they felt his presence and wished to avoid any encounter. "The Masterharper wants my opinion on your knowledge of musical theory."

Menolly was given to understand by the tone of his voice that the Masterharper relied on Master Morshal's opinion in this and other far more important matters.

And she also gathered the distinct impression that Morshal didn't expect her to know very much.

Menolly was sorry she had eaten so heartily because the food was beginning to weigh uneasily in her stomach. Morshal was obviously already predisposed against her.

"Pssst! Menolly!" A hoarse whisper attracted her attention to one side. Piemur ducked out from behind a taller boy, jerked his thumb upward in an easily interpreted gesture of encouragement. He rolled his eyes at the oblivious Morshal, grinned impudently and then popped out of sight in his group.

But the gesture heartened her. Funny-looking kid, Piemur was, with his tangle of tight black curls, missing half a front tooth and by far the smallest of the apprentice lot. How kind of him to reassure her.

When Menolly realized that Master Morshal must be taking her to the archroom, she sent a mental command to the fire lizards to stay quiet or go find a sunny roof until she called them again. There wasn't so much as a rustle or a chirp when she and Morshal entered. With a resigned attitude, he seated himself on the only backed chair at the sandtable. As he didn't indicate that she could seat herself, she remained standing.

"Now, recite for me the notes in a C major chord," he said.

She did so. He regarded her steadily for a moment, and blinked.

"What notes would comprise a major fifth in C?"

When she had answered that, he began to fire questions at her, irritable if she paused, however briefly, to reply, but Petiron had drilled her too often the same way. Morshal's bored expression was disconcerting but, as his queries became more and more complex, she suddenly realized that he was taking examples from various traditional Sagas and Ballads. Once he mentioned the signature and which chord, it was simple enough for her to visualize the record hide and recite from memory.

Suddenly he grunted and then murmured in his throat. Abruptly he asked her if she'd been taught the drum.

When she admitted some knowledge, he asked tedious questions about basic beats in each time factor. How would she vary the beat? Now, as to finger positions on a tenor pipe, what closures did one make for a chord in F? He took her through scales again. She could have demonstrated more quickly, but he gave her no chance to suggest it.

"Stand still, girl," he said testily as she shifted her throbbing feet. "Shoulders back, feet together, girl, head up." He heard a soft twitter, but as he'd been glaring at Menolly, it was obvious she hadn't opened her lips. He glanced about, to seek the source, as Menolly silently reassured Beauty and urged silence. "Don't slouch. What was my question?"

She told him, and he continued the barrage. The more she answered, the more he asked. Her feet were aching so that she had to ask permission to sit, if only briefly. But, to her amazement, before she could, Morshal abruptly stabbed a finger at the stool next to him. She hesitated, not quite believing the gesture.

"Sit! sit! sit!" he said in an excess of irritation at her delay. "Now, let's see if you know anything about writing down what you've been repeating so glibly."

So she'd been answering correctly, and he was annoyed because she knew so much. Her flagging spirits lifted, and as Master Morshal dictated musical notations, her fingers drove the pointer quickly over the sands. In her mind, a different, kinder voice dictated; and the exercise became a game, rather than an examination by a prejudiced judge.

"Well, move back so I can see what you've written." Morshal's testy voice recalled her to the present.

He peered at her inscriptions, pursed his lips, humphed and sat back. He gestured peremptorily for her to smooth the sand surface and rapidly gave her another set of chords. They included some difficult modulations and time values, but after the first two, she recognized the "Riddle Song" and was very glad Petiron had made her learn the haunting tune.

"That's enough of that," Master Morshal said, drawing his overtunic about him with quick, angry motions. "Now, have you an instrument?"

"Yes, sir."

"Then get it and that third score from the top shelf. Over there. Be quick about it."

Menolly hissed to herself as she stepped on her throbbing feet. Sitting had not relieved the swelling, and her feet felt thick at the ankles and stiff.

"Hurry up, girl. Don't waste my time."

Beauty gave a soft hiss, too, from her perch on the top shelf, unlidding her eyes, and from the rustling sounds in the same general area, Menolly knew the other fire lizards had roused. With her back to Master Morshal, she gestured to Beauty to close her eyes and be quiet. She cringed at the thought of Master Morshal's probable reaction to fire lizards.

"I said to hurry, girl."

She shuffled to the place where she had laid the gitar and hurried back with instrument and music. The Master took the hides, his lips twitching with annoyance as he turned the thick leaves. This was new copying, Menolly saw, for the hide was almost white and the notes clear and easily read. The hide edges were neatly trimmed, too, the lines going from margin to margin, to be sure, but no notes lost in decayed edges.

"There! Play me that!" The music was slid across the sandtable with—Menolly thought, somewhat shocked—complete disregard for the value of the work.

By some freak of chance, Master Morshal had chosen the "Ballad of Moreta's Ride." She'd never manage the verse chords as written, and he'd fault her if she couldn't.

"Sir, my . . . " she began, holding out her left hand.

"I want no excuses. Either you can play it as written or I assume that you are unable to perform a traditional work to a creditable standard."

Menolly ran her fingers across the strings to see if the tuning had held.

"Come, come. If you can read written scores, you can play them."

That was assuming a lot, Menolly thought to herself. But she struck the opening chords and, mindful that he was undoubtedly waiting for her to falter, she played the so well-known Ballad according to the score before her, rather than by rote. There were variations in the chords: two of which were easily managed, but she flubbed the fourth and fifth because her scarred hand would not stretch.

"I see, I see," he said, waving her to stop, but he looked oddly pleased. "You cannot play accurately at tempo. Very well, that is all. You are dismissed."

"I beg your pardon, Master Morshal . . ." Menolly began, again extending her hand as explanation.

"You what?" He glared at her, his eyes wide with incredulity that she seemed to be defying him. "Out! I just dismissed you! What is the world coming to when *girls* presume to be harpers and pretend to compose music! Out! Great shells and stars!" His voice changed from scold to panic. "What's that? What are they? Who let them in here?"

Already making her way down the steps, Menolly lost her anger with him at the fright in his voice. His anger had roused her friends, and since she was apparently in danger, they had rushed to protect her, by squeaking and diving at him. She laughed as she heard the slamming of a heavy door, and as instantly regretted the scene. Master Morshal would be against her, and that would not make her life easy in the Harper Hall. "Nothing to fear from harpers?" Was that what T'gellan had said last night? Maybe not *fear,* but certainly she was going to have to be cautious with them. Perhaps she ought not to have been so knowledgeable about music; that had irritated him. But wasn't that knowledge what he was testing? Once again, she wondered if there really was a place for her here? *Presume to be a harper?* No, she hadn't, and it was up to Master Robinton, wasn't it? Were Master Morshal and Master Domick part of the conventional procedures Master Robinton had mentioned? Even if she needn't have much to do with them, she sensed their antagonism and dislike.

She sighed and turned on the landing for the second flight and stopped. Piemur was in the hall, motionless, his eyes enormous as he followed the excited flitting of the fire lizards. Lazy and Uncle had subsided to the banister.

"I'm not seeing things?" he asked her, watching Lazy and Uncle with apprehensive gaze. From the hand held rigid at his side, the forefinger indicated the two fire lizards.

"No, you're not. The brown one is Lazy, and the blue is Uncle."

His eyes followed the flight of the others a moment longer, trying to count. Then they popped out further as Beauty landed daintily on Menolly's shoulder, in her usual position.

"This is Beauty, the queen."

"Yes, she is, isn't she?" Piemur kept staring as Menolly descended to the floor level.

Beauty stretched her neck, her eyes whirling gently as she returned his look. Suddenly she blinked her eyes, and so did Piemur, which made Menolly giggle.

"No wonder Camo was cracking his shell over her." Then Piemur shook himself, all over, like a fire lizard shedding seawater. "I was sent to bring you to Master Shonagar."

"Who's he?" asked Menolly, weary enough from the session with Master Morshal.

"Old Marshface give you a hard time? Don't worry about it. You'll like Master Shonagar; he's my Master, he's the Voice Master. He's the best." Piemur's face lit up with real enthusiasm. "And *he* said that if you can sing half as well as your fire lizards do, you're an assss . . . atest . . .?"

"Asset?" It amused Menolly to be so considered by anyone.

"That's the word. And he said that it didn't really matter if you croaked like a watchwher, so long as you could get the fire lizards to sing. Do you think she likes me?" he added, for he hadn't stopped staring at Beauty. Nor had he moved.

"Why not?"

"She keeps staring at me so, and her eyes are whirling." He gestured absently with one hand.

"You're staring at her."

Piemur blinked again and looked at Menolly, smiling shyly and giggling a bit self-consciously. "Yeah, I was, wasn't I? Sorry about that, Beauty. I know it's rude, but I've always wanted to see a fire lizard! Hey, Menolly, c'mon," and now Piemur moved off at a half-run, gesturing urgently for Menolly to follow him across the courtyard. "Master Shonagar's waiting, and I know you're new here, but you don't ever keep a master waiting. And say, can you keep them from following us, 'cause they might sing, and Master Shonagar did say it was you he wanted to hear sing today, not them again."

"They'll be quiet if I ask them to."

"Ranly, he sat across the table from you, he's from Crom and he's so smart, he says they only mimic."

"Oh no, they don't."

"Glad to hear that, because I told him they're just as smart as dragons, and he wouldn't believe me." Piemur had been leading her toward the big hall where the chorus had been practicing that morning. "Hurry up, Menolly. Masters hate to be kept waiting, and I've been gone awhile tracking you down."

"I can't walk fast," Menolly said, gritting her teeth at the pain of each step.

"You sure are walking funny. What's the matter with your feet?"

Menolly wondered that he hadn't heard that tidbit of news. "I got caught away from the cave just at Threadfall. I had to run for safety."

Piemur's eyes threatened to bulge out of their sockets. "You ran?" His voice squeaked. "Ahead of Thread?"

"I ran my shoes off my feet and the skin as well."

Menolly had no chance to speak further because Piemur had brought her to the hall door. Before she could adjust her eyes to the darkness within the huge room, she was told not to gawk but come forward at a proper pace, he detested dawdling.

"With respect, sir, Menolly's feet were injured out-running Thread," said Piemur, just as if he'd always been in possession of this truth. "She's not the dawdling kind."

Now Menolly could see the barrel-shaped figure seated at the massive sandtable opposite the entrance.

"Proceed at your own pace then, for surely a girl who outruns Thread has learned not to dawdle." The voice flowed out of the darkness, rich, round, with the r's rolled and the vowel sounds pure and ringing.

The other fire lizards swooped in through the open door, and the Master's eyes widened slightly. He regarded Menolly in mock surprise.

"Piemur!" The single word stopped the boy in his tracks, and the volume, which startled Menolly, caused Piemur to flick her a grin. "Did you not convey my message accurately? The creatures were *not* to come."

"They follow her everywhere, Master Shonagar, only she says they'll be quiet if she tells them to."

Master Shonagar turned his heavy head to regard Menolly with hooded eyes.

"So tell them!"

Menolly detached Beauty from her shoulder and ordered them all to perch themselves quietly. And not to make a single sound until she said they could.

"Well," remarked Master Shonagar, turning his head slightly to observe the obedience of the fire lizards. "That is a welcome sight, surrounded as I generally am by mass disobedience." He glared narrow-eyed at Piemur, who had had the temerity to giggle, and, at Master Shonagar's stare, tried to assume a sober expression. "I've had enough of your bold face, Piemur, and your dilatory manner. Take them away!"

"Yes, sir," said Piemur cheerfully, and twisting about on his heels, he marched himself smartly to the door, pausing to give Menolly an encouraging wave as he skipped down the steps.

"Rascal," said the Master in a mock growl as he flicked his fingers at Menolly to take the stool opposite him. "I'm given to believe that Petiron ended his days as Harper at your Hold, Menolly."

She nodded, tacitly reassured by his unexpected willingness to address her by name.

"And he taught you to play instruments and to understand musical theory?"

Menolly nodded again.

"In which Masters Domick and Morshal have examined you today." Some dryness in his tone alerted her, and she regarded him more warily as he tilted his heavy head sideways on his massive shoulders. "And did Petiron," and now the bass voice rolled with a hint of coming displeasure, so that Menolly wondered if her original assessment of this man was wrong and he was just as prejudiced as cynical Domick and soured Morshal, "did he have the audacity to teach you how to use your voice?"

"No, sir. At least, I don't think he did. We . . . we just sang together."

"Ha!" And the huge hand of Master Shonagar came down so forcefully on the sand table that the drier portions jumped in their frames. "You just sang together. As you sang together with those fire lizards of yours?"

Her friends chirped inquiringly.

"Silence!" he cried, with another sand-displacing thump on the table.

Somewhat to Menolly's surprise, because Master Shonagar had startled her again, the fire lizards flipped their wings to their backs and settled down.

"Well?"

"Did I just sing with them? Yes, I did."

"As you used to sing with Petiron?"

"Well, I used to sing descant to Petiron's melody, and the fire lizards usually do the descant now."

"That was not precisely what I meant. Now, I wish you just to sing for me."

"What, sir?" she asked, reaching for the gitar slung across her back.

"No, not with that," and he waved at her impatiently. "Sing, not concertize. The voice only is important now, not how you mask vocal inadequacies with pleasant strumming and clever harmony. I want to hear the voice. . . . It is the voice we communicate with, the voice which utters the words we seek to impress on men's minds, the voice which evokes emotional response; tears, laughter, sense. Your voice is the most important, most complex, most amazing instrument of all. And if you cannot use that voice properly, effectively, you might just as well go back to whatever insignificant hold you came from."

Menolly had been so fascinated by the richness and variety of the Master's tones that she didn't really pay heed to the content.

"Well?" he demanded.

She blinked at him, drawing in her breath, belatedly aware that he was waiting for her to sing.

"No, not like that! Dolt! You breathe from here," and his fingers spread across his barrel-width midsection, pressing in so that the sound from his mouth reflected that pressure. "Through the nose, so . . ." and he inhaled, his massive chest barely rising as it was filled, "down the windpipe," and he spoke on a single musical note, "to the belly," and the voice dropped an octave. "You breathe from your belly . . . if you breathe properly."

She took the breath as suggested and then expelled it because she didn't know what to sing with all that breath.

"For the sake of the Hold that protects us," and he raised his eyes and hands aloft as if he could grasp patience from thin air, "the girl simply sits there. Sing, Menolly, sing!"

Menolly was quite willing to, but he had so much to say before she could start or think of what to sing.

She took another quick breath, felt uncomfortable seated, and without asking, stood and launched into the same song that the apprentices had been singing that morning. She had a brief notion of showing him that he wasn't the only one who could fill the hall with resounding tones, but some fragment of advice from Petiron came to mind, and she concentrated on singing intensely, rather than loudly.

He just looked at her.

She held the last note, letting it die away as if the singer were moving off, and then she sank down onto the stool. She was trembling, and now that she'd stopped singing, her feet began to throb in a dull beat.

Master Shonagar only sat there, great folds of chin billowing down his chest. Without lifting his hand, he tilted his body backward and stared at her from under his fleshy and black-haired brows.

"And you say that Petiron never taught you to use your voice?"

"Not the way you did," and Menolly pressed her hands demonstratively against her flat belly. "He told me always to sing with my gut and heart. I can sing louder," she added, wondering if that's why Shonagar was frowning.

He waggled his fingers. "Any idiot can bellow. Camo can bellow. But he *can't* sing."

"Petiron used to say, 'If you sing loud, they only hear noise, not sound or song.'"

"Ha! He told you that? My words! My words exactly. So he did listen to me, after all." The last was delivered in an undertone to himself. "Petiron was wise enough to know his limitations."

Silently Menolly bridled at the aspersion. From the window ledge, Beauty hissed, and Rocky and Diver echoed her sentiment. Master Shonagar raised his head and regarded them in mild perplexity.

"So?" and he fixed his deep eyes on her. "What the mistress feels the pretty creatures echo? And you loved Petiron and will hear no ill-word against him?" He leaned forward slightly, wagging a forefinger at her. "Know this, Menolly who runs, we all have limitations, and wise is he who recognizes them. I meant," and he settled back into his chair, "no disrespect for the departed Petiron. For me that was praise." He tilted his head again. "For you, the best thing possible; for Petiron had sense enough not to meddle but to wait until I could attend to your vocal education. Temper and refine what is natural—and produce . . ." now Master Shonagar's left eyebrow was jerking up and down, the one arching while the other remained unmoved, so that Menolly was fascinated by his control, ". . . produce a well-placed, proper singing voice." The Master exhaled hugely.

Then Menolly took in the sense of what he'd been saying, no longer distracted by his facial contortions.

"You mean, I *can* sing?"

"Any idiot on Pern can sing," the Master said disparagingly. "No more talk. I'm weary." He began brushing her away from him. "Take those other sweet-throated freaks along with you, too. I've had enough of their baleful looks and assorted noises."

"I'll see that they stay . . ."

"Stay away? No." Shonagar's eyebrows rose sharply. "Bring them. They learn from example, one assumes. So you will set them a good example." A distant look clouded his face, and then a slow smile tugged up the corners of his mouth. "Go, Menolly. Go now. All this has wearied me beyond belief."

With that, he leaned his elbow on the sandtable so heavily that the opposite end left the floor. He cushioned his head against his fist and, while Menolly watched bemused, began to snore. Although she didn't think any human could fall asleep so quickly, she obeyed the implicit dismissal and, beckoning to her fire lizards, quietly departed.

Chapter 4

Harper, your song has a sorrowful sound
Though the tune was written as gay.
Your voice is sad and your hands are slow,
And your eye meeting mine turns away.

Menolly would have liked to find someplace to curl up and sleep herself, but Beauty began to creel softly. Silvina had said something about saving scraps, so Menolly crossed the courtyard to the kitchen door. She couldn't see either Silvina or Camo with all the coming and going. Then she saw the half-wit staggering in from the storage rooms, his arms clasping a great round yellow cheese. He saw her, grinned and deposited the cheese on the only clear space at one of the worktables.

"Camo feed pretty ones? Camo feed?"

"Camo, get on with that cheese, there's a good fellow," said the woman Menolly remembered as Abuna.

"Camo must feed." And the man had grabbed up a bowl, unceremoniously dumping its contents onto the table, and marched back to the storeroom.

"Camo! Come back and take care of this cheese!"

Menolly was sorry she'd come to the kitchen, but Abuna saw her.

"So you're the problem with him. Oh, all right. He'll be no use till he's helped you feed those creatures! But keep them out of my kitchen!"

"Yes, Abuna. I'm sorry to bother you—"

"And so you should be in the middle of getting ready the supper but . . ."

"Camo fed pretty ones? Camo feed pretty ones?" He was back trailing gobbets of meat from an overfull bowl.

"Not in my kitchen, Camo. Outside with you. Outside now. And send him back in when they've et, will you, girl? One thing he can do is get the cheese ready!"

Menolly assured Abuna, and smiling at Camo, drew him out of the kitchen and up the steps. Beauty and the others immediately converged on them. The two Aunties and Uncle again perched on convenient portions of Camo. The man's face was ecstatic, and he stood rigid, as if the slightest motion on his part would discourage his unusual guests, as the other fire lizards swooped to snatch food or clung to him long enough to eat directly from the bowl. Beauty, Rocky and Diver fed by preference from Menolly's hands, but the bowl was soon empty.

"Camo get more? Camo get more?"

Menolly caught him, forcing him to look at her. "No, Camo. They've had enough. No more, Camo. Now you must work on the cheese."

"Pretty ones leave?" Camo's face became a mask of tragedy as he watched one after the other of the fire lizards circle lazily up to the gable points of the hall. "Pretty ones leave?"

"They're going to sleep in the sun now, Camo. They're not hungry anymore. You go back to the cheese now." She gave him a gentle shove toward the kitchen. He went, bowl in both hands, staring back over his shoulder at the fire lizards so intently that this time he did bang right into the doorframe, corrected his direction without ever taking his eyes from the fire lizards, and disappeared into the kitchen.

"Could I help feed them? Maybe? Once?" asked a wistful voice at her elbow. Startled, she whirled to see Piemur, fringe of hair damp about his face and a line of rearranged dirt on each side of his neck up to his ears.

Other lads and some of the journeymen were beginning

to drift across the courtyard to the Hall. "Rascal," Master Shonagar had called Piemur, and Menolly agreed, for a gleam lurked in Piemur's eyes for all his plaintive voice.

"Got a bet on with Ranly?"

"Bet on?" Piemur gave her a searching look. Then he chuckled. "A small guy like me, Menolly, has got to stay a jump ahead of the big ones, like Ranly, or they put on me in the dorm at night."

"So what did you put up with Ranly?"

"That you'd let me feed the fire lizards because they like me already. They do, don't they?"

"You really are a rascal, aren't you?"

Piemur's grin became a calculated grimace, and he shrugged admission of the charge.

"I've already got Camo falling over himself to feed . . ."

". . . 'Pretty Beauty,'" and Piemur mimicked the older man's thick voice perfectly, "'Feed pretty Beauty . . .' Oh, don't worry Menolly, Camo and me are friends. He won't object to me helping, too."

As if that had settled the matter, Piemur grabbed Menolly's hand to pull her up the steps. "Hey, you don't want to be late for the table again," he said, leading her toward the dining hall.

"Menolly!"

The two halted at the sound of the Harper's voice and turned to see him descending the stairs from the upper level.

"How's the day gone for you, Menolly? You've seen Domick, Morshal and Shonagar, have you? I must make you known to Sebell, too, very soon. Before the eggs hatch!" The Masterharper grinned, much as Piemur had just done, in anticipation of the event. "And this scamp has attached himself to you, has he? Well, maybe you can keep him out of trouble for awhile. Ah, Brudegan, a word with you before supper."

"Quick . . ." Piemur had her by the arm and was hurrying her into the dining hall so that betwixt the Harper and Piemur, it looked to Menolly as if neither wished her to meet Journeyman Brudegan, whose practice her fire lizards had interrupted. "Sebell's a real clever fellow," Piemur added in such a casual fashion that Menolly berated herself for imagining things. "He's to get the other egg." Piemur whistled in his teeth. "You think you got troubles? Sebell's only just walked the tables—"

"Walked the tables?" Menolly was startled.

"That's what we say when you've been promoted a grade. It happens at supper. If you're an apprentice, a journeyman stands by your seat and then walks you to your new place." He was pointing from the long tables to the oval ones at the far end of the dining hall. "And a master escorts a journeyman from them to the round table. But it'll be a long time before any of that happens to me," he said, sighing. "If it ever does."

"Why? Don't all apprentices become journeymen?"

"No," replied the boy with a grimace. "Some get sent home as useless. Some get dull jobs around here, helping journeymen or masters, or sent to a smaller crafthall elsewhere."

Maybe that was what the Masterharper had in mind for her, helping a journeyman or a master in some hold or crafthall. That made good sense, at least, but Menolly sighed. A sigh echoed by Piemur.

"How long have you been here?" Menolly asked. He looked a poorly grown nine or ten Turns, the age at which boys were customarily apprenticed, but he sounded as if he'd been in the Hall a long time.

"Two Turns I've been apprenticed," he answered with a grin. "I got taken in early on account of my voice." He said that without the least bit of conceit. "Now, look, you go on over there where the girls sit. And don't worry. You rank 'em."

Without explaining that, he darted in between the first and second tables. Menolly tried not to hobble as she moved to the benches he had indicated, keeping her shoulders back, her head up, and walking slowly so as to disguise her pain-footed gait. She was aware of, and tried to ignore, the overt and covert glances of the boys already in position at the tables. She'd better let Piemur help her feed the fire lizards: keeping on his good side might be as important as staying in the Harper's good graces.

The seats evidently reserved for the girls were marked by flaps of cushion on the hard wood. She took the end position, away from the fiercest heat of the hearth fire and stood politely waiting.

The girls entered the dining hall together. Together in more than one sense, for all regarded her steadily as they crossed to the table. Their unity was also maintained in their blank expressions. Menolly swallowed against the dryness in her throat, glanced around her, anywhere but at the fast approaching girls. She caught Piemur's eyes, saw him grin impishly, and she had to smile back.

"You're Menolly?" asked a quiet voice. The girls were ranged beyond their spokesman, again in a line that betokened unity.

"She couldn't be anyone else, could she?" asked the dark girl just behind her.

"My name is Pona, my grandfather is Lord Holder of Boll." She held out her right hand, palm up, and Menolly, who had never had an opportunity to make the gesture of formal greeting, covered it with hers.

"I am Menolly," and, remembering Piemur's comment about rank, she added, "my father is Yanus, Sea Holder of Half-Circle Sea Hold."

There was a startled murmur of surprise from the others.

"She ranks us," said someone, rebellious and astonished.

"There's rank in the Harper Hall?" asked Menolly, disturbed and wondering what other elements of courtesy she might unwittingly have neglected. Hadn't Petiron always told her that the Harper Craft, in particular, laid stress on skill and musical achievement rather than natal rank? But Piemur had said, "You rank 'em."

"Half-Circle is not the oldest seahold. Tillek is," said the dark-complexioned girl, rather crossly.

"Menolly is daughter, not niece," said the girl who had mentioned outranking. She now extended her hand, less grudgingly, Menolly thought. "My father is Weaver Craftmaster Timareen of Telgar Hold. My name is Audiva."

The dark-complexioned girl was about to name herself, her hand extended, when a sudden shuffling of feet alerted them all, and they took their places at the bench as everyone in the hall stood straight and looked forward. Menolly was then facing a tall boy whose slightly protuberant eyes were bulging with interest on the little scene he had just witnessed. Looking over his left shoulder and through a gap, she saw Piemur, rolling his eyes as far to his right as possible. Menolly tried peering in the same direction and decided it must be the Harper's table that Piemur watched. Then everyone was jumping over the benches to get seated, and she hastened to do the same.

Heavy pitchers of a thick, meaty, hot soup were passed, and trays of the yellow cheese, which Camo must eventually have taken care of, as well as baskets of crusty bread. Evidently meals were reversed here in the Harper Craft Hall, with the heaviest meal in the middle of the day. Menolly ate hungrily and quickly until she realized that the girls were all taking half-spoonsful and breaking their bread and cheese into dainty bite-sized portions. Pona and Audiva watched her surreptitiously, and one of the other girls tittered. So, thought Menolly grimly, her table manners differed from theirs? Well, to change would mean admitting that hers were faulty. She did slow down, but she continued to eat heartily, making no bones about asking for more while the girls were still but halfway through their first serving.

"I understand that you were privileged to attend the latest Hatching at Benden Weyr," Pona said to Menolly with all the air of one conferring a favor by such conversation.

"Yes, I was there." *Privileged?* Yes, she supposed it would be considered a privilege.

"I don't suppose you can remember who made Impression?" Pona was vitally interested.

"Some of them, yes. Talina of Ruatha Hold is the new queen's weyrwoman . . ."

"You're certain?"

Menolly glanced beyond her to Audiva and saw merriment in her eyes.

"Yes, I'm certain."

"Too bad those three candidates from your grandfather's Hold didn't Impress, Pona. There'll be other times," said Audiva.

"Who else do you remember?"

"A lad from Master Nicat's Craft Hall Impressed a brown . . ." For some reason that seemed to please Pona. "Master Nicat also received two of the fire lizards' eggs."

Pona turned her head to stare haughtily at Menolly. "How ever did it come about that *you* . . ." and Menolly was made intensely aware of her unworthiness ". . . have nine fire lizards?"

"She was in the right place at the right time, Pona," said Audiva. "Luck doesn't recognize rank and privilege. And it's thanks to Menolly that there were fire lizard eggs for Master Robinton and Master Nicat."

"How do you know that?" Pona sounded surprised but her tone lost its affectedness.

"Oh, I had a word or two with Talmor while you were busy trying to make up to Jessuan and Benis."

"I never . . ." Pona was evidently as quick to take offense as give it, but she lowered her tone at Audiva's warning hiss.

"Don't worry, Pona. Just so long as Dunca doesn't *catch* you flipping your skirts at a son of the Hold, I'll hold my peace."

Whether Audiva was subtly deflecting Pona from pestering Menolly with snide questions or not, Menolly didn't know, but the girl from Boll ignored her for the rest of the meal. As Menolly had been taught that it was impolite to talk through or around someone, she couldn't converse with the apparently friendly Audiva, and the boy beside her was talking to his mates, his back to her.

"My uncle of Tillek says that fire lizards are going to be

nothing more than pets, and I thought pets weren't allowed in the cottages . . ." said the dark girl, her mouth setting primly, as she cast a sideways look toward Menolly.

"The Masterharper doesn't rate fire lizards as pets, Briala," said Audiva in her droll way, and she winked at Menolly over Pona's head. "Of course, you've only got one at Tillek Hold."

"Well, my uncle says the Weyrmen are spending too much time on these creatures when they ought to get down to basic problems and go after Thread on the Red Star. That's the only way to stop this dreadful menace."

"What are the dragonriders supposed to do?" asked Audiva scornfully. "Even you should know that dragons can't go *between* blind."

"They ought to just flame the Red Star clean of Thread, that's what."

"Could they really?" asked the girl beyond Briala, her eyes round with amazement and a sort of hopeful horror.

"Oh, don't be ridiculous, Amania," said Audiva in disgust. "No one's ever been to the Red Star."

"They could *try* to get there," replied Pona. "That's what my grandfather says."

"Who's to say the first dragonmen didn't try?" asked Audiva.

"Then why isn't there a Record of the attempt?" demanded Pona with haughty condescension.

"They'd certainly have written a song about it if they had," said Briala, pleased to see Audiva confounded.

"Well, the Red Star is not our problem," said Audiva.

"Learning songs is." Briala's voice had a wailing edge to it. "And *when* are we going to have a chance to learn that music Talmor set us today? We've got rehearsal tonight, and it'll go on and on because those boys are always—"

"The boys? Just like you to blame it on the boys, Briala," said Audiva. "You had plenty of time this afternoon to practice your lessons, same as the rest of us."

"I had to wash my hair, and Dunca had to let out the seams of my red gown. . . ."

"If you'd stop. . . . Oh, not redfruit again?" Pona sounded aggrieved, but Menolly eyed the basket of delicacies with surprised delight.

Pona might affect indifference, but she was quick to snatch the curiously shaped fruit from the basket when it was passed to her. Menolly took hers and ate it quickly, getting as much of the sweet, tangy juice as possible. She wished she had the courage to lick her fingers the way the boys were doing. But the girls were so stuffy and mannered, she knew they'd stare if she did.

Suddenly the demands of the day, the excitements and tensions, sapped the last of Menolly's energy. She found it almost unbearable to have to sit at the table amid so many unknown people, unable to guess what more might be asked of her before she could seek the quiet and solitude of her bed. She worried about her fire lizards, and then tried not to, for fear they would seek her out. She was conscious of her throbbing feet; her hand ached, and the scar begged to be scratched. She shifted on the bench, wondering why they were held here at table. Restlessly she craned her neck to peer around at the Harper's table. She couldn't see Master Robinton but the others were laughing, obviously enjoying an aftermeal conversation. Was that why everyone was being held so long? Until the masters had stopped talking?

She longed for the peace of her cave near the Dragon Stones. Even for the little cubicle in her father's Sea Hold. She'd usually been able to slip away to it without accounting to anyone for her disappearance. At least once the day's work was done. And somehow, she'd never thought of the Harper Craft Hall being so . . . so populated, with so much to be done and doing, and all the masters and Silvina and. . . .

She was caught unawares and had to struggle to her feet as the others rose more gracefully to theirs. She was so relieved to be able to go that at first she didn't realize no one was leaving the benches but masters and journeymen. Pona's hiss caught her attention before she'd moved more than a few strides. Embarrassed, she stood with all the girls glaring at her as if she had committed a far more heinous crime than moving out of turn. She edged back toward her vacated place. Then, as soon as the apprentices and the girls began to saunter out of the dining hall, she sat down again. She did not want to be among people, especially all these strange people who had odd notions and different manners, and seemingly, no sympathy for the newcomer. The Weyr had been as big and well-populated, but she had felt at home there, with friendly glances and uncritical, smiling faces.

"Your feet hurting again?" It was Piemur asking, his brows contorted in a worried scowl.

Menolly bit her lip.

"I guess I'm just suddenly very tired," she said.

He wrinkled his nose drolly and then twitched it to one side. "I'm not surprised, your first day here and all, and having the masters giving you a poke and prod. Look, you can lean on my shoulder across to Dunca's. I can still get back in time for rehearsal . . ."

"Rehearsal? Do I have to be somewhere else now?" Menolly fought an almost overwhelming desire to weep.

"Shouldn't think so, your first day here. Unless Master Shonagar said something? No? Well, they can hardly have sorted out what your standard is, even if you couldn't play note one. And you know, you look ruddy awful. Awful tired, I mean. C'mon, I'll help you."

"But you have a rehearsal . . ."

"Don't you worry your head about me, Menolly." He grinned mischievously. "Sometimes it's an astest . . . asset . . . to be small," and he made a weaving motion with his hand, then squared his shoulders and stood, radiating innocent attention. He was so comic that Menolly giggled.

She rose, excessively grateful to him. He rattled on about the rehearsal for the usual spring affair at Fort Hold. The rehearsal was usually fun because Brudegan was in charge this season. *He* was good at explaining exactly what he wanted you to do, so if you listened sharp, you didn't make mistakes.

The swift spring evening was settling over the complex

of Hold and Hall so there were very few passers-by. Piemur's physical presence and his chatter, blithely ignoring her silence, were more supportive than his bony shoulder, but she couldn't have made the walk without it. Menolly was grateful that she'd only the short flight of steps to go. The fire lizards chirped sympathetically at her from the window ledge outside her fast-shuttered room.

"You're okay now, with them," said Piemur, grinning up at the fire lizards. "I'll dash off. You'll be fine in the morning, Menolly, with a good night's rest under your ear. That's what my foster-mother always told us."

"I'm sure I will, Piemur, and thank you so much . . ."

Her words trailed off because he was dashing and out of earshot. She opened the door, calling tentatively for Dunca, but there was no answer, nor any sign of the plump cotkeeper. Grateful for that unexpected mercy, Menolly began to climb the steep steps, one at a time, pulling herself along by the railing and taking as much pressure off her feet as she could. Halfway up, Beauty appeared, chirruping encouragement. Rocky and Diver joined her on the top step and added their comforting noises.

With a sense of utmost relief, Menolly closed the door behind her. She hobbled to the bed and sank down, fumbling with the ties of the sleeping furs, not really aware of the scratching on the closed shutters until Beauty let out an authoritative squawk. Fortunately, Menolly only had to stretch out her arm to open the shutters. Aunties One and Two fell in, catching themselves by wing just off the floor, scolding her soundly as they flew about the room. Lazy, Brownie and Uncle entered with more dignity and Mimic waddled to the window edge, yawning.

Menolly remembered to rub the salve on her feet, though they were so tender, tears jumped to her eyes. Briefly she wished that Mirrim was there, with her brisk chatter and gentle touch. Feet were indeed very awkward to tend yourself. She rubbed the other stuff into her hand scar, restraining the urge to scratch the itching tissue.

She slipped out of her clothes and under the sleeping furs, only vaguely aware that the fire lizards were making themselves comfortable about her. *Nothing to fear from harpers,* huh? T'gellan's comment mocked her. As she fell deeply asleep, she wondered if envy was akin to fear?

Chapter 5

My nightly craft is winged in white;
A dragon of night-dark sea.
Swiftborn, dreambound and rudderless;
Her captain and crew are me.
I sail a hundred sleeping tides
Where no seaman's ever been
And only my white-winged craft and I
Know the marvels we have seen.

The next day did not start propitiously for Menolly. Her sleep was broken by shrieks: Dunca's, the girls', and the fire lizards'. Dazed, Menolly at first tried to calm the fire lizards swooping about the room, but Dunca, standing in the doorway, would not be quiet; and her terror, whether assumed or real, only stimulated the fire lizards into such aerial acrobatics that Menolly ordered them all out the window.

This only changed the tone of Dunca's screams because the woman was now pointing at Menolly's nudity until she could snatch up the discarded shirt and cover herself.

"And where were you all night?" Dunca demanded in a sobbingly angry voice. "How did you get in? When did you get in?"

"I was here all night. I got in by the front door. You weren't in the cottage." Then, seeing the look of complete disbelief on Dunca's plump face, Menolly added, "I came here directly after supper. Piemur helped me across the court."

"He was at rehearsal. Which was just after supper," said one of the girls crowding in at the door.

"Yes, but he got there out of breath," Audiva said, frowning, "I remember Brudegan rounding him on it."

"You must always inform me when you come in," said Dúnca, by no means pacified.

Menolly hesitated and then nodded her head in acquiescence; it was useless to argue with someone like Dunca, who had obviously made up her mind not to like Menolly and to pick every fault possible.

"When you are washed and decently attired," and the tone of Dunca's voice suggested that she doubted Menolly was capable of either, "you will join us. Come, girls. There is no reason for you to delay your own meal."

As the girls filed obediently past the open doorway, most of the faces reflected Dunca's disapproval. Except Audiva who winked solemnly and then grinned before she schooled her features into a blank expression.

By the time Menolly had attended to her feet, had a quick wash, dressed and found the small room where the other girls were eating, they were almost finished. As one, they stared critically at her before Dunca brusquely motioned her to take the empty seat. And as one, they all watched her so that she felt doubly awkward about the simple acts of chewing and swallowing. The food tasted dry and the klah was cold. She managed to finish what had been set before her and mumbled thanks. She sat there, looking down at her plate, only then noticing the fruit stains on her tunic. So, they had reason to stare. And she had nothing to change into while this top was washed, except her old things from her cave days.

Though she had eaten, she was still conscious of hunger pangs. The fire lizards were waiting to be fed! She doubted that Dunca would supply her need, but her responsibility to her friends gave her the courage to ask.

"May I be excused, please? The fire lizards must be fed. I have to go to Silvina . . ."

"Why would you bother Silvina with such a detail?" demanded Dunca, her eyes popping slightly with indignation. "Don't you realize that she is the headwoman of the entire Harper Craft Hall? The demands on her time are enormous! And if you don't keep those creatures of yours under proper control. . . ."

"You startled them this morning."

"I'm not having that sort of carry-on every morning, frightening my girls with them flying at such dangerous speeds."

Menolly refrained from pointing out that it had been Dunca's screaming that had alarmed the fire lizards.

"If you can't control them. . . . Where are they now?" She looked wildly about her, her eyes bulging with alarm.

"Waiting to be fed."

"Don't get pert with me, girl. You may be the daughter of a Sea Holder, but while you are in the Harper Craft Hall and in my charge, you are to behave yourself. We'll have no ranking here."

Half-torn between laughter and disgust, Menolly rose. "If I may go, please, before the fire lizards come in search of me . . ."

That sufficed. Dunca couldn't get her out of the cot fast enough. Someone sniggered, but when Menolly glanced up she wasn't sure if it had been Audiva or not. It was a small encouragement that someone had recognized Dunca's hypocrisy.

As she stepped out into the crisp morning air, Menolly realized how stuffy the cot had been and glanced over her shoulder. Sure enough, all the shutters, except her own, were closed tight. As she crossed the wide court, she received morning grins and greetings from the farmholders making their way to the fields, from apprentices dashing to their masters. She looked about her for her fire lizards and saw one wheeling down behind the outer wing of the Craft Hall. As she walked under the arch, she saw the others clinging to the kitchen and dining hall ledges. Camo was in the doorway, a great bowl in the crook of his left arm, a hunk of something dangling from his right hand as he tried to entice the fire lizards to him.

She was halfway across the courtyard before she realized that it was much easier to walk on her feet today. However, that was one of the few good things that happened. Camo was chastized by Abuna for trying to coax the fire lizards to eat when he should have been delivering the cereal to the dining hall (for the fire lizards would not eat from his hands until Menolly arrived). Then the fire lizards were frightened away when the apprentices and journeymen came tearing out of the dining hall, filling the courtyard with yells and shrieks and wild antics as they made their way to their morning classes. Menolly looked vainly for Piemur, and then, as abruptly, the courtyard was clear. Except for some older journeymen. One of them paused by her, officiously demanding to know why she was hanging about the yard. When she said that she hadn't been told where to go, he informed her that she obviously should be with the other girls and to get herself there immediately. As he gestured in the general direction of the archroom, Menolly assumed that was where the girls met.

She reached the archway room to find the girls already practicing scales on their gitars with a journeyman, who told her she was late, to get her instrument and see if she could catch up with the others. She mumbled an apology, found her precious gitar, and took a stool near the others. But the chords were basic and even with her injured hand she had no trouble with the drill. Not so the others. Pona seemed unable to bridge strings with forefinger: the joint kept snapping up; and although the journeyman, Talmor, patiently showed her an alternative chording, she couldn't get to it fast enough to keep the rhythm of the exercise. Talmor had great patience, Menolly thought, and idly ran silent fingers down the neck of her gitar, doing his alternative placement. Yes, it was a bit awkward if you were after speed, but not as impossible as Pona was making it out to be.

"Since you are so good at it, Menolly, suppose you demonstrate the exercise. In the time . . . " and Talmor directed the beat.

She caught it with her eyes, keeping her head still, for

Petiron abhorred a musician who had to use unnecessary body motion to keep a rhythm going. She went through the chords on the scale as directed and then saw Audiva regarding her with fierce intent. Pona and the others glowered.

"Now use the regular fingering," Talmor said, coming over to stand by Menolly, his eyes intent on her hands.

Menolly executed the run. He gave a sharp nod of his head, eyed her inscrutably, and then returned to Pona, asking her to try it again, though he outlined a slower time. Pona mastered the run the third time, smiling with relief at her success.

Talmor gave them another set of scales and then brought out a large copy of a piece of occasional music. Menolly was delighted because the score was completely new to her. Petiron had been, as he phrased it, a teaching Harper, not an entertainer, and though she had learned the one or two occasional pieces of music he had in his possession, he had never acquired more. The Sea Holder, Menolly knew, had preferred to sing, not listen; and most occasional music was instrumental. In the bigger Holds, Petiron had told her, the Lord Holders liked music during the dinner hour and at night when they entertained guests in conversation rather than song.

This was not a difficult piece, Menolly realized, scanning it and silently fingering the one or two transitional chords that might be troublesome.

"All right, Audiva, let's see what you can make of it today," Talmor said, smiling at the girl with encouragement.

Audiva gulped, exhibiting a nervousness that puzzled Menolly. As Audiva began to pick out the chords, nodding her head and tapping one foot at a much slower rhythm than the musical notation required, Menolly's perplexity grew. Well, she thought, charitably, maybe Audiva was a new student. If she was, she was far more competent than Briala, who apparently had trouble just reading the music.

Talmor dismissed Briala to the table to copy the score for later practice. Pona was no improvement on the other two. The sly-faced, fair-haired girl played with great banging against the gitar belly, at time, but with many inaccuracies. When it was finally her own turn, Menolly's stomach was roiled by frustrated listening.

"Menolly," said Talmor at the end of a sigh that expressed his own frustration and boredom.

It was such a relief to play the music as it should be that Menolly found herself increasing the time and emphasizing the chords with a variation of her own in the strum.

Talmor just looked at her. Then he blinked and exhaled heavily, pursing his lips together.

"Well, yes. You've seen it before?"

"Oh, no. We had very little occasional music in Half-Circle. This is lovely."

"You played that cold?"

Only then did Menolly realize what she'd done: made the other girls look inadequate. She was aware of their cold, chill silence, their hostile stares. But not to play one's best seemed a dishonesty that she had never practiced and could not. Belatedly she recognized that she could have hedged: with her scarred hand she could have faltered, missed some of the chordings. Yet it had been such a relief, after their limping renditions, to play the music as it was meant to be played.

"I was the last to go," she said in a lame effort to retrieve matters, "I'd more time to study it, and see. . . ." She'd started to say, "see where they went wrong."

"Yes, well, so you did," Talmor said, so hastily that Menolly wondered if he'd also realized what a break she'd made. Then he added in a rush of impatience and irritation. "Who told you to join this class? I'd rather thought . . ." A snigger interrupted his query, and he turned to glare at the girls. "Well?" he asked Menolly.

"A journeyman . . ."

"Who?"

"I don't know. I was in the courtyard, and he asked me why wasn't I in class. Then he told me to come here."

Talmor rubbed the side of his jaw. "Too late now, I suppose, but I'll inquire." He turned to the other girls.

"Let's play it in . . ." The girls were staring pointedly at the doorway, and he looked about. "Yes, Sebell?"

Menolly turned, too, to see the man to whom the other coveted fire lizard egg had gone. Sebell was a slender man, a hand or so taller than herself: a brown man, tanned skin, light brown hair and eyes, dressed in brown with a faded Harper apprentice badge half-hidden in the shoulder fold of his tunic.

"I've been looking for Menolly," he said, gazing steadily at her.

"I thought someone ought to be. She was misdirected here." Talmor sounded irritated, and he gestured sharply for Menolly to go to Sebell.

Menolly slipped from the stool, but she was uncertain what to do about the gitar and glanced questioningly at Sebell.

"You won't need it now," he said so she quietly put it away on the shelf.

She felt the girls staring at her, knew that Talmor was watching and would not continue the lesson until she had gone, so it was with intense relief that she heard the door close behind her and the quiet brown man.

"Where was I supposed to be?" she asked, but he motioned her down the steps.

"You got no message?" His eyes searched her face carefully although his expression gave no hint of his thoughts.

"No."

"You did breakfast at Dunca's?"

"Yes . . ." Menolly couldn't suppress her distaste for that painful meal. Then she caught her breath and stared at Sebell, comprehension awakening. "Oh, she wouldn't have. . . ."

Sebell was nodding, his brown eyes registering an understanding of the matter. "And you wouldn't have known yet to come to me for instructions . . ."

"You . . ." Hadn't Piemur said something about Sebell walking the tables, to become a journeyman? ". . . sir?" she added.

A slow smile spread across the man's round face.

"I suppose I do rate a 'sir' from a mere apprentice, but the Harper is not as strict about such observances as other masters. The tradition here is that the oldest journeyman under the same master is responsible for the newest apprentice. So you are my responsibility. At least while I'm in the Hall and I'm enjoying a respite from my journeyings. I didn't have the chance to meet you yesterday, and this morning . . . you didn't arrive as planned at Master Domick's . . ."

"Oh, no." Menolly swallowed the hard knot of dismay. "Not Master Domick!" Even Piemur was careful not to annoy him. "Was Master Domick very . . . upset?"

"In a manner of speaking, yes. But don't worry, Menolly, I shall use the incident to your advantage. It doesn't do to antagonize Domick unnecessarily."

"Not when he doesn't like me anyhow." Menolly closed her eyes against a vision of Master Domick's cynical face contorted with anger.

"How do you construe that?"

Menolly shrugged. "I had to play for him yesterday, I know he doesn't like me."

"Master Domick doesn't like anyone," replied Sebell with a wry laugh, "including himself. So you're no exception. But, as far as studying with him is concerned . . ."

"I'm to study with him?"

"Don't panic. As a teacher, he's top rank. I know. In some ways I think Master Domick is superior, instrumentally, to the Harper. He doesn't have Master Robinton's flare and vitality, nor his keen perception in matters outside the Craft." Although Sebell was speaking in his customary impersonal way, Menolly sensed his complete loyalty and devotion to the Masterharper. "You," and there was a slight emphasis on the pronoun, "will learn a great deal from Domick. Just don't let his manner fuss you. He's agreed to teach you, and that's quite a concession."

"But I didn't come this morning . . ." The magnitude of that truancy appalled Menolly.

Sebell gave her a quick reassuring grin. "I said that I can turn that to your advantage. Domick doesn't like people to ignore his instructions. It is not *your* worry. Now, come on. Enough of the morning has been lost."

He had directed her up the steps into the Hall, and to her surprise opened the door into the Great Hall. It was twice the size of the dining hall, three times the size of the Great Hall at Half-Circle. Across the far end was fitted a raised and curtained platform that jutted into the floor space. Tables and benches were piled haphazardly against the inner walls and under windows. Immediately to her right were a collection of more comfortable chairs arranged in an informal grouping about a small round table. To this area Sebell motioned her and seated himself opposite her.

"I've some questions to put to you, and I can't explain why I need to have this information. It is Harper business, and if you're told that, you'll be wise to ask no further. I need your help . . ."

"*My* help?"

"Strange as that might seem, yes," and his brown eyes laughed at her. "I need to know how to sail a boat, how to gut a fish, how to act like a seaman . . ."

He was ticking off the points on his fingers, and she stared at his hands.

"With those, no one would ever believe you had sailed . . ."

He examined his hands impersonally. "Why?"

"Seamen's hands get gnarled quickly from popping the joints, rough from salt water and fish oil, much browner than yours from weathering . . ."

"Would anyone but a seaman know that?"

"Well, *I* know it."

"Fair enough. Can you teach me to act, from a distance," and his grin teased her, "like a seaman? Is it hard to learn to sail a boat? Or bait a hook? Or gut a fish?"

Her left palm itched, and so did her curiosity. Harper business? Why would a journeyman harper need to know such things?

"Sailing, baiting, gutting . . . those are a question of practicing . . ."

"Could *you* teach me?"

"With a boat and a place to sail, yes . . . with hook and bait, and a few fish." Then she laughed.

"What's funny?"

"Just that . . . I thought when I came here, that I'd never need to gut a fish again."

Sebell regarded her sardonically for a long moment, a smile playing at the corners of his mouth. "Yes, I can appreciate that, Menolly. I was landbred and thought I'd done with walking about. Just don't be surprised at anything you're asked to do here. The Harper requires us to play many tunes for our Craft . . . not always on gitar or pipe. Now," and he went on more briskly, "I'll arrange for the boat, the water and the fish. But when?" At this requisite, he whistled softly through the slight gap between his two front teeth. "Time will be the problem, for you have lessons, and there are the two eggs . . ." He looked her squarely in the eye then, and grinned. "Speaking of which, have you any idea what color mine might be?"

She smiled back. "I don't think you can really be as sure with fire lizard eggs as you can with the dragon's, but I kept the two largest ones for Master Robinton. One ought to be a queen, and the other should turn out to be a bronze at least."

"A bronze fire lizard?"

The rapt expression on Sebell's face alarmed her. What if both eggs produced browns? Or greens? As if he sensed her apprehension, Sebell smiled.

"I don't really care so long as I have one. The Harper says they can be trained to carry messages. And sing!" He was a great teaser, this Sebell, thought Menolly, for all his quiet manner and solemn expressions, but she felt completely at ease with him. "The Harper says they can get as attached to their friends as dragons do to their riders."

She nodded. "Would you like to meet mine?"

"I would, but not now," he replied, shaking his head ruefully. "I must pick your brains about the seaman's craft. So, tell me how goes a day at a Sea Hold?"

Amused to find herself explaining such a thing in the

Harper Hall, Menolly gave the brown journeyman a drily factual account of the routine that was all she'd known for so many Turns. He was an attentive listener, occasionally repeating cogent points, or asking her to elaborate others. She was giving him a list of the various types of fish that inhabited the oceans of Pern when the tocsin rang again and her explanation was drowned by shouts as apprentices erupted into the courtyard on their way to the dining hall.

"We'll wait until the stampede has settled, Menolly," Sebell said, raising his voice above the commotion outside, "just give me that rundown on deep water fishes again."

When Sebell escorted her to her place, the girls treated her with a stony silence, emphasized by pursed lips, averted eyes and then sniggers to each other. Buoyed by Sebell's reassurances, Menolly ignored them. She concentrated on eating the roast wherry and the crusty brown tubers, bigger than she'd ever seen and so fluffy inside their crust that she ate more of them than bread.

Since the girls were so pointedly snubbing her, Menolly looked about the room. She couldn't spot Piemur, and she wanted him to come help her feed the fire lizards in the evening. She'd better strengthen what friendships she could within the Harper Hall.

The gong again called their attention to announcements; and to her surprise, Menolly heard her own name called to report to Master Oldive. Immediately the girls fell to whispering among themselves, as if such a summons was untoward, though she couldn't imagine why, unless they were doing it to frighten her. She continued to ignore them. And then the gong released the diners.

The girls remained where they were, pointedly not looking in her direction, and she was forced to struggle from the bench.

"And where in the name of the first shell were you this morning?" asked Master Domick, his face set with anger, his eyes slitted, his voice low but projected so that the girls all cowered away from him.

"I was told to go to—"

"So Talmor informed me," and he brushed aside her explanation, "but *I* had left word with Dunca for you to report to me."

"Dunca told me nothing, Master Domick," Menolly flicked a glance beyond him to the girls and saw in their smug expression the knowledge that they, too, had known there'd been a message for her, which Dunca had deliberately neglected to pass on.

"She said she did," said Master Domick.

Menolly stared back at him, bereft of any response and heartily wishing for Sebell to produce his assistance.

"I realize," Domick went on sarcastically, "that you've been living holdless and without authority for some time, but while you are an apprentice here, you will obey the masters."

In the face of his wrath, Menolly bowed her head. The next moment, Beauty came diving into the room, with two bronze and two brown shapes right behind her.

"Beauty! Rocky! Diver! Stop it!"

Menolly jumped in front of Domick, arms outstretched, protecting him from the onslaught of winged retaliation.

"What do you mean, disobeying me? Attacking Master Domick? He's a Harper! Behave yourselves."

Menolly had to shout because the girls, seeing the fire lizards swooping down, screamed and tried variously to get under the table or off the benches, overturning them; anywhere away from the fire lizards.

Domick had sense enough to stand still, incredulous as he was at the attack. Despite the girls' shriek, Menolly had the lungs to be heard when she wished to.

Twittering, Beauty circled once and then came to Menolly's shoulder, glaring balefully at Domick from behind her mistress. The others lined up on the mantel, wings still spread, hissing, their jeweled eyes whirling, looking ready and quite willing to pounce again. As Menolly stroked Beauty to calmness, she struggled with an apology to Domick.

"Back to work, you! The rest of you, along to your sections," Domick said, raising his own voice to energize the stragglers in the dining hall who had observed the strange attack, and the boys who were clearing the tables. "I'd forgot about your loyal defenders," he told Menolly in a tight but controlled voice.

"Master Domick, will you ever forgive . . ."

"Master Domick," said another voice near the floor, and Audiva crawled from under the table. Domick extended a hand to help the girl to her feet. She glanced toward the entrance, then gave Menolly a brief nod. "Master Domick, Dunca told Menolly nothing about your message, but *we* all knew about it. Fair's fair." With one more glance at Menolly, she hurried across the dining hall to catch up with the other girls in the courtyard.

"How did you contrive to alienate Dunca?" asked Domick, his expression sullen but less fierce.

Menolly gulped and glanced at the fire lizards.

"Oh, them! Yes! I can quite see her point." There was no flexibility in Master Domick's attitude. "They do not, however, intimidate me."

"Master Domick—"

"That's enough, girl. Since you haven't the native intelligence to be tactful, I shall have to—"

"Master Domick—" Sebell came hurrying up.

"I know, I know," and the Master cut off the journeyman's explanation. "You do seem to acquire some champions at any rate. Let's hope the end result is worth the effort. I'll see you tomorrow morning, promptly after breakfast, in my study, which is on the second level to the right, fourth door on the outside. You will take your pipes this afternoon to Master Jerint for the first hour. I'm told you made the pipes yourself in that cave of yours? Good! Then the second hour you're to see Master Shonagar. Now, get yourself off to Master Oldive. His office is at the top of the steps on the inside, to your right. No, Sebell, you do not need to hover about her so protectingly. I'm not so lost to common sense as to punish her for being the victim of envy." He gestured imperatively at the journeyman to accompany him and then strode out of the hall. Sebell gave her a quick nod and followed.

"Pssst!" Attracted by the sound, Menolly looked down and saw Piemur crouched under the table.

"Is it safe to come out?"

"Aren't you supposed to be in chore section?"

"Yeah, but never mind. I've got a few seconds leeway. Hey, those fribbles have it in for you, don't they? Or maybe Dunca *made* them not tell you?"

"How much did you overhear?"

"All of it." Piemur grinned, getting to his feet. "I don't miss much around here."

"Piemur!"

"Menolly, can I help you feed the fire lizards tonight?" he asked, eyeing Beauty warily.

"I was going to ask you."

"Great!" He beamed with pleasure. "And don't worry about *them*," he added, jerking his head toward the door, meaning the girls. "You're much nicer'n them."

"You just want to make friends with my fire lizards . . ."

"Too right!" His grin was impudence itself, but Menolly felt that he'd have been her friend without Beauty and the others. "Gotta scamper, or I'll be put on. See you!"

She made her way to Master Oldive's office. He had the hard-gum ball for her and showed her how to exercise her hand around it.

"Not," he said, giving her the grimace of his smile, "that your hand will lack exercise of other sorts around here. How much does it ache?"

She mumbled something, so he gave her a stern look and laid a small pot in her hand.

"There is only one excuse on this planet for the existence of that odorous plant known as numbweed, which is to ease pain. Use it when needed. The salve is mild enough to give you relief without loss of sensitivity."

Beauty, who'd observed everything from her perch on Menolly's shoulder, gave an admonitory chirp, as if agreeing with Master Oldive. The man chuckled, eyeing the little queen.

"Things are lively with you lot about, aren't they?" he said, addressing the fire lizard directly. She chittered in response, turning her head this way and that as if looking him over. "How much larger will she grow?" he asked Menolly. "I understand yours are not long out of the shell."

Menolly coaxed Beauty from her shoulder to her forearm so that Master Oldive could examine her closely.

"What's this? What's this?" he asked, glancing from Beauty to Menolly. "Patchy skin?"

Menolly was horrified. She'd been so engrossed in her own problems that she hadn't been taking proper care of her fire lizards. And here was Beauty, her back skin flaking. Probably the others were in trouble, too.

"Oil. They need to be oiled. . . ."

"Don't panic, child. The matter is easily taken care of," and with one long arm, he reached to the shelving above his head, and without seeming to look, brought down a large pot. "I make this for the ladies of the Hold, so if your creatures don't mind smelling like females fair . . ."

Shaking her head, Menolly grinned with relief, remembering the stinking fish oil she'd used first for the fire lizards at the Dragon Stones cave. Master Oldive scooped up a fingertip of the ointment and gestured toward Beauty's back. At Menolly's encouraging nod, he gently smoothed the stuff on the patchy skin. Beauty arched her back appreciatively, crooning with relief, and then she stroked her head against his hand in gratitude.

"Most responsive little creature, isn't she?" Master Oldive said, pleased.

"Very," but Menolly was thinking of Beauty's deplorable attack on Master Domick.

"Now, I'll have a look at your feet. Hmmm. You've been on them too much; there's quite a bit of swelling," he said sternly. "I want you off your feet as much as possible. Did I not make that clear?"

Beauty squeaked angrily.

"Is she agreeing with me or defending you?" asked the Master.

"Possibly both, sir, because I had to stand a lot yesterday. . . ."

"I suppose you did," he said, more kindly, "but do try to keep off your feet as much as possible. Most of the masters will be understanding." He dismissed her then, giving her the extra jars and reminding her to return the next day after dinner.

Menolly was glad the Master had an inside office, or he'd have seen her trudging across the courtyard after her pipes; but there was no other way, if she was to report with them to Master Jerint. And she didn't wish to offend another master today.

The chore sections were at work in the courtyard, sweeping, cleaning, raking and doing the general heavy drudgery to keep the Harper Hall in order. She was aware of furtive glances in her direction but affected not to notice them.

The door to the cot was half-closed when she reached it, but Menolly clearly heard the voices raised inside.

"She's an *apprentice*," Pona was shouting in strident and argumentative tones. "He *said* she was an *apprentice*. She doesn't belong with *us*. We're not apprentices! We've rank to uphold. She doesn't belong in here with us! Let her go where she does belong . . . with the apprentices!" There was a vicious, hateful edge to Pona's voice.

Menolly drew back from the doorway, trembling. She lay flat against the wall, wishing she were anywhere but here. Beauty chirped questioningly in her ear and then stroked her head against Menolly's cheek, the perfumed salve a sweetness in Menolly's nostrils.

One thing was certain: Menolly did not want to go into the cottage for her pipes. But what would happen if she went to Master Jerint without them? She *couldn't* go into the cot. Not now. Her fair swirled about, deprived of their customary landing spot by the closed shutters of Menolly's disputed room, and she wished with all her heart that she could consolidate her nine fire lizards into one dragon and be borne aloft, and *between*, back to her quiet cave by the Dragon Stones. She did belong there because she'd made it *her* place. Hers alone! And really, what place was there for her in the Harper Hall, much less the cot? She might be called an apprentice, but she wasn't part of their group either. Ranly had made that plain at the dining table.

And Master Morshal didn't want her to "presume" to be a harper. Master Domick would as soon she disappeared, for all he'd been willing to teach her. She *had* played well for him, scarred hand and all. She was certain of that. And she was clearly a far better musician than the girls. No false modesty prompted that evaluation.

If her only use at the Harper Hall was to instruct people on being bogus seamen or turning fire lizard eggs, someone else could as easily perform those services. She'd managed to alienate more people than she'd made friends, and the few friends she'd acquired were far more interested in her fire lizards than they were in her. Briefly she wondered what welcome she would have received if she hadn't brought the fire lizards or the two eggs with her. Then there would have been no fire lizard song for the Masterharper to rewrite. And he'd apologized to her for that. The Masterharper of Pern had apologized to her, Menolly of Half-Circle Sea Hold, for improving on her song. Her songs were what he needed, he said. Menolly took in a deep breath and expelled it slowly.

She did have music in the Harper Hall, and that was important! There might not be girl harpers, but no one had ever said there couldn't be girl song-crafters and that mightn't be a bad future.

Not to think of that now, Menolly, she chided herself. Think what you're going to do when you appear before Master Jerint with no pipes. He might seem absentminded, but she doubted very much if he really was. The pipes were in her room, on the little press, and nothing, not even obedience to, and love of, the Masterharper would force her into the cot while those girls were raging on about her.

Beauty took off from her shoulder, calling to the other fire lizards, and when they were all midair above her, they disappeared. Menolly pushed herself away from the cot's wall and started back to the Harper Hall. She'd think of something to say to Master Jerint about the pipes.

The fire lizards exploded into the air above her, squealing so shrilly that she looked up in alarm. They were grouped in a tight cluster, hovered just a split second while her eye took in their unusual formation, and then they parted. Something dropped. Automatically she held out her hands, and the multiple pipes smacked into her palms.

"Oh, you darlings. I didn't know you could do that!" She clutched the pipes to her, ignoring the sting of her hands. Only the stiffness in her feet prevented her from dancing with the joy of relief and the discovery of this unexpected ability of her friends. How clever, clever they were, going to her room and bringing her the pipes. No one could ever again say in her presence that they were just pets and nuisances, good for nothing but trouble!

"The worst storm throws up some wood on the beach," her mother used to say; mostly to soothe her father caught holdbound during a storm.

Why, if she hadn't needed the pipes so badly, and if the girls hadn't been so nasty, she'd never have discovered how very clever her fire lizards could be!

It was with a considerably lightened heart that she entered Master Jerint's workshop. The place was unexpectedly empty. Master Jerint, bent over a vise attached to his wide and cluttered worktable, was the only occupant of the big room. As she could see that he was meticulously glueing veneer to a harp shaft, she waited and waited. And waited until, bored, she sighed.

"Yes? Oh, the girl! And where have you been this long time? Oh, waiting, I see. You brought your pipes with you?" He held out his hand, and she surrendered them.

She was a bit startled by the sudden intensity of his examination. He weighed the pipes in his hand, peered closely at the way she had joined the sections of reed with braided seaplant; he poked a tool into the blow and finger holes. Muttering under his breath, he brought the pipes over to the rank of windows and examined them minutely in the bright afternoon sun. Glancing at her for permission, he arranged his long fingers appropriately and blew on the pipes, his eyebrows arching at the pure clear tone.

"Sea reeds? Not fresh water?"

"Fresh water, but I cured them in the sea."

"How'd you get this dark shine?"

"Mixed fish oil with sea grass and rubbed it in, warm. . . ."

"Makes an interesting hint of purple in the wood. Could you duplicate the compound again?"

"I think so."

"Any particular type of sea grass? Or fish oil?"

"Packtail," and despite herself, Menolly winced at having to mention the fish by name. Her hand twitched. "And shallow-water sea grass, the sort that clings to sandy bottoms rather than rock."

"Very good." He handed her back the pipes, gesturing for her to follow him to another table where drum rings and skins of varying sizes had been laid out, as well as a reel of the oiled cord necessary to secure drum hides to frame. "Can you assemble a drum?"

"I can try."

He sniffed, not critically—reflectively, Menolly thought —and then motioned for her to begin. He turned back to his patient woodworking on the harp.

Knowing that this was likely another test, Menolly examined each of the nine drum frames carefully for hidden flaws, for the dryness and hardness of the wood. Only one did she feel worth the trouble, and the drum would be a thin, sharp-sounding instrument. She preferred a drum with deep full notes, one that would cut through male voices in a chorus and keep them on the beat. Then she reminded herself that here she would scarcely have to worry about keeping singers in time. She set to work, putting the metal clips on the frame edge to hold the skin. Most of the hides were well cured and stretched, so that it was a matter of finding one the proper size and thinness for her drum frame. She softened the chosen hide in the tub of water, working the skin in her hands until it was flexible enough to draw across the frame. Carefully she made slits and skewered the hide to the clips, symmetrically, so that one side wasn't pulled tighter than another lest it make an uneven tone along the outside of the drum and a sour one in the center. When she was sure she had the hide evenly placed, she lashed it around the frame, two fingers from the edge of the surface. When the hide dried, she'd have a taut drum.

"Well, you do know some of the tricks of the trade, don't you?"

She nearly jumped out of her own hide at the sound of Master Jerint's voice right by her elbow. He gave her a little wintry smile. She wondered how long he'd been standing there watching her. He took the drum, examining it minutely, humphing to himself, his face making a variety of contortions that gave her no real idea of his opinion of her handiwork.

He put the drum carefully on a high shelf. "We'll just let that dry, but you'd better get yourself off to your next class. The juniors are about to arrive, I hear," he added in a dry, unamused tone.

Menolly became immediately conscious of exterior noise; laughter, yells and the dull thudding of many booted feet. Dutifully she made her way to the chorus room where Master Shonagar, seemingly not having moved since she'd left him the day before, greeted her.

"Assemble your friends please, and have them dispose themselves to listen," he told her, blinking a bit as the fire lizards swept into the high ceilinged hall. Beauty took up her favorite position on Menolly's shoulder, "You!" And one long fat forefinger pointed directly to the little queen. "You will find another perch today." The forefinger moved inexorably toward a bench. "There!"

Beauty gave a quizzical cheep but obediently retired when Menolly silently reinforced the order. Master Shonagar's eyebrows ascended into his hair line as he watched the little fire lizard settle herself, primly flipping her wings to her back, her eyes whirling gently. He grunted, his belly bouncing.

"Now, Menolly, shoulders back, chin up but in, hands

together across your diaphragm, breathe in, from the belly to the lungs . . . No, I do not want to see your chest heaving like a smith's bellows . . ."

By the end of the session, Menolly was exhausted: the small of her back and all of her midriff muscles ached, her belly was sore, and she felt that dragging nets for offshore fishing would have been child's play. Yet she'd done no more than stand in one spot and attempt, in Master Shonagar's pithy phrase, to control her breathing properly. She'd been allowed to sing only single notes, and then scales of five notes, each scale done on the breath, lightly but in true tone and on pitch. She'd have gutted a whole net of packtail with less effort, so she was intensely grateful when Master Shonagar finally waved her to a seat.

"Now, young Piemur, come forward."

Menolly looked around in surprise, wondering how long Piemur had been sitting quietly by the door.

"The other morning, Menolly, our ears were assailed by pure sound, in descant to a chorus. Piemur here seems of the opinion that the fire lizards will sing for or with anyone. Do you concur?"

"They certainly sang the other morning, but I was singing, too. I do not know, sir."

"Let us conduct a little experiment then. Let us see if they will sing when invited to do so."

Menolly winced a little at his phrasing, but Piemur's wry smile told her that this was Master Shonagar's odd version of humor.

"Supposing I just sing the melody of the chorus we were doing the other morning," said Piemur, "because if you sing *with* me, they're still singing with you and not along with me?"

"Less chatter, young Piemur, more music," said Master Shonagar, sounding extremely bass and impatient.

Piemur took a breath, properly, Menolly noticed, and opened his mouth. To her surprise and delight, a true and delicately sweet sound emerged. Her astonishment registered in the twinkle in Piemur's eyes, but his voice reflected none of his inner amusement to her reaction.

Belatedly she encouraged her fire lizards to sing. Beauty flitted to her shoulder, wrapping her tail lightly around Menolly's neck as she peered toward Piemur, cocking her head this way and that as if analyzing the sound and Menolly's command. Rocky and Diver were less restrained. They flew from their perch on the sandtable and, rearing to their haunches, began to sing along with Piemur. Beauty gave a funny scolding sound before she sat up, one forepaw resting lightly on Menolly's ear. Then she took up the descant, her fragile voice rising sure and true above Piemur's. His eyes rolled in appreciation and, when Mimic and Brownie joined in, Piemur backed up so that he could see all of the singing fire lizards.

Anxiously, Menolly glanced at Master Shonagar, but he sat, his fingers shading his eyes, engrossed in the sounds, giving absolutely no indication of his reception. Menolly made herself listen critically, as the Master was undoubtedly doing, but she found little to criticize. She hadn't taught the fire lizards how to sing: she had only given them melody to enjoy. They had enjoyed it, and were expressing that enjoyment by participation. Their voices were not limited to the few octaves of the human voice. Their piercingly sweet tones resonated through their listeners. She could feel the sound in her ear bones, and, from the way Piemur was pressing behind his ears, he felt it as well.

"There, young fellow," said Master Shonagar as the echo of the song died away, "that'll put you in your place, won't it?"

The boy grinned impudently.

"So they will warble with someone besides yourself," the Master said to Menolly.

Out of the corner of her eye, Menolly saw Piemur reach out to stroke Rocky who was nearest him. The bronze immediately rubbed his head along Piemur's hand, whether in approval of the singing or in friendship was irrelevant, judging by the charmed expression on the boy's face.

"They're used to singing because they like it, sir. It's difficult to keep them quiet when there's music about."

"Is that so? I shall consider the potentialities of this phenomenon," and with a brusque wave, Master Shonagar dismissed them all. He settled his head against his propped arm and almost immediately began to snore.

"Is he really asleep? Or shamming?" Menolly asked Piemur when they were out in the courtyard.

"Far's anyone's been able to tell, he's asleep. The only thing that'll wake him is a flat tone or meals. He never goes out of the chorus hall. He sleeps in a little room at the back. Don't think he could climb steps anyway. He's too fat. Hey, you know, Menolly, even in scales, you got a pretty voice. Sort of furry."

"Thanks!"

"Don't mention it. I like furry voices," Piemur went on, undismayed by her sarcasm. "I *don't* like high, thin, screechy ones like Briala or Pona . . ." and he jerked his thumb toward the cot. "Say, hadn't we better feed the fire lizards? It's nearly suppertime, and they look kinda faded to me."

Menolly agreed, as Beauty, riding on her shoulder, began to creel piteously.

"I sure hope that Shonagar wants to use the fire lizards with the chorus," Piemur said, kicking at a pebble. Then he laughed, pointing to the kitchen. "Look, Camo's ready and waiting."

He was there, one thick arm wrapped about an enormous bowl, heaped high with scraps. He had a handful raised to attract the fire lizards who spiraled in on him.

Uncle and the two green Aunties had decidedly adopted Camo as their feeding perch. They took so much of his attention that he didn't notice that Rocky, Lazy and Mimic draped themselves about Piemur to be fed. It certainly made it easier to apportion the scraps fairly, with three people feeding. So, when she caught Piemur glancing about the courtyard to see if anyone was noticing his new task, Menolly suggested that he'd be needed on a permanent basis if that didn't get him into any trouble with the masters.

"I'm apprenticed to Master Shonagar. *He* won't mind! And I sure as shells don't." Whereupon Piemur began to stroke the bronze and the two browns with an almost proprietary affection.

As soon as the fire lizards had finished gobbling, Menolly sent Camo back into the kitchen. There had been no loud complaints from Abuna, but Menolly had been conscious of being watched from the kitchen windows. Camo went willingly enough, once she assured him that he'd be feeding the fire lizards again in the morning. Sated, the nine lazily spiraled upward to the outer roof of the Hall, to bask in the late afternoon sun. And not a moment too soon. They were only just settling themselves when the courtyard became full of boys and men filing into the Hall for their supper.

"Too bad you gotta sit with them," Piemur said, jerking his head at the girls seated at their table.

"Can't you sit opposite me?" asked Menolly, hopefully. It would be nice to have someone to talk to during the meal.

"Naw, I'm not allowed anymore."

"Not allowed?"

Alternating between sour disgust and pleased recollection, Piemur gave a shrug. "Pona complained to Dunca, and she got on to Silvina . . ."

"What did you do?"

"Oh, nothing much," Piemur's shrug was eloquent enough for Menolly to guess that he'd probably been downright wicked. "Pona's a sorry wherry hen, you know, rank-happy and pleased to pull it. So I can't sit near the girls anymore."

She might regret the prohibition, but it enhanced her estimation of Piemur. As she reluctantly made her way toward the girls, it occurred to her that all she had to do to avoid sitting with them was to be late to meals. Then she'd have to sit where she could. That remedy pleased her so much that she walked more resolutely to her place and endured the hostility of the girls with fortitude. She matched their coldness with stony indifference and ate heartily of the soup, cheese and bread and the sweet pasty that finished the simple supper. She listened politely to the evening announcements of rehearsal times and the fact that Threadfall was expected midday tomorrow. All were to hold themselves close to the Hall, to perform their allotted tasks before, during and after Fall. Menolly heard, with private amusement, the nervous whispering of the girls at the advent of Threadfall and permitted herself to smile in disdain at their terror. They couldn't *really* be that afraid of a menace they'd known all their lives?

She made no move to leave the table when they did, but she was sure that she caught Audiva's wink as the girl followed the others out. When she judged them well away, she rose. Maybe she'd be able to get back into the cot again without confronting Dunca.

"Ah, Menolly, a moment if you please." The cheery voice of the Masterharper sang out as she reached the entrance. Robinton was standing by the stairs, talking to Sebell, and he gestured for Menolly to join them. "Come and check our eggs for us. I know Lessa said it would be a few more days but . . ." and the Harper shrugged his anxiety. "This way . . ." As she accompanied the two men to the upper level, he went on. "Sebell says that you're a mine of information." He grinned down at her. "Didn't ever think you'd have to talk fish in a Harper Hall, did you?"

"No, sir, I didn't. But then, I don't think I really knew what does go on in a Harper Hall."

"Well said, Menolly, well said," and the Harper laughed as well as Sebell. "The other crafts can jibe that we want to know too much about what is not strictly our business, but I've always felt knowledge of matters minor or major makes for better understandings. The mind that will not admit it has something more to learn tomorrow is in danger of stagnating."

"Yes, sir." Menolly caught Sebell's eye, anxiously hoping that the Harper had not heard the minor—or was it major—matter about her missing her scheduled lesson with Domick. An almost imperceptible shake of the brown man's head reassured her.

"Give me your opinion of our eggs, Menolly, for I must be out and about a great deal, but I don't wish to risk the Hatching without me in attendance. Right, Sebell?"

"Nor do I wish two fire lizards instead of the one I'm entitled to have."

The two men exchanged knowing glances as Menolly obediently checked the eggs in their sand-filled, warm pots. She turned each one slightly so that the colder side faced the heat of the glowing embers on the hearth. Robinton added a few more blackstones and then eyed her expectantly.

"Well, sir, the eggs are hardening, but they are not hard enough to hatch today or tomorrow."

"So, will you check again tomorrow morning for me, Menolly? I must be away, although Sebell will always know where I can be reached."

Menolly assured the Masterharper that she would keep a watchful eye on the eggs and inform Sebell if there were any alarming changes. The Harper walked her back through his study to the door.

"Now, Menolly, you've played for Domick, been thoroughly catechized by Morshal and sung for Shonagar. Jerint says your pipes are quite allowable, and the drum is well-constructed and should dry out sound. The fire lizards will sing sweetly with others than yourself, so you've accomplished a very great deal in your first days here. Hasn't she, Sebell?"

Sebell agreed, smiling at her in a quiet, kind way. She wondered if either man knew how Dunca and the girls felt about her presence in the Harper Hall.

"And I can leave the matter of the eggs in your good hands. That's grand. That's very good, indeed," the Masterharper said, combing his fingers through his silvered hair.

For a fleeting moment, his usually mobile face was still, and in that unguarded moment, Menolly saw signs of strain and worry. Then he smiled so cheerfully that she wondered if she'd only imagined his weariness. Well, she could certainly spare him anxiety about the fire lizards.

She'd check them several times during the day, even if it made her late to Master Shonagar.

As she returned to the cot, pleased that there was some small way in which she could serve the Masterharper, she recalled what he'd said about fish in a Harper Hall. For the first time, Menolly realized that she'd never really thought about life in a Harper Hall—except as a place where music was played and created. Petiron had spoken hazily about apprentices and his time as a journeyman, but nothing in detail. She had imagined the Harper Hall as some magical place, where people sang all conversations, or earnestly copied Records. The reality was almost commonplace, up to and especially including Dunca and the spiteful Pona. Why she had considered all Harpers, and harper people, above such pettiness, endowed with more humanity than Morshal or Domick had shown her, she did not know. She smiled at her naivety. And yet, Harpers like Sebell and Robinton, even cynical Domick, were above the ordinary. And Silvina and Piemur were basically good, and certainly had been kind to her. She was in far better circumstances than she'd ever enjoyed in Half-Circle, so she could put up with a little unpleasantness, surely.

It was as well she had reached this conclusion because, no sooner was she inside the door, than Dunca pounced on her with a list of grievances. Menolly received a tirade about her fire lizards, how dangerous and unreliable the creatures were, how they must behave themselves or Dunca would not tolerate them, that Menolly had better realize how little rank mattered in Dunca's cot and that, as the newcomer, she must behave with more deference to those who had been studying far longer at the Harper Craft Hall. Menolly's attitude was presumptuous, uncooperative, unfriendly and discourteous, and Dunca was not having a tunnel-snake in her cot where the girls were as friendly and as considerate of one another as any fosterer could wish.

After the first few sentences, Menolly realized that she could put forth no defense of herself or her friends acceptable to Dunca. All she could do was say "yes" and "no" at appropriate intervals, when Dunca was forced to stop for breath. And every time Menolly thought the woman must surely have exhausted the subject, she would surge onto another imagined slight until Menolly seriously considered calling Beauty to her. The appearance of the fire lizard would certainly curtail the flow of abuse, but would irrevocably destroy any possibility of getting into Dunca's fair record.

"Now, have I made myself plain?" Dunca asked unexpectedly.

"You have," and since Menolly's calm acceptance momentarily robbed Dunca of speech, the girl flew up the steps, ignoring the stiffness of her feet and grinning at the explosive and furious reprimands Dunca made at her retreat.

Chapter 6

The tears I feel today
I'll wait to shed tomorrow.
Though I'll not sleep this night
Nor find surcease from sorrow.
My eyes must keep their sight:
I dare not be tear-blinded.
I must be free to talk
Not choked with grief, clear-minded.
My mouth cannot betray
The anguish that I know.
Yes, I'll keep my tears till later:
But my grief will never go.
                    Menolly's "Song for Petiron"

Beauty woke her at sunrise. The other fire lizards were awake, too, though one thing was sure, no one else in the cot was awake yet.

Last night, when Menolly had reached the relative safety of her room, she had closed and barred the door, and then opened the shutters to admit her friends. She had recovered her composure by oiling their patchy skin with Master Oldive's salve. This was the first opportunity she'd had since they'd left the cave by the Dragon Stones to tend and fondle each one. They, too, were communicative. She got many impressions from them, mostly that they'd been bathing daily in the lakes above Fort Hold, which weren't much fun because there weren't any waves to sport in. Menolly caught pictures from their minds of great dragons and of a Weyr, differing in shape from Benden. Beauty's pictures were the sharpest. Menolly had enjoyed her quiet evening with them; it had made up for Dunca's irrational attitudes.

Now, as she became aware of the early morning stillness, she knew she'd have time to do a few tasks for herself. She could get a bath and wash the fruit stains out of her tunic. It ought to dry quickly on the window ledge in the morning sun. There should be time before Threadfall, for she remembered that would occur today.

Quietly she unbarred the door, listening in the corridor, and heard only the faintest echo of a snore. Probably Dunca. Adjuring her fire lizards to silence, she walked noiselessly down the steps to the bathing room at the back of the first level. She'd always heard of the thermal pools in the big Holds and Weyrs, but this was her first experience with them. The fire lizards came clustering in behind her, and she hushed their excited twitterings at the sight of the waist-high trough of steaming water. Menolly dipped her fingers in the pleasant warm water, checked to see if there were sandsoap and then, throwing her clothes on the floor, slipped into the bath.

The water was delightfully warm and soft to her skin, a change from the harsh sea or the mineral-heavy water in Half-Circle Sea Hold. Menolly submerged completely and came up, shaking her hair. She'd wash all over. One of the others pushed Auntie Two into the bath, and she let out a high-pitched squeal of protest and fright, then paddled happily about in the warm water. The next thing Menolly knew, all the fire lizards were splashing about, their talons unexpectedly catching her bare skin or tangling in her hair. She hushed them often and sternly, because she wasn't sure how far noise carried from the bathing room: all she'd need, after last night, was for Dunca to come charging in, roused from her night's rest by her least-wanted guests.

Menolly sandsoaped all of the fire lizards thoroughly, rinsed them well, got herself, her hair and finally her clothes well washed, then got back to her room without anyone the wiser for her early morning activity. She was oiling a rough patch on Mimic's back when she heard the first stirrings outside: the cheery greetings of the herdsmen going to attend their beasts who would be hold-bound today with Threadfall due. She wondered how Fall would affect the business of the Harper Hall: probably the apprentices and journeymen were required to assist the holders in flame-thrower details. Thank goodness no one had asked her what she'd done after Fall in Half-Circle. She heard the slamming of a door below and decided that Dunca was up. Menolly slipped into her only other clothes, the patched tunic and trousers of her cave days. They were at least clean and neat.

They were not, however, it was pointed out to Menolly at the breakfast table, suitable attire for a young lady living in Dunca's cot. When Menolly explained that she had only the one other change, which was now drying, Dunca let out a shriek of outrage and demanded to know where the clothes were drying. Menolly was emphatically told that she had committed yet another unwitting sin by hanging her washing—like the commonest field worker—on the window ledge. She was ordered to bring down the offending garments, still damp, and shown by the fuming Dunca where such laundry was to be hung, in the inner recesses of the cot. Where, Menolly was sure, they would take days to dry and smell musty besides with no air to freshen them.

Very much aware of her disgrace and destitute condition, Menolly finished her breakfast as quickly as possible. But when she rose from the table, Dunca demanded to know where she thought she was going.

"I must feed my fire lizards, Dunca, and I was told to report to Master Domick this morning . . ."

"No message was received by me to such effect." Dunca drew herself up in officious disbelief.

"Master Domick told me yesterday."

"He made no mention of such instructions to me." Dunca's manner implied that Menolly was making up the order.

"Probably because yesterday's message went astray."

And, while Dunca stammered and stuttered, Menolly slipped out of the room and out of the cot, trotting across the road, the fire lizards gracefully swirling above her head until they were sure she was headed toward the Harper Hall. Then they disappeared.

They were perched on the window ledges when she reached the kitchen corner, their eyes whirling redly in anticipation of breakfast. There seemed to be more than the usual amount of confusion in the kitchen, but Camo, once he caught sight of her, immediately put down the side of herdbeast he'd been lugging and left the carcass, its legs obscenely dropping across the passage, while he disappeared back into the storeroom. He emerged with yet a bigger bowl, scraps spilling down its sides as he jogged to meet her. Suddenly he gave a startled cry; and Menolly, peering in the window, saw that Abuna, wooden spoon upraised, was chasing after him. He slithered by, but her dress got caught on the extruding legs of the carcass.

Menolly ducked into the space between the windows, fervently hoping that Camo's preoccupation with the feeding of fire lizards was not going to cause a major breach with Abuna. There might be nothing to fear from harpers, but the women in the Harper Hall were certainly possible enemies.

"Menolly, am I too late . . ." Piemur came charging across the courtyard from the apprentice dormitory, his boots half-fastened, his tunic laces untied and his face and hair showing signs of half-hearted washing.

Before he could assemble his clothing properly, Rocky, Lazy and Mimic attached themselves to him: Camo came out of the kitchen to be assaulted by his three; and the three humans were exhorted by shrill hungry creelings to be fed.

Camo's great bowl was finally emptied, and as if on cue, Abuna's voice rose to command Camo back to his duties. Menolly hurriedly thanked the man and pushed him urgently down the kitchen steps, assuring him that he'd saved quite enough food for the pretties, that the pretties could not stuff in another mouthful.

When the breakfast gong sounded, Menolly stayed in the kitchen corner until the courtyard was cleared of the hungry harpers. She had to see Master Domick, for which interview she would need her gitar. She went to the archroom to collect it and lingered there, since everyone was still eating. She tuned the gitar, delighting afresh in its rich sweet tone. She attempted some of the bridges from the music she'd played in the abortive lesson with the girls, stretching and stretching against the pull of the scar until her hand muscles went into a spasm of cramping. All of a sudden, she remembered her other chore; to check the fire lizard eggs. But, if the Masterharper were still asleep. . . . No way of telling from here. She ran lightly down the steps, pleased that her feet were less stiff and tender this morning. She paused in the main hall, listening, and heard the distinctive sound of the Masterharper's voice at the round table. So she hurried up the steps and down the corridor to his room.

The fire lizard pots were warm on the side away from the fire, so they'd obviously just been turned. She uncovered each egg and checked the shells for hardness, for any sign of cracking or striation. They were fine. She gently covered them with sand and replaced the lids.

As she emerged from the Masterharper's rooms, she heard Master Domick's voice on the steps. With him were Sebell, carrying a small harp, and Talmor, gitar slung across his back.

"There she is," Sebell said. "You checked the eggs, Menolly?"

"I did, sir. They're fine."

"Come this way, then, step lively now . . . if you can. . . . " Domick said, frowning as he belatedly recalled her disability.

"My feet are nearly as good as new now, sir," she told him.

"Well, you're not to run any races with Thread today, hear?"

Menolly wasn't certain, as she followed the three men into the study, if Domick were teasing her or not. He sounded so sour, it was difficult to tell, but Sebell caught her eye and winked.

Domick's study, well-lit by huge baskets of glows, was dominated by the biggest sandtable Menolly had ever seen, with all its spaces glass-covered, though she politely averted her eyes from the inscriptions. Domick might not like people peering at his music. The shelves were jammed with loose record hides, and thin, white-bleached sheets of some substance evenly cut along the edges. She tried to get a closer look at them, but Master Domick called her to attention by telling her to take the middle stool.

Sebell and Talmor were already settling themselves before the music rack and tuning their instruments. So she took her place and cast a quick glance at the music before them. With a thrill of surprise, she saw that it was for four instruments, and no easy read.

"You're to play second gitar, Menolly," Domick said, with the smile of one who is conferring a favor. He picked up a metal pipe with finger stops, one of the flutes that Petiron had told her were used by more accomplished pipers. She politely suppressed her curiosity, but she couldn't control her delighted surprise when Domick ran a test scale. It sounded like a fire lizard's voice.

"You'll need to look through the music," he said, observing her interest.

"I will?"

Master Domick cleared his throat. "It *is* customary with music you've never seen before." He tapped the music with his pipe. "That," and his tone was very acid, "is no children's exercise. Despite your display for Talmor yesterday, you will not find this easy to read."

Rebuked, she skimmed the music, trying an alternative chording in one measure to see which would be easier on her hand at that tempo. The complexity of the chording was so fascinating that she forgot she was keeping three harpers waiting. "I beg your pardon." She turned the music back to the beginning and looked at Domick for him to give them the beat.

"You're ready?"

"I think so, sir."

"Just like that?"

"Sir?"

"Very well, young woman, at the beat," and Domick sternly tapped out the time with a strong stamp.

It had been fun, always, for Menolly to play with Petiron, particularly when he let her improvise around his melody. It had been a pleasure yesterday to see new music in Talmor's lesson, but now, the stimulation of playing with three keen and competent musicians gave her such impulsion that she seemed to be an irrelevant medium for fingers that had to play what her eager eyes saw. She was lost completely in the thrall of the music, so that when the rushing finale ended, she suffered a shock as keen as pain.

"Oh, that was marvelous. Could we play it again?"

Talmor burst out laughing, Domick stared at her, and Sebell covered his eyes with his hands as he bowed his head over his harp.

"I didn't believe you, Talmor," Domick said, shaking his head. "And I'd played with her myself. True, only basic things. I didn't think she was up to any demanding standard."

Menolly inhaled sharply, worried that she had somehow erred, as she had with the girls the previous day.

"And I know," Domick went on in that tight, dry tone, "that you can't ever have seen that piece of music before . . ."

Menolly stared at the Master. "It was fascinating. The interweaving of melody from flute to harp and gitar. I'm sorry about this section," and she flipped back the sheets. "I should have used your chords but my hand . . ."

Domick stared at her until her voice trailed off. "Did Sebell warn you what would happen this morning?"

"No, sir, only to say that I mustn't fail to come today."

"Enough, Domick. The child's worried sick that she's done something wrong. Well, you haven't, Menolly," Talmor said, patting her hand encouragingly. "You see," he went on, glaring in a good-natured fashion at Domick, "he just finished writing it. You've played the fingers off Sebell and me. Domick's panting for breath. And you've managed to plow through one of Domick's tortuous inventions with . . . well, I did hear one faulty chording besides the one you just pointed out, but, as you say, your hand . . ."

Now Sebell lifted his head, and Menolly stared at him because his eyes were overflowing with tears. But at the same time, he was laughing! Convulsed with mirth he wagged an impotent finger at Domick, unable to speak.

Domick batted irritably at Sebell's hand and glared at both journeymen. "That's enough. All right, so the joke's on me, but you'll have to admit that there was good precedent for my skepticism. Anyone can play solo . . ." He turned on the bewildered Menolly. "Did you play a great deal with Petiron? Or any of the other musicians at Half-Circle?"

"There *was* only Petiron who could play properly. Fishing leaves a man's hands too stiff for any fine music." She flicked a glance at Sebell. "There were a few drummers and stickmen. . . ."

Her reply set Sebell laughing again. He hadn't seemed the sort, Menolly thought, being so calm and quiet. To be sure he was laughing without roaring but . . .

"Suppose you tell me exactly what you did do at Half-Circle Sea Hold, Menolly. Musically, that is. Master Robinton's been too busy to confer with me at any length."

Domick's words implied that he had the right to know whatever it was she might tell Master Robinton, and she saw Sebell nodding his head in permission. So she thought for a moment. Would it be proper, now, to tell the Harpers that she had taught the children after Petiron had died and before the new Harper had come? Yes, because Harper Elgion must have told Master Robinton, and *he* hadn't chided her for stepping into a man's duties. Further, Master Domick had taunted her with telling the truth once before. Rather than antagonize him for any reason, she had best be candid now. So she spoke of her situation at Half-Circle Sea Hold: how Petiron had singled her out when she was old enough to learn Teaching Ballads and Sagas. He had taught her to play gitar and harp, "to help with the teaching," she assured her listeners, "and with the evening singing." Domick nodded. And how Petiron had shown her all the music he had, "but he'd only three pieces of occasional music because he said there wasn't need for more. Yanus, the Sea Holder, wanted music to sing to, not listen to."

"Naturally," Domick replied, nodding again.

And Petiron had taught her how to cut and hole reeds to make pipes, to stretch skin on drum frames, large and small, the principles involved in making a gitar or small harp, but there was no hardwood in the Sea Hold for another harp, and no real need for Menolly to have either harp or gitar. Two Turns ago, however, she'd had to take over the playing of the Teaching because Petiron's hands had become crippled with the knuckle disease. And then, of course, and now Menolly felt the lump of grief rising in her throat, she'd done all the teaching when Petiron had died because Yanus realized that the young must be kept up in their Teaching Ballads and Songs since he knew his duty to the Weyr, and she was the only person in the Hold who could be spared from the fishing.

"Of course," Domick had said. "And when you cut your hand?"

"Oh, the new Harper, Elgion, had arrived so I . . . wasn't required to play anymore. And besides," she held her hand up explanatorily, "it was thought I'd never be able to play again."

She wasn't conscious of the silence at first, her head bent, her eyes on her hand, rubbing the scar with her right thumb, because the intensive playing had caused it to ache again.

"When Petiron was here at the Hall, there was no finer musician, no better instructor," Master Domick said quietly. "I had the good fortune to be his apprentice. You've no need ever to be ashamed of your playing. . . ."

"Or of your joy in music," Sebell added, no laughter in his eyes now as he leaned toward her.

Joy in music! His words were like a release. How could he have known so acutely!

"Now that you're at the Harper Hall, Menolly, what would you like best to do?" Master Domick asked her, his tone so casual, so neutral that Menolly couldn't think what answer he expected of her.

Joy in music. How could she express that? In writing the kind of songs Master Robinson needed? How would she know what he needed? And hadn't Talmor said that Domick had composed the magnificent quartet they had just played? Why did Master Robinson need another composer if he already had Domick in the Hall?

"You mean, play or sing, or teach?"

Master Domick widened his eyes and regarded her with a half-smile. "If that's what you wish?"

"I'm here to learn, aren't I?" She avoided his taunt.

Domick acknowledged that that was true enough.

"So I'll learn the things I haven't had the chance to learn before because Petiron told me there were a lot of things he couldn't teach me. Like how to use my voice properly. That's going to take a lot of hard work with Master Shonagar. He only lets me breathe and sing five-note scales . . ." Talmor grinned so broadly at her, his eyes dancing as if he knew so exactly her feelings that she took encouragement from him. "I'd really love. . . ." Then she hesitated because of what Domick might say and she dreaded his clever-edged tongue.

"What do you really want, Menolly?" asked Sebell kindly.

"You're frightening her, Domick," Talmor said at the same time.

"Nonsense, are you frightened of me, Menolly?" He sounded surprised. "It's having to train idiots that sours me, Menolly," said Master Domick, but his voice was suddenly gentler. "Now tell *me* what facet of music appeals to you most?"

He caught her gaze and would not release her eyes, but his phrasing had given her the answer.

"What appeals to me most? Why, playing like this, in

a group." She got the words out in a rush, gesturing at the rack in front of her. "It's so beautiful. It's such a challenge, to hear the interweaving harmonies and the melody line changing from instrument to instrument. I felt as if I was . . . was flying on a dragon!"

Domick looked startled and blinked, a slow pleased smile lighting his otherwise dour face.

"She means it, Domick," Talmor said in the pause that followed.

"Oh, I do. It's the most exciting thing I've ever played. Only . . ."

"Only what?" urged Talmor when she faltered.

"I didn't play it right. I should have studied the music longer before I started playing because I was so busy watching the notes and time changes that I didn't, I couldn't, follow the dynamic markings. . . . I *am* sorry."

Domick brought his hand against his forehead in an exasperated smack. Sebell dissolved again into his quiet laughter. But Talmor just howled, slapping his knee and pointing at Domick.

"In that case, Menolly, we will play it again," Domick said, raising his voice to drown the amusement of the others. "And this time . . ." he frowned at Menolly, an expression which no longer distressed her because she knew that she had touched him, "watching those dynamic signs, which I put in for very good reason. Now, on the beat . . ."

They did not play the music through. Domick stopped them, time and again, insisting on a retard here, a variation of the designated time here, a better balance of the instruments in another section. In some respects, this was as satisfying as playing for Menolly, since Domick's comments gave her insights to the music as well as its composer. Sebell had been right about her studying with Domick. She had a lot to learn from a man who could write music like this, pure music.

Then Talmor began to argue interpretation with Domick, an argument cut short by the eerie sound that began softly and increased in volume and intensity so that it was almost unbearable in the closed room. Abruptly her fire lizards appeared.

"How did they get in here like that?" Talmor demanded, hunching his shoulders to protect his head as the study got overcrowded with nervous fire lizards.

"They're like dragons, you know," Sebell said, equally wary of claw and wing.

"Tell those creatures to settle down, Menolly," commanded Domick.

"The noise bothers them."

"That's only the Threadfall alarm," said Domick, but the men were putting down their instruments.

Menolly called her fire lizards to order, and they settled on the shelves, their eyes wheeling with alarm.

"Wait here, Menolly," Domick said as he and the others made for the door. "We'll be back. That is, I will . . ."

"And I," "I, too," said the others, and then they all stamped out of the room.

Menolly sat uneasily, aware that the Hall was preparing for Threadfall, as she had prepared for the menace all her conscious years. She heard racing feet in the corridors, for the door was half ajar. Then the clanging of shutters, the squeal of metal, many shouts and a gradual compression of air in the room. The sudden throb as the great ventilating fans of the Hall were set into motion for the duration of Threadfall. Once again, she found herself wishing to be back in the safety of her seaside cave. She had always hated being closed in at Half-Circle Sea Hold during Threadfall. There never seemed to be enough air to breathe during those fear-filled times. The cave, safe but with a reassuringly clear view of the sea, had been a perfect compromise between security and convention.

Beauty chirped inquiringly and then sprang from the shelf to Menolly's shoulder. She wasn't nervous at being closed in, but she was very much aware of Thread's imminence, her slim body taut, her eyes whirling.

The clatter and clangs, the shouts and stampings ceased. Menolly heard the low murmur of men's voices on the steps as Domick and the two journeymen returned.

"Granted that your left hand won't do octave stretches yet," Domick said, addressing Menolly but more as if he were continuing a conversation begun with the two journeymen, "how much harp instruction did Petiron give you?"

"He had one small floor harp, sir, but we'd such a desperate time getting new wire, so I sort of learned to . . ."

"Improvise?" asked Sebell, extending his harp to her.

She thanked him and politely proffered the gitar in its place, which he, with equally grave courtesy, accepted.

Domick had been riffling through music on the shelves and brought over another score, worn and faded in spots but legible enough, he said, for the purpose.

Menolly rubbed her fingertips experimentally. She'd lost most of the harp-string calluses, and her fingers would be sore but perhaps. . . . She looked up at Domick and receiving permission, plucked an arpeggio. Sebell's harp was a joy to use, the tone singing through the frame, held between her knees, like liquid sound. She had to shift her fingers awkwardly to make the octave run. Despite the fact that her scar made her wince more than once, she became so quickly involved in the music that the discomfort could be ignored. She was a bit startled when she reached the finale to realize that the others had been playing along with her.

"In the slow section," she asked, "is the major seventh chord accented throughout? The notation doesn't say."

"Whether it is or not must wait for another day," Domick said, firmly taking the harp from her and handing it back to Sebell. "You'll live to play harp another time, Menolly. No more now." He turned her left hand over so she was forced to notice that the scar had split and was bleeding slightly from the tear.

"But . . ."

"*But* . . ." Dominick interrupted her more gently than he usually spoke, "it's time to eat. Everyone has to eat sometime, Menolly."

They were all grinning at her and, emboldened by the rapport she'd had with them during their practice, she smiled back. Now she smelled the aroma of roasted meat and spices and was mildly astonished to feel her stomach churning with hunger. To be sure, she hadn't eaten much at the cot, with everyone glaring at her so.

Some of her elation with the morning's satisfying work was dampened by the realization that she'd have to sit with the girls. But that was a small blemish on the pleasure of the hours gone past. To her surprise, however, there were no girls at the hearth table, and the great metal doors of the Hall were locked tight, the windows shuttered, the dining hall lit by the great central and corner baskets of glows; in some obscure way, the hall looked more friendly than she'd seen it before.

Everyone else was seated, though her quick glance did not show Master Robinton to be in his customary place at the round table. Master Morshal was and frowned at her until Master Domick gave her a shove toward her place as he drew out his own chair. Sebell and Talmor seemed in no way abashed as they went late to the oval journeymen's tables. But Menolly felt more conspicuous than ever as she walked awkwardly toward the hearth table. And it wasn't her imagination: every eye in the room was on her.

"Hey, Menolly," said a familiar voice in a harsh but carrying whisper, "hurry up so we can get fed." She saw Piemur slapping the empty place beside him. "See?" he said to his neighbor, "I told you she wouldn't be hiding in the Hold with the others." Then he added, under the cover of the noise of everyone taking their seats, "You aren't afraid of Thread, are you?"

"Why should I be?" Menolly was being truthful, but it obviously stood her in good credit with the boys near enough to hear her reply. "And I thought you said you weren't supposed to sit at the girls' table?"

"They're not here, are they? And you said you wanted someone to talk to. So here I am."

"Menolly?" asked the boy with the protuberant eyes who usually sat opposite her, "do fire lizards breathe fire like dragons and go after Thread?"

Menolly glanced at Piemur to see if he were back of the question. He shrugged innocence.

"Mine never have, but they're young."

"I told you so, Brolly," replied Piemur. "Dragonets in the Weyrs don't fight Thread, and fire lizards are just small dragons. Right, Menolly?"

"They do seem to be," she said, temporizing slightly, but neither debater noticed.

"Then where are they now?" Brolly wanted to know, slightly sneering.

"In Master Domick's study."

The meat reached them and further discussion was suspended. Today Menolly blithely speared four slices of juicy meat to her plate. She reached for bread, beating Brolly's grab for some. And she dished Piemur some of the redroots, which he wasn't going to take. He was much too small not to eat properly.

Whether it was Piemur's company or the absence of the girls, or both, Menolly didn't know, but suddenly she was included in the table conversations. The boys opposite her had question after question about her fire lizards: how she had accidentally discovered the queen's clutch in the sand; how she'd saved the hatchlings from destruction by Thread; how she had found enough food to support their voracious appetites; how she'd dragged a wherry from the mire to provide oil for her fire lizards' patchy skins. She sensed that the boys gradually became reconciled to her possession of so many fire lizards because it was obviously no gather day to take care of them. They had the most bizarre theories about fire lizards and a few unsubtle queries about when would her queen fly to mate and how soon would there be a clutch and how many in it.

"The masters and journeymen would get first crack anyhow," Piemur said, disgruntled.

"It ought to be free choice, the way the dragons choose their riders," said Brolly.

"Fire lizards aren't quite the same as dragons, Brolly," said Piemur, glancing at Menolly for support. "Look at Lord Groghe. What dragon would've picked him if it had had another choice?"

The boys shushed him, glancing nervously about to see if anyone had overheard his indiscreet remark.

"The Weyrs have control of the fire lizards any road," said Brolly. "You can just bet the Weyrs're going to hand 'em out where they'll keep the Lord Holders and Craft Masters happy."

Menolly sighed for the truth of that surmise.

"Yes, but you can't *make* a fire lizard stay with you if you're mean to him," said Piemur flatly. "I heard that Lord Meron's disappears for days."

"Where do they go?" asked Brolly.

As Menolly didn't know, she was just as glad that the eerie sound, which Domick had said was the Thread alarm, sounded, effectively ending the conversation.

"That means Thread is directly over us," said Piemur, hunching his shoulders and pointing toward the ceiling.

"Look at that!" And Brolly's startled exclamation made everyone turn about.

On the mantel behind her were ranged all nine fire lizards, their eyes sparkling with rainbow reflections of intense agitation, their wings spread, talons unsheathed. They were hissing, retracting and extending their tongues as if licking imaginary Thread from the air.

Menolly half rose, glancing toward the round table. She saw Domick nodding permission to her as he, too, got to his feet. He was gesturing to someone at the journeymen's tables.

"The alarm chorus would be appropriate, Brudegan," he called as he crossed to the hearth, a wary eye on the fire lizards.

Menolly motioned to Beauty, but the little queen ignored her, rising to her haunches and starting to keen a piercing series of notes, up and down an almost inaudibly high octave. The others joined her.

"For the sake of our ears, Menolly, can you get your creatures to sing *with* the chorus now? Brudegan, where's your beat?"

Feet began to stamp, one, two, three, four, and suddenly the fire lizards' keen was covered by the mass chorus. Beauty fanned her wings in surprise, and Mimic backwinged himself off the mantel, only missing a drop to the floor by claws biting into the wood.

> "Drummer, beat, and piper, blow,
>   Harper, strike, and soldier, go . . ."

sang the massed voices. Menolly joined in, singing directly to the fire lizards. She was aware of Brudegan, then Sebell and Talmor coming to stand beside her, but facing the boys. Brudegan directed, cueing in the parts, the descant on the refrain. Above the male voices, pure and piercingly thrilling, rang the fire lizards' tone, weaving their own harmonies about the melody.

The last triumphant note echoed through the corridors of the Harper Hall. And from the doorway to the outer hall, there came a sigh of pleasure. Menolly saw the kitchen drudges, an utterly entranced Camo among them, standing there, every face wreathed with smiles.

"I'd say that a rendition of 'Moreta's Ride' might be in order, if you think your friends would oblige us," Brudegan said, with a slight bow to Menolly and a gesture to take his place.

Beauty, as if she understood what had been said, gave a complacent chirp, blinking the first lids across her eyes so that those nearest laughed. That startled her, and she fanned her wings as if scolding them for impudence. That prompted more laughter, but Beauty was now watching Menolly.

"Give the beat, Menolly," said Brudegan, and because his manner indicated that he expected her obedience, she raised her hands and sketched the time.

The chorus responded at the upstroke, and she experienced a curious sense of power as she realized that these voices were hers to direct. Beauty led the fire lizards in another dizzy climb of sound, but they sang the melody, octaves above the baritones who introduced the first stanza of the Ballad, to the muted humming of the other parts. The baritones, Menolly felt, were not really watching her: she signaled for more intensity because, after all, the Ballad told of a tragedy. The singers gave more depth to their part. Menolly had often led the evening sings at the Half-Circle Sea Hold, so conducting was not new to her. It was the quality of the singers, their responsiveness to her signals, that made as much difference as chalk from cheese.

Once the baritones had finished telling of the dread sickness in the land, which had struck with incredible speed across the breath of Pern, the full chorus quietly introduced the refrain, of Moreta secluded with her queen, Orlith, who is about to clutch in Fort Weyr, while the healers from all holds and Weyrs try to isolate the form of the disease and find a cure. The tenors take up the narration, with increasing intensity, the basses and baritones emphasizing the plight of the land, herdbeasts left untended, wherries breaking into crops as holders, crafters, dragonfolk alike are consumed by the dread fever.

A bass sings the solo of Capiam, Masterhealer of Pern, who isolates the illness and suggests its cure. Those dragonriders who are still able to stay on their beasts, fly to the rain forests of Nabol and Ista, to find and deliver to Capiam the all-important seeds that contain the cure, some riders dying with the effort as they complete their task.

A dialogue between baritone, Capiam, and the soprano; Moreta was sung, Menolly was only vaguely cognizant, by Piemur. Excitement builds as Moreta, once Orlith has clutched, is the only healthy dragonrider at the Fort and one of the few immune to the disease. It is up to her to deliver the medicine. Moreta, pushing herself and her queen to the limits of their endurance, flies *between* from hold to hold, crafthall to cot, from Weyr to Weyr. The final verse, a dirge with keening descant, this time so appropriately rendered by the fire lizards that Menolly waved the humans silent, ended in the sorrowful farewell of a world to its heroines as Orlith, the dying Moreta on her back, seeks the oblivion of *between*.

Such a deep silence followed the soft final chord that Menolly shook off the spell of the song with difficulty.

"I wonder if we could ever repeat that again," Brudegan

said slowly, thoughtfully, after a further moment of almost unendurable silence. A sigh of release from the thrall of the music spread through the hall.

"It's the fire lizards," said the very soft voice of the usually impudent Piemur.

"You're right, Piemur," Brudegan replied, considering the suggestion, and there was a murmur of assent from the others.

Menolly had taken a seat, her knees shaking and her insides gripped by a rhythmic shuddering. She took a sip of the klah remaining in her cup; cold or not, it helped.

"Menolly, do you think they'd sing like that again?" Brudegan asked, dropping to the bench beside her.

Menolly blinked at him, as much because she hadn't had time to recover from the extraordinary experience of directing a trained group as because he, as journeyman, was asking the advice of the newest arrival in the Harper Craft Hall.

"They sang fine with me yesterday, sir," said Piemur. Then he giggled. "Menolly told Master Shonagar that it's hard to keep 'em quiet when you *don't* want 'em singing. Right, Menolly?" Piemur chortled again, all his impudence revived. "That's what happened the other morning, sir, when you didn't know who was singing."

To Menolly's relief, Brudegan laughed heartily, evidently reconciled. Menolly managed a shy and apologetic smile for that untoward incident, but the chorus leader was watching the fire lizards now. They were preening their wingtips or glancing about the room at all the people, oblivious to the sensation they had just caused.

"Pretties sing pretty," said Camo, appearing beside Menolly and Brudegan, a pitcher of steaming klah in one hand. He poured some into each empty cup, and then Menolly noticed that the drink was being served throughout the hall.

"You liked their singing, eh, Camo?" asked Brudegan, taking a judicious sip from his mug. "Sing higher than Piemur here, and he's got the best voice we've had in many a Turn. As if he didn't know it." Brudegan reached across the table to ruffle Piemur's hair.

"Pretties sing again?" asked Camo plaintively.

"They can sing any time they like for all of me," Brudegan replied, nodding to Menolly. "But right now, I want to get some practice done. We've that big chorale work to polish properly before Lord Groghe's entertainment." With a sigh, he pushed himself to his feet and tapped an empty klah pot for silence. "Don't stop them if they feel like singing, Menolly," he added, inclining his head toward the fire lizards. "Now then, you lot. We'll begin with the tenor solo, Fesnal, if you please . . ." And Brudegan pointed to one of the journeymen who rose to his feet.

Listening to the rehearsal was not quite the same involving experience as directing. Then, Menolly had felt herself to be an extension of the choral group. Now she found it objectively interesting to observe Brudegan's direction, and to think what she would do with the same passages. About the time she decided that he was an exceedingly clever director, she realized that she'd been setting herself in comparison with a man in every way superior in experience and training.

Menolly almost laughed aloud. Yet, she reflected, this was what life should be in a Harper Hall: music, morning, noon, afternoon and evening. She couldn't have enough of it, and yet, she could now see the logic of afternoons spent on other chores. Her fingertips ached from the harp strings, and her scar felt hot and pulsed. She massaged her hand, but that was too painful. She'd left the jar of numbweed in the cot, which meant she'd have to wait until after Threadfall to get easement. She wondered if the girls knew what went on in the Harper Hall during Threadfall. Hadn't Piemur said they were up at the Hold during Fall? She shrugged; she was far happier to be here.

Once more the eerie alarm cut through other sounds. Brudegan abruptly ended the practice, thanking his chorus members for their attention and hard work. Then he stood back politely as a tall older journeyman walked quietly to the fireplace, raising his hands unnecessarily for attention.

121

"Everyone remembers his duties now?" There was a murmur of assent. "Good. As soon as the doors are open, join your sections. With luck and Fort Weyr's usual efficiency, we'll be back in the Hall by suppertime . . ."

"I've meatrolls for the outside crews," announced Silvina, standing up at the round table. "Camo, take the tray and stand by the door!"

A second weird hooting, and then the clang and ring of metal and a ponderous creaking. Menolly half wished that she were in a position to see the Hall doors working as light began to flood the outer hallway. A cheer went up, and the boys surged toward the entrance, some going across the tide to take meatrolls from Camo's patiently held tray.

Then the dining hall shutters clanked back, the afternoon sunlight an assault on eyes accustomed to the softer illumination from glow baskets.

"Here they come! Here they come!" rose the shout, and the flow toward the door became a scramble, despite the attempts of masters and journeymen to keep an orderly pace.

"We can see as well from the windows, Menolly. Come on!" Piemur tugged at her sleeve.

The fire lizards reacted to the excitement, streaking through the open windows. Menolly saw the spiral of dragons descending in wings to the ground beyond the Hall courtyard. Truly they made a magnificent sight. The sky seemed to be as clogged with dragons as just recently it must have been with Thread. The boys let out a cheer, and Menolly saw the dragonriders lifting their arms in response to the hurray! She might have lost her fear of Thread, of being caught out holdless, but she would never lose that lift of heart at the sight of the great dragons who protected all Pern from the ravages of Thread.

"Menolly!"

She whirled at the sound of her name and saw Silvina standing there, a slight frown creasing her wide forehead. For the first time since morning, Menolly wondered what she had done wrong now.

"Menolly, has nothing been forwarded to you from Benden Weyr in the way of clothes? I know that Master Robinton dragged you out of there with scant time to assemble yourself . . ."

Menolly could say nothing, realizing that Dunca had complained about her tattered trousers to Silvina. The headwoman was giving her clothes a keen scrutiny.

"Well, for once," and Silvina's admission was grudging, "Dunca is right. Your clothes are worn to the woof. Can't have that. You'll give the Harper Craft a bad name, wandering about in rags, however attached to them you may be."

"Silvina, I . . ."

"Great shells, child, I'm not angry with *you!*" And Silvina took Menolly's chin firmly in her hand and made her look eye to eye. "I'm furious with myself for not *thinking!* Not to mention giving that Dunca a chance to snipe at you! Only don't go repeating *that,* please, for Dunca's useful to me in her own way. Not that you talk much anyhow. Haven't heard you put two sentences together yet. There now! What have I said to distress you? You just come along with me." And Silvina took Menolly firmly by the elbow and marched her toward the complex of storage rooms at the back of the Harper Hall on the kitchen level.

"There's been so much excitement these days, I haven't any more wit about me than Camo. But then, every apprentice is supposed to come with two decent sets of clothing, new or nearly new, so it never occurred to me. And you having come from Benden Weyr, I thought . . . though you weren't there long enough, now, were you?"

"Felena gave me the skirt and tunic, and they took my measure for boots . . ."

"And Master Robinton threw you a-dragonback before you could say a word. Well now, let's just see," and Silvina unlocked a door, flipped open a glow basket to illuminate a storeroom stacked from floor to ceiling with bolts of cloth, clothing, boots, hides made or uncut, sleeping furs and rolls of tapestries and rugs. She gave Menolly another appraising look, turning her from side to side. "We've more that's suitable for boys and men from the Weaver and Tanner Halls . . ."

"I'd really prefer trousers."

Silvina chuckled kindly. "You're lanky enough to wear them well, I must say, and since you're to be using an instrument, trousers will be handier than skirts. But you ought to have some finery, child. It does lift the spirit and there're gathers . . ." She was sorting through folded skirts of black and brown, which she replaced disdainfully. "Now this . . ." and she pulled out a bolt of rich, dark red fabric.

"That's too fine for me . . ."

"You'd have me dress you in drudges' colors? Even they have something good!" Silvina was scornful. "You may not be proud in yourself, Menolly. In point of fact, your modesty has done you great service, but you will kindly consider the change in your circumstances. You're not the youngest child in a family of an isolated Sea Hold. You're an apprentice harper, and *we*"—Silvina tapped her chest smartly with her fingers—"have appearances to maintain. You will dress yourself as well as, and if I've my way, better than, those fumble-fingered females, or those musical midgets who will never be more than senior apprentices or very junior journeymen. Now, a rich red will become you. Ah, yes, this will suit you well," she said holding the red up against Menolly's shoulder. "Until I can have that made up, trous will have to do," and she held up a pair of dark blue hide pants to Menolly's waist. "You're all leg. And here." She shoved a pair of close-woven blue-green trousers at Menolly. "This should match the leather pants, and it does," she said tossing to Menolly a dark blue jerkin. "Put that lot on the chest there and try on this wherhide jacket. Yes, that's not too bad a fit, is it? Here's a hat and gloves. And tunics. Now these," and from another chest Silvina extracted breast bands and underpants, snorting as she passed them to Menolly. "Dunca was quite incensed that you'd no under-things at all." Silvina's amusement ended as she saw Menolly's face. "Whyever are you looking so stricken?

Because you wore your underthings out? Or because Dunca's pried into your affairs? You can't honestly be worried what that fat old fool thinks or says or does? Yes, you can and you are and you would!"

Silvina pushed Menolly backward until she sat abruptly on the chest behind her while Silvina, hands on her hips, regarded her with a curiously intense expression.

"I think," said Silvina slowly, in a very gentle voice, "that you have lived too much alone. And not just in that cave. And I think you must have been terribly bereft when old Petiron died. He seems to have been the only one in your Hold who understood what's in you. Though why he left it so long to tell Master Robinton I simply don't understand. Well, in a way I do, but that's neither here nor there. One thing certain, you're not staying on in that cot. Not another night . . ."

"Oh, but Silvina—"

"Don't 'oh but Silvina' me," the woman said sharply, but her expression was mocking, not stern. "Don't think I've missed Pona's little tricks, or Dunca's. No, the cot is the wrong place for you. I thought so when you first arrived, but there were other reasons for plunking you there at first. So we'll take the long view, as should be done, and shift you here. Oldive doesn't want you on your feet so much, and sure as Fall'll come again, the fire lizards are as unhappy at Dunca's as she is to have them. The old fool! No, Menolly," and now Silvina was angry with Menolly, "it is not your fault! Besides which, as a full harper apprentice, you really haven't anything to do with the paying students. Further, you ought to be near those fire lizard eggs until they hatch. So, you're staying here in the Hall! And that's the end of the matter." Silvina got to her feet. "Let's just gather these clothes, and we'll settle you right now. Back in the room you had the first night. It's handy to the Harper's and all—"

"That's much too grand a place for me!"

Silvina gave her a droll look. "I could, of course, move all the furniture out, take down the hangings, and give you an apprentice's cot and a fold stool . . ."

"I'd feel better about it . . ."

Silvina stared at her so that Menolly broke off, flustered.

"Why, you numbwit. You think I meant that?"

"Didn't you? Because the things in that room are far too valuable for an apprentice." Silvina was still staring at her. "Having nine fire lizards is causing enough trouble. The room would be just grand, and if I've only the furnishings of any other apprentice, why, that's proper, isn't it?"

Silvina gave her one more long, appraising look, shaking her head and laughing to herself.

"You're right, you know. Then none of the others could quibble about the change. But an apprentice's cot is narrow, and you've the fire lizards to consider."

"Two apprentice cots? If you have them to spare—?"

"Done! We'll tie the legs together and heap the rushes high."

Which is what they did. Without the rich hangings and heavy furniture, the chamber was echoingly empty. Menolly insisted that she didn't mind; but Silvina said it wasn't up to her because who was headwoman in this Hall? Hangings that Silvina had removed for shabbiness were recovered from storage, and Menolly was told that she could mend them when she had free time. Several small rugs were spread on the floor. A long table from the apprentices' study (with a leg mended after being damaged in a brawl), a bench and a small press for storage gave the room some homeyness. Silvina said that the place looked heartlessly plain but certainly no one could fault it for not displaying an apprentice's lowly state.

"Now then, that's settled. Yes, Piemur, you were looking for me?"

"No, Silvina. It's Menolly I'm after. For Master Shonagar. She's dead late for her lesson."

"Nonsense, there're no regular lessons on a Threadfall day. He should know that as well as anyone," Silvina said, taking Menolly by the arm as she started to leave the room.

"That's what I told him, Silvina," said Piemur, grinning from ear to ear, "but he asked me when had Menolly been assigned to a section. And, of course, I know she hasn't, so he said that she'd have nothing better to do with her time so she'd better learn something constructive. So . . ." And Piemur shrugged his helplessness in the face of such logic.

"Well, girl, you'd better go then. We're all settled here anyway. And you, Piemur, you pop over to Dunca's. Ask Audiva, politely, too, you imp, to bundle up Menolly's things . . . including the skirt and tunic Menolly washed today. What else did you have there, Menolly?"

Silvina smiled as if she knew perfectly well that Menolly was grateful not to have to return to the cot.

"Master Jerint has my pipes so there's only the medicines."

"Off with you, Piemur, and mind you make sure it's Audiva."

"I'd've asked for her anyhow, Silvina!"

"Bold as brass you are," Silvina called after him as he scampered down the steps. "A good lad at heart. You've heard him sing? He's younger than I like to have them in the Hall, but he does hold his own, rascal that he is, and where else should he be with a glorious treble voice like that? Planting tubers or herding the beasties? No, for such originals as Piemur and yourself, you're better here. Off with you now, before Master Shonagar starts bellowing. We don't really need a claxon with him in the Hall, so we don't."

Silvina had walked Menolly down the steps and now gave her a gentle shove toward the open Hall doors as she turned toward the kitchen. Menolly watched her for a moment, suffused by an inarticulate gratitude and affection for Silvina's understanding. The woman wasn't at all like Petiron, and yet Menolly knew that she could go to Silvina, as she had to Petiron, when she was perplexed or in difficulties. Silvina was like . . . like a storm anchor. Menolly, trotting obediently across the yard to Master Shonagar, smiled at such a seamanly metaphor for a land-bound woman.

Master Shonagar did roar and bellow and carry on, but,

buoyed by Silvina's courtesies, Menolly took the berating in silence until he made her promise faithfully that whatever else happened to her during the morning hours, the afternoon was his. Otherwise he'd never make a singer of her. So she was to report to him, please and thank you, through Fall, fog or fire, for how else was she to be a credit to his skill or the Craft Hall that had been pleased to exhibit its secrets for her edification and education?

Chapter 7

Don't leave me alone!
A cry in the night,
Of anguish heart-striking,
Of soul-killing fright.

The restlessness of the fire lizards about her woke Menolly from a deep sleep. She wished irritably that they didn't insist on sleeping with her; it had been an exciting and trying day, and she'd had a hard enough time getting to sleep. Her hand ached so from the day's playing that she'd had to slather the scar with numbweed to dull the pain. Beauty's tail twitched violently against Menolly's ear. She nudged the little queen, hoping to stir her out of whatever dream disturbed her. But Beauty was awake, not dreaming: her eyes, yellow and whirling with anxiety. All the fire lizards were awake and unusually alert in the dark of the night.

Seeing that Menolly's eyes were open, Beauty crooned, a half-fearful, half-worried sound. Rocky and Diver minced up Menolly's legs and crouched on her stomach, extending their heads toward her. Their eyes, too, were whirling with the speed and shade of fear. The rest, cuddling close against her, crooned for comfort.

Propping herself up on one elbow, Menolly peered toward the open windows. She could just distinguish the Fort Hold fire heights, black against the dark sky. It took her some time to locate the dark bulk of the watch dragon.

He was motionless, so whatever distressed the fire lizards did not apparently concern him.

"Whatever is your problem, Beauty?"

The little queen's croon increased its intensity. First Rocky, then Diver, added their notes. Aunties One and Two crept up and nuzzled to get under Menolly's left arm. Lazy, Mimic and Uncle burrowed into the fur at her right side, their twined tails latching fiercely onto her wrist while Brownie piteously paced across her feet. They were afraid.

"What's gotten into you?" Menolly couldn't for the life of her imagine anything within the Harper Craft Hall that would menace them. Covet them, yes; injure them, no.

"Shush a minute and let me listen." Beauty and Rocky gave little spurting sounds of fear, but they obeyed her. She listened as hard as she could, but the only sounds on the night air were the comfortable murmur of men's voices and an occasional laugh from the Hall beneath her. It wasn't as late as it had first seemed to her then, if the masters and older journeymen were still chatting.

Gently disengaging tails, Menolly slipped from her sleeping furs to the window. Several rectangles of light shone on the stones of the courtyard, two from the Great Hall and one above it, from Robinton's quarters, beyond hers.

Beauty gave a worried cheep and flew to Menolly's shoulder, wrapping her tail tightly around the girl's neck and burrowing into her hair, the slender little body trembling. The others set up an anxious clamor from the furs, so Menolly hurriedly returned to them. They were panic-stricken. The Masterharper might not approve of Silvina's moving her into this room if her fire lizards disturbed his studies at night. She tried to quiet them with a soft song, but now Beauty's voice rose querulously above her lullaby. Menolly gathered all of the fire lizards against her. Their tails twined about her arms so firmly that she couldn't use her hands to stroke them.

Now she felt a confused sense of imminent danger; clearly all the fire lizards were responding to a mutually experienced threat. Menolly fought against the panic their fear stirred in her.

"You're being ridiculous. What can harm us in the Harper Hall?"

Beauty on one side, Rocky on the other, stroked her face urgently with their heads, cheeping in mounting distress. Through their touch and minds, she got the distinct impression that they were reacting to a fear beyond them, beyond the walls, at a distance.

"Then how could it hurt you?"

Suddenly their terror erupted in her with such intensity that she cried out.

"Don't!" Her injunction was spontaneous. She tried to throw up her arms to protect herself from this unknown danger, but her hands were lizard-bound. Their fear was completely and utterly hers. And, incoherently, she repeated the cry, "Don't! DON'T!"

In her mind, out of nowhere, Menolly received an indelible impression of turbulence: savage, ruthless, destructive; a pressure inexorable and deadly; churning masses of slick, sickly gray surfaces that heaved and dipped. Heat as massive as a tidal wave. Fear! Terror! An inarticulate longing!

A scream, heard in her mind, a scream like a knife upon raw nerves!

"DON'T LEAVE ME ALONE!"

Menolly didn't think she had cried out. She was, as far as she could think sanely, certain that she hadn't heard the cry, but she knew that the words had been spoken at the extreme of someone's anguish.

Simultaneously the door to her room burst open, and the watch dragon on the Hold fire heights let out a shriek so like the one in her mind that she wondered if the dragon had called before. But dragon's don't speak.

"Menolly! What's wrong?" Master Robinton was striding across the floor to her. The fire lizards took wing, darting out one window and back in the next, maniacal with fear.

131

"The dragon!" Menolly pointed, diverting Robinton's eyes to the window, to prove that she wasn't alone in alarm. They both saw the watch dragon launching himself, riderless, into the sky, bulging his distress. Robinton and Menolly heard, on the night air, the faint echo of answering bugles, a moment of silence and then the eerie screech of an hysterical watchwher from the Fort Hold court.

"Is every winged thing in the Hold out of its mind?" asked Robinton. "What made you scream, Menolly? 'Don't' what?"

"I don't know," Menolly cried, tears streaming down her face. She experienced a profound grief now and hugged herself against the chill of an awe-filled panic she couldn't explain and yet had experienced so profoundly. "I just don't know."

Robinton ducked as Beauty, leading the others, swooped past him and out the window. The queen was screaming at the others to follow. Menolly saw them outlined briefly by the light of the Masterharper's window and then the entire fair disappeared. Before Menolly, frightened for fear the fire lizards had gone completely from her, could tell Master Robinton, Domick came charging into the room.

"Robinton, what's going on—"

"Quiet, Domick!" The Masterharper's stern voice interrupted. "Whatever has frightened Menolly has also alarmed the watch dragon, and even the dead could hear that watchwher's howling. Furthermore, the dragon went *between*, without his rider!"

"What?" Domick was startled, no longer angry.

"Menolly," said Robinton, his hands warm and firm on her shoulder, his voice kindly calm, "take a deep breath. Now, take another . . ."

"I can't. I can't. Something terrible is happening," and Menolly was appalled at the sobs that tore at her, the cold terror that made her tremble so violently in the grip of this unknown disaster. "It's something terrible . . ."

Others were crowding into her room now, roused by

her involuntary cries. Someone said loudly that there wasn't anything stirring in the court or on any of the roads. Another remarked that it was ridiculous to be startled out of a sound sleep by an hysterical child, trying to attract attention.

"Hold your silly tongue, Morshal," said Silvina, pushing through the crowd to Menolly's bed. "Better still, get off to your beds. All of you. You're no help here."

"Yes, if you'd please leave," said Robinton in a voice as close to anger as anyone had ever heard in him.

"It isn't the eggs hatching, it is?" Sebell asked anxiously.

Menolly shook her head, struggling to control herself and to stop the spasmodic shudders of fear that were depriving her of voice and wit enough to explain what was so inexplicable.

Silvina was soothing her. "Her hands are ice cold, Robinton," she said, and Menolly clung to the woman, as Robinton slipped to the other side of the double cot to support her shuddering body. "And these aren't hysterical tremors . . ."

Abruptly the spasms eased, then ceased completely. Menolly went limp against Silvina, gasping for breath, forcing herself to breathe as deeply as Robinton again urged her to do.

"Whatever was wrong has stopped," she said, spent.

Silvina and the Harper eased her against the bed rushes, Silvina drawing the fur up to her neck.

"Did the fire lizards take a fit?" the headwoman asked, glancing about the now-bright room. "They're not here . . ."

"I saw them go *between*. I don't know where. They were so afraid. It was incredible. There was nothing I could do."

"Take your time and tell us," said the Masterharper.

"I don't know all of it. I woke because they were so restless. They usually sleep quietly. And they got more and more frightened. And there wasn't anything . . . nothing . . . I could *see* that . . ."

"Yes, yes, but something caused them to react." Robinton had captured her hand and was stroking it reassuringly. "Tell us the sequence."

"They were frightened out of their wits. And it got to me, too. Then," and Menolly swallowed quickly against that flash of vivid impression, "then, in my mind, I was aware of something so dangerous, so terrible, something heaving, and gray and deadly. . . . Masses of it . . . all gray and . . . and . . . terrible! Hot, too. Yes, the heat was part of the terror. Then a longing. I don't know which was the worst . . ." She clutched at the comforting hands and could not keep back the sobs of fright that rose from her guts. "I wasn't asleep either. It wasn't just a bad dream!"

"Don't talk anymore, Menolly. We can hope the terror has passed completely."

"No, I have to tell you. That's part of it. I'm supposed to tell. Then . . . I heard, only I didn't hear . . except that it was as clear as if someone had shouted it right in this room . . . right inside my head . . . I heard something scream, 'Don't leave me alone!' "

The muscles in her body relaxed all at once now that she had spoken of the weight of terror.

" 'Don't leave me alone'?" The Harper repeated the words half to himself, puzzling over the significance of the phrase.

"It's all gone now. Being afraid, I mean . . . and . . ."

The fire lizards swooped back into the room, aiming for the bed, but some of them dipped and darted for the window ledges, away from Master Robinton and Silvina, twittering, but only with surprise, not fear. Beauty and the two bronzes landed on the foot of the double cot, chirping at Menolly with little calls that sounded so normally inquisitive that Menolly let out an exasperated exclamation.

"Don't scold them, Menolly," said the Masterharper. "See if you can determine where they've just been."

Menolly beckoned to Beauty, who obediently crawled up to her arm and permitted Menolly to stroke her head and body.

134

"She's certainly not bothered by anything now."

"Yes, but where did she go?"

Menolly raised Beauty to her face, looking into the idly whirling eyes, laying the back of her hand against Beauty's cheek. "Where'd you go, pet? Where have you just been?"

Beauty stroked Menolly's hand, gave a smug chirrup, cocking her dainty head to one side. But an impression reached Menolly's mind, of a Weyr Bowl, and many dragons and excited people.

"I think they've been back to Benden Weyr. It must be Benden! They don't know Fort Weyr well enough to be that vivid. And whatever happened involved many dragons and lots of excited people."

"Ask Beauty what frightened her."

Menolly stroked the little queen's head for a moment longer, to reassure her, because the question was sure to upset the little fire lizard. It did. Beauty launched herself from Menolly's arm so violently that her talons scratched deep enough to draw blood.

"A dragon falling in the sky!" Menolly gasped out the picture. "Dragons don't fall in the sky."

"She scratched you, child . . ."

"Oh, that's nothing, Master Robinton, but I don't think we'll get anything more out of her."

Beauty was clinging to the fireplace, chittering irritably, her eyes wheeling angrily orange.

"If something has happened at Benden Weyr, Master Robinton," remarked Silvina in a dry tone of voice, "they won't be overlong in sending for you." Silvina had to raise her voice to counteract the excited cries of the other fire lizards, who were reacting to Beauty's scolding. "We'd best not upset the creatures any further now. And I'm getting you a dose, young lady, or you'll never sleep tonight from the look of your eyes."

"I didn't mean to disturb everyone . . ."

Silvina gave her an exasperated snort, dismissing the need for an apology, although Menolly couldn't help but see, as Silvina opened the door, that harpers were lingering in the corridor. Menolly heard Silvina berating them and telling them to get off to their beds, what did they think they knew about fire lizards?

"The strangest aspect to this incident, Menolly," said the Masterharper, his forehead creased with thought lines, "is that the dragon reacted, too. I've *never* seen a dragon—short of a mating flight—go off without his rider. I shouldn't wonder," and Robinton smiled wryly, "if we don't have T'ledon over here demanding an explanation from you for the disappearance of his dragon."

The notion of a dragonrider compelled to ask her for advice was so absurd that Menolly managed a weak smile.

"How's that hand? You've been playing a lot, I hear," and the Harper turned her left hand over in his. "That scar's too red. You have been doing too much. Make haste a little more slowly. Is it painful?"

"Not much. Master Oldive gave me some salve."

"And your feet?"

"So long as I don't have to stand too much or walk too far . . ."

"Too bad your fire lizards can't combine to give you one little dragonpower."

"Sir?"

"Yes?"

"I think I ought to tell you . . . my fire lizards can lift things. They brought me my pipes the other day . . . to spare me the walk . . ." she added hastily. "They took it from my room at the cot, all in a cluster, and then dropped it into my hands!"

"Now that is very interesting. I didn't realize they had so much initiative. You know, Brekke, Mirrim and F'nor have got theirs to carry messages on a collar about their necks . . ." The Masterharper smiled with amusement, ". . . though they aren't always good about arriving promptly."

"I think you have to make certain *they* know how urgent the matter is."

"Like having your pipes for Master Jerint?"

"I didn't wish to be late, and I can't walk fast."

"We'll let that stand as the reason then, Menolly," said Robinton gently, and when Menolly glanced up at him startled, she saw the kind understanding in his eyes and flushed. He stroked her hand again. "What I don't *know*, I sometimes guess, knowing the way people interact, Menolly. Don't keep so much bottled inside, girl. And do tell me anything unusual that your fire lizards do. That's far more important than *why* they did it. We don't know much about these tiny cousins of the dragons, and I have a suspicion they'll be very important creatures to us."

"Is the little white dragon all right?"

"Reading my mind, too, Menolly? Little Ruth is all right," but the Harper's heavy, slightly hesitant tone gave the lie to his reassurance. "Don't fret yourself about Jaxom and Ruth. Just about everyone else on Pern does." He placed her hand back on the furs with a final pat.

Silvina returned, offering Menolly the mug she'd brought, and stood over her while she downed the dose, gagging a little at the bitterness.

"Yes, I know. I made it strong on purpose. You need to sleep. And Master Robinton, there's a messenger from the Hold for you below. Urgent, he said, and he's out of breath!"

"Sleep yourself out, Menolly," the Harper said as he rapidly left the room.

"Trouble?" Menolly asked Silvina, hoping to be told something.

"Not for you, or because of you, m'girl." Silvina chuckled, pushing the sleeping fur under Menolly's chin. "I understand that Groghe, Lord of Fort Hold, experienced the same unnerving nightmare, as he calls it, that you did and has sent for Master Robinton to explain it to him. Now rest and don't fuss yourself."

"How could I? You must have doubled that dose of fellis juice," said Menolly, relaxed and tactless in the grip of the drug. She couldn't keep her eyes open and effortlessly drifted to sleep to the sound of another chuckle from Silvina. One last thought let her slip easily into unconsciousness: Lord Groghe's fire lizard had reacted, so *she* wasn't hysterical.

She awoke slightly at one point, not quite conscious of her surroundings but aware of a rumbling voice, a treble response, and hungry creelings. When she woke completely later, there was an empty bowl on the floor, and her friends were curled up about her in slumbering balls, wing-limp. The gnawing in her stomach suggested that she had slept well into the day, and the hunger was all her own. If the fire lizards had been that starved, they'd've been awake. Doubtless Camo and Piemur had done her the favor of feeding her friends. She grinned; Piemur and Camo must have been delighted at the chance.

The shutters were open and, with no sounds of music or voices, she guessed it must be afternoon and the Hall's population dispersed to their various chores. The watch dragon was back on the fire heights.

She sat upright in bed as the memory of the previous night's terror shattered her pleasant somnolence. At the same moment there was a tap on her door, and before she could answer, Silvina entered, carrying a small tray.

"My timing's very good," she said, pleased and smiling. "Do you feel rested?"

Menolly nodded in reply and thanked Silvina for the hot klah she was handed. "But, if I can be bold, you don't look as if you slept at all." Silvina's eyes were dark-circled and red-shot.

"Well, you're right and you're not bold, but I'm on my way to my bed, I can assure you, as soon as I've straightened up for Robinton. Now . . ." and Silvina nudged Menolly's hip so the girl made room for her to sit on the bed, "you ought to hear what disturbed your friends last night. No one else will think to tell you with the Harper away. Also, I've just checked the eggs, and I think you should take a look at them. . . . Not, however, until you've finished your klah," and Silvina put a restraining hand on Menolly's shoulder. "I want your wits in place and not fellis-fuddled."

"What happened?"

"The bare bones of the matter are that F'nor, brown

Canth's rider, took it into his head to go to the Red Star last night . . ."

Menolly's gasp woke the fire lizards.

"Mind your thoughts, girl. I don't want them turning hysterical again, thank you." Silvina waited until the creatures had settled back into their naps.

"That's what seems to have set the fire lizards off, at any rate. And not just yours. Robinton said that anyone who has a fire lizard had the same trouble you did, only with your having nine, it was intensified. What happened was that Canth and F'nor went *between* to the Red Star. . . . Yes, small wonder you were terrified. What you told us about grayness and all that hideous heat and churning, that's what's on the Red Star. No one could land there!" She paused, gave a smug grunt. "That'll shut up the Lord Holders for wanting to *go* there!"

"Canth and F'nor?" Menolly felt fear stab coldly up her throat, and she remembered the scream.

"They're alive, but only just. And when you said, 'Don't leave me alone'? What you heard . . . and it had to be through your fire lizards . . . was Brekke calling out to F'nor and Canth." Silvina broke her narrative for effect. "Somehow they got back. Well, partway back from the Red Star. It must have been the most incredible sight . . ." Silvina's tired eyes narrowed, reconstructing that vision. "The reason the hold dragon took off was to help land Canth. It was like a path, Robinton tells us, of dragons in the air, catching Canth and F'nor, and braking their fall. They were both senseless, of course. Robinton says there isn't a scrap of hide left on Canth; as if some mighty hand had sanded his skin away. F'nor is not much better, for all he wore wherhide."

"Silvina, how could my fire lizards know what was happening at Benden Weyr?"

"Ramoth called the dragons . . . the Benden queen can do that, you know. Your fire lizards have been at Benden Weyr. Perhaps they heard her, too," Silvina dismissed that part of the mystery impatiently.

"But, Silvina, my fire lizards were afraid long before

Ramoth called the Fort dragon, even before I heard Brekke call."

"Why, that's right. Ah well, we'll find the answer to that mystery in due time. We always do at the Harper Hall. If dragons can talk to dragons across distance, why can't fire lizards?"

"Dragons think sense," Menolly said, gently scratching her waking queen's little head, "and these beauties don't. At least not often."

"Babies don't make sense, and your fire lizards aren't all that long out of the shell. But think on it, Menolly. Camo doesn't make much sense, but he does have feelings."

"Was it he who fed my fire lizards this morning so I could sleep?"

"He and Piemur. Camo fussed and fussed before breakfast until I had to send him up here, with Piemur, to shut his moans." Silvina's chuckle was half amusement, half remembered irritation. "Nag, nag, nag about 'pretties hungry,' 'feed pretties.' Piemur said you didn't wake. Did you?"

"No." But the matter of fire lizard intelligence was more urgent in Menolly's estimation. "I suppose being at Benden Weyr might explain their reaction."

"Not entirely," Silvina replied briskly. "Lord Groghe's little friend responded, too. It wasn't hatched at Benden and has never been there. There may well be more to these creatures than being silly pets after all. And making idiots of men who fancy themselves as good as dragonriders."

"I've finished my klah. Shall we see the eggs now?"

"Yes, by all means. If his egg should hatch without the Harper, we'd never hear the end of it."

"Is Sebell about?"

"Hovering!" Silvina's grimace was so maliciously expressive that Menolly laughed. "How're your feet today?"

"Only stiff."

"Just remember that that salve doesn't do you any good in the jar."

"Yes, Silvina."

"Don't you 'yes, Silvina' me meekly, m'girl," and there was unexpected warmth and affection in the woman's tone. Menolly smiled shyly back as the headwoman left the room.

She dressed quickly in one of the new tunics and the blue wherhide trousers, plumped up the rushes in their bag and smoothed the sleeping fur over all.

Silvina had just finished tidying up the Harper's room when Menolly entered, Beauty winging in gracefully behind her. She landed on Menolly's shoulder and, as Menolly checked both eggs, peered with equally curious interest. She chirped a question at Menolly.

"Well?" drawled Silvina, "now that you experts have conferred. . . ."

Menolly giggled. "I don't think Beauty knows anymore than I do. She's never seen eggs hatch, but they are a good deal harder. They've been kept so nicely warm. I don't know for sure, but I suspect they'll hatch at any time now."

Silvina drew in her breath sharply, startling Beauty. "That Harper! The problem will be keeping track of him." She gave the rush bag a final poke and twitched the sleeping fur straight. "If Lord Groghe," and Silvina jerked her head toward the Fort Hold palisade, "isn't sending for him, F'lar is. Or Lord Lytol for that white dragonet."

"If he wants to Impress his fire lizard, he'll have to make a choice, won't he?"

Silvina gaped at Menolly for a long moment and then burst out laughing.

"Might be the best thing that's happened since the queens were killed," Silvina said, mopping laugh tears from her eyes. "The man's had no more than a few hours sleep a day. . . ." Silvina gestured toward the study room, flicking her fingers at the scattered piles of records, the scrawls on the sandtable's surface, the half-empty wine sack with its pouring neck collapsed ludicrously to one side. "He won't miss the Impression of his fire lizard!

But isn't there some sign to tell if the Hatching is imminent? The dragonmen can tell. And what the Harper's doing is really urgent."

"When Beauty and the others hatched, the old queen and her flight hummed, sort of deep in the throat . . ." Menolly said cautiously, after a moment's thought.

Silvina nodded encouragingly.

"This isn't Beauty's clutch, so I don't know if she'll react, though the dragons at Benden Weyr hummed for Ramoth's clutch. So it seems logical that the fire lizards would react the same way."

Silvina agreed. "There'd be a slight interval in which we could track the Harper down? Supposing we can't get him to stay put here for the next day or two?"

Menolly hesitated, reluctant to agree to a conclusion achieved by guesswork.

"And they eat anything when they hatch?" asked Silvina who appeared content with the supposition.

"Just about." Menolly remembered the sack of spider-claws, not the easiest of edibles, that had gone down the throats of her newly hatched friends. "Red meat is best."

"That will please Camo," Silvina said cryptically. "Now I think you'd best stay here. Well, what's wrong with that? Robinton would give up more than the privacy of his quarters to have a fire lizard. He's even threatened to forego his wine . . ." Silvina had a snort for that unlikely sacrifice. "Well, what is wrong with you?"

"Silvina . . . it's afternoon, isn't it?"

"Yes, indeed."

"I'm pledged to go . . . I must go . . . to Master Shonagar. He was very insistent . . "

"Oh, he was, was he? And will he explain to Master Robinton that your voice is more important than the Harper's fire lizard? Oh, don't get yourself in a pucker. Sebell can sit in for you. And you tell your fire lizards to stand by . . ." Silvina walked to the open window and peered down into the courtyard. "Piemur! Piemur, ask Sebell to step up to the Harper's room, will you? Menolly? Yes, she's awake and here. No, she can't attend Master Shonagar until Sebell arrives. Yes? Well, go through the choir hall *to* the journeymen's quarters and give Master Shonagar *my* message. Menolly answers to Master Robinton first, me second and *then* any of the other masters who require her attention."

Menolly fretted about Master Shonagar's certain wrath while Silvina made her wait until Piemur had found and returned, at a run, with Sebell.

"They're hatching?" Sebell slithered to a stop in the doorway, breathing hard, his face flushed and anxious.

"Not quite yet," Menolly said, ready to speed to Master Shonagar but unwilling to brush impolitely past the journeyman blocking the entrance.

"How will I know?"

"Menolly says the fire lizards hum," replied Silvina. "Shonagar insists on her presence now."

"He would! Where's the Harper?"

"At Ruatha Hold by now, I think," Silvina said. "He went off to Benden Weyr when the dragonrider came for him. He said he'd stop off to see Mastersmith Fandarel at Telgar . . ."

Sebell's eyes went from Silvina to Menolly in surprise, as if Silvina were being indiscreet.

"More than any other, saving yourself, Menolly will need to know how many tunes a harper, much less *the* Harper, plays," she said. "I'll send more klah and . . ." now she chuckled, "have Camo lay about with that hatchet of his on the meat."

Menolly told the fire lizards to stay by Sebell, and then she scurried down the steps and across the courtyard to the chorus hall.

Despite Silvina's reassurance, Menolly was apprehensive as she made her tardy arrival before Master Shonagar. But he said nothing. That made her dereliction harder. He kept looking at her until she nervously began to shift her weight from foot to foot.

"I do not know what it is about you, young Menolly, that you can disrupt an entire Craft Hall, for you are not presumptuous. In fact, you are immodestly modest. You do not brag nor flaunt your rank nor put yourself forward. You listen, which I assure you is a pleasure and relief, and you learn from what you are told, which is veritably unheard of. I begin to entertain hope that I have finally discovered, in a mere slip of a girl, the dedication required of a true musician, an artist! Yes, I might even coax a real voice out of your throat." His fist came down with an almighty wallop on the sandtable, the opposite end flapping onto its supports. She jumped. "But even I cannot do much if you are not *here!*"

"Silvina said . . ."

"Silvina is a wonderful woman. Without her the Hall would be in chaos and our comfort ignored," Master Shonagar said, still in a loud tone. "She is also a good musician . . . ah, you didn't know that? You should make the occasion to listen to her singing, my dear girl. . . . *But,*" again the voice boomed, Master Shonagar's belly bouncing, although the rest of him seemed stationary, "I thought I had made it plain that *you are to be here without fail* every single day!"

"Yes, sir!"

"Come fog, fire or Fall! Have I made myself plain enough?"

"Yes, sir!"

"*Then . . .*" and his voice dropped to normal proportions, "let us begin with breathing . . ."

Menolly fought the desire to giggle. She mastered it by breathing deeply and then settled quickly to the discipline of the lesson.

When Master Shonagar had dismissed her with a further injunction to be on time not the next day, which was a rest day and he needed his rest, but the day following, the work parties were back from their chores. To her surprise, she was greeted by many of the boys as she raced past them to get back to the fire lizard eggs. She answered, smiling, unsure of names and faces but inwardly warmed by their recognition. As she took the steps to the higher level two at a time, she wondered if the boys all knew about the previous night's disturbance. Probably. News spreads faster in this Craft Hall than Thread could burrow.

The sounds of soft gitar strumming reached her ears as

she got to the upper hall. She slowed down, out of breath anyhow, and arrived at the Harper's quarters still breathing heavily, much as Sebell had done. He glanced up, grinned understandingly, and held up a hand to reassure her. Then his hand gestured to the sandtable. All her fire lizards were there, crouched, watching him.

"I've had an audience. What I can't tell is if my music has pleased them."

"It has," Menolly told him, smiling. She extended her arm for Beauty, who immediately glided to her. "See, their eyes tell you . . . the green is dominant, which is sleeping pleasure. Red means hunger, blue and green are sort of general shades, white means danger, and yellow is fright. The speed of the eye whirling tells you how intensely they feel about something."

"What about him then?" And Sebell pointed to Lazy whose eyes were first-lidded.

"He's called Lazybones for good reason."

"I wasn't playing a lullaby."

"Except when he's hungry, he's that way. Here," and Menolly scooped Lazy up from the sandtable and deposited him on Sebell's arm. Startled, the man froze. "Stroke his eye ridges and the back joints of the wings. There! See? He's crooning with delight."

Sebell had obeyed her instructions, and now Lazy collapsed about the journeyman's forearm, locked his claws loosely about the wrist and stretched his head across the back of Sebell's hand. Sebell caressed him, a shy and delighted smile on his face.

"I hadn't thought they'd be so soft to the touch."

"You have to watch for patchy skin and oil it well. I did a thorough job on these the other evening, but you can see where I'll have to do them again. Just stay there . . ." And Menolly quickly went down the hall to her room for the salve, Beauty complaining at the jouncing on her shoulder.

As they spread salve on the fire lizards, Sebell grew more confident of his handling of the creatures. He wore a half-smile, as if surprised to find himself at such a task.

"Do all fire lizards sing?" he asked, oiling Brownie.

"I don't really know. I suppose mine learned simply because I used to sing to them in the cave." Menolly smiled to herself, remembering the fire lizards perched attentively on the ledges about the cave, their little heads turning from side to side to catch the sounds of music.

"Any audience being better than none?" asked Sebell. "Did anyone think to tell you that Lord Groghe's little queen has recently started to sing along with the Hold Harper?"

"Oh no!"

"If Groghe could carry a tune," Sebell went on, enjoying her dismay, "it'd be understandable. Don't worry about it, Menolly. I heard also that Groghe's delighted." Then Sebell's expression altered subtly.

"I'll bet Lord Groghe wasn't so happy about last night, was he?" she hesitated, then blurted out. "Do you think Canth and F'nor will live?"

"They have much to live for, Menolly. Brekke needs them to stay alive. She's lost her queen already. She'll make them live. We'll know more when the Harper returns."

Camo entered the room, carrying a heavily laden tray. His thick-featured face changed from ludicrous anxiety to beams of joy as he saw first the fire lizards and then Menolly.

"Pretty ones hungry? Camo has food?" And Menolly saw two huge pans of meat in pieces among the other dishes on the tray.

"Thank you for feeding the pretties this morning, Camo."

"Camo very quiet. Very quiet." The man bobbed at Menolly in such a fashion that the pitcher of klah splashed.

Sebell deftly relieved him of the tray and set it on the sandtable center board.

"You're a good man, Camo," the journeyman said, "but go to the kitchen now. You must help Abuna. She needs you."

"Pretty ones hungry?" The disappointment was writ large on Camo's face.

"No, not now, Camo," Menolly said gently, smiling up at him. "See, they're asleep."

Camo turned himself in a circle toward the sandtable and then the window ledges where several of the fire lizards were sprawled on the sun-warmed stone, glistening with their recent oiling.

"We'll feed them again tonight, Camo."

"Tonight? Good. Don't forget? Promise? Promise? Camo feed pretties?"

"I promise, Camo," Menolly said with extra fervor. The wistful, piteous way in which the poor man asked her to promise suggested that too many promises made to Camo were conveniently forgotten.

"Now," Sebell said as the man shuffled from the room, "Silvina said you'd no time for more than klah when you woke. If I remember Shonagar's lessons, you'll be starved."

To Menolly's delight, there was redfruit on the tray as well as meatrolls, klah, cheese, bread and a sweet conserve. Sebell ate lightly, more to keep her company than because he was hungry, though he said he'd been studying. To prove that, he rattled off the names and descriptions of the fish she had given him the other morning.

"Did I remember them all correctly?" he asked, peering at her as she stared at him in amazement.

"Yes, you did!"

"Think I can pose as a seaman now?"

"If you only have to name fish!"

"If only . . ." he paused dramatically, making a grimace for that restriction. "I had a chat with a bronze dragonrider I know at Fort Weyr. He's agreed to take us, on the quiet, to any body of water that you feel is adequate to teach me how to sail."

"Teach you how to sail!" Menolly was appalled. "In one easy lesson, like those fish names?"

"No, but I don't think I'll actually have to sail. I should know the fundamentals and leave . . ." he grinned at her, ". . . the doing to the experts in the craft."

She breathed a sigh of relief for she liked Sebell, and she'd been distressed to think that he might be foolhardy enough to attempt sailing on the ocean by himself. Yanus had often said that no one ever really learned all there was to know about the sea, the winds and the tides. Just when one got confident, a squall could make up and smash a ship to splinters.

"I do feel, that to be convincing, I'd better know how to gut fish as well. That seems a more integral part of the craft than actual sailing. So that will take priority in your instruction. N'ton said he could acquire some fresh fish for me with no problems."

Again Menolly suppressed her curiosity as to why a journeyman harper needed to be conversant with the seacraft.

"Tomorrow's a rest day," Sebell continued. "There may even be a gather if the weather holds, which to my landsman's eye, seems likely. So, if the fire lizards break shell, and if we can disappear circumspectly, perhaps some day after that . . ."

"I can't miss my lessons with Master Shonagar . . ."

"Has he got you dithering so soon?"

"He is so emphatic . . ."

"Yes, he usually is. But he really knows how to build a voice, if that's any consolation to you. I could always play an instrument . . ." and Sebell grinned in reminiscence, ". . . but I never thought I'd make a singer. I was terrified I'd be sent away from the Hall . . ."

"*You* were?"

"Oh, indeed I was. I'd wanted to be a harper since I learned my first Ballads. I'm landsman bred, so harpering is very respectable. My foster father gave me all the assistance I needed, and our Hold Harper was a good technician, not very creative," and Sebell waggled a hand, "but capable of teaching the fundamentals throughly. I thought myself a right proper musician . . . until I got here." Sebell uttered a self-deprecating noise at his boyish pretensions. "Then I learned just how much more there is to harpering than playing an instrument."

Menolly grinned with complete understanding. "Just

like there's more to being a seaman than knowing how to gut a fish and trim sail?"

"Yes. Exactly. Which reminds me, Domick did excuse you from this morning's session, but he hasn't excused you from the work. . . .So, we might as well put waiting time to use. Incidentally, my compliments on your manner with Domick yesterday. You struck exactly the right note with him."

"I never play flat."

Sebell gave her a wide-eyed stare. "I didn't mean, playing." He stared at her a moment more. "You mean, you really like that sort of music? You weren't dissembling?"

"That music was brilliant. I've never heard anything like it." Menolly was a bit disconcerted by Sebell's attitude.

"Oh, I guess it would seem so to you. I only hope you have the same opinion several Turns from now after you've had to endure more of Domick's eternal search for pure musical forms." He gave a mock shudder. "Here . . ." and he spread out sheets of new music. "Let's see how you like this. Domick wants you to play first gitar, but you're to learn the second as well."

The occasional music for two gitars was extremely complex, switching from one time value to another, with chording difficult enough for uninjured hands. She and Sebell had to work out alternative fingering for the passages that her left hand could not manage. The repetitive theme had to dominate, but it swung from one gitar part to the other. They had gone through two of the three sections before Sebell called a break, laughing at his surrender as he stretched and kneaded tired fingers and shoulders.

"We won't get this music note-perfect in one sitting, Menolly," he protested when she wanted to finish the third movement.

"I'm sorry. I didn't realize . . ."

"Will you stop apologizing for the wrong things?"

"I'm sor— Well, I didn't mean to . . ." She had to rephrase what she wanted to say as Sebell laughed at her attempt to obey his injunction. "This sort of music is a challenge. It really is. For instance here . . ." and she turned to a quick time passage that had been extremely difficult to finger.

"Enough, Menolly. I'm bone tired, and why you aren't . . ."

"But you're a journeyman harper . . ."

"I know but this joureyman harper cannot spend all his time playing . . ."

"What do you do? Besides cross-craft."

"Whatever the Harper needs me to do. Primarily I journey . . . looking among the youngsters in hold and craft to see if there're any likely ones for the Craft Hall. I bring new music to distant harpers . . . your music most recently—"

"My music?"

"First to flush you out because we didn't know you were a girl. Second, because they were exactly the songs we need."

"That's what Master Robinton said."

"Don't sound so surprised . . . and meek. Admittedly it's nice to have one modest apprentice in this company of rampant extroverts . . . what's the matter?"

"Why isn't music like Master Domick's—"

"*Your* music can be played easily and well by any half-stringed harper or fumble-fingered idiot. Not that I'm maligning your songs. It's just that they're an entirely different kettle of fish—to use a seamanly metaphor—to Domick's. Don't you judge your songs against his standard! More people have already *listened* to your melodies and liked them, than will ever hear Domick's, much less like them."

Menolly swallowed. The very notion that her music was more acceptable than Domick's was incredible, and yet she could appreciate the distinction that Sebell was making. Domick was a musician's composer.

"Of course, we need music like Master Domick's, too. It serves a different purpose, for the Hall, and the Craft. He knows more about the art of composing—which you have to learn—"

"Oh, I know I do." Then, because the problem had been weighing heavily on her conscience, she spilled the words out in a rush. "What do I do, Sebell, about the fire lizard song? Master Robinton rewrote it, and it's much, much better. But he's told everyone that *I* wrote it."

"So? That's the way the Harper wishes it to be, Menolly. He has his reasons." Sebell reached out to grip her knee and give her a little shake. "And he didn't change the song much. Just sort of . . ." Sebell gestured with both hands, compressing the space between them, ". . . tightened it up. He kept the melody as you'd written it, and that's what everyone is humming. What you have to do now is learn how to polish your music without losing its freshness. That's why it's so important for you to study with Domick. He has the discipline: you have the originality."

Menolly could not reply to that assessment. There was a lump in her throat as she remembered the beatings she'd taken for doing exactly what she was now encouraged to do.

"Don't hunch up like that," Sebell said, almost sharply. "What's the matter? You've gone white as a sheet. Shells!" This last word came out as an expletive and caused Menolly to look in surprise at the journeyman. "Just when I didn't want to be interrupted . . ."

She followed the line of his gaze and saw the bronze dragon circling down to land beyond the courtyard.

"That's N'ton. I've got to speak to him, Menolly, about our teaching trip. I'll be right back." He was out of the room at a trot, and she could hear him taking the steps in a clatter.

She looked at the music they'd been playing, and Sebell's words echoed through her mind. "He has the discipline; you have the originality." "Everyone's been humming it." People liking her twiddles? That still didn't seem possible, although Sebell had no more reason to lie to her than the Masterharper when he'd said that her music was valuable to him. To the Harper Craft. Incredible! She struck a chord on the gitar, a triumphant, incredible chord, and then modulated it, thinking how undisciplined that musical reaction had been.

They were still twiddles, her songs, unlike the beautiful, intricate musical designs that Domick composed. But if she studied hard with him, maybe she could improve her twiddles into what she could honestly call music.

Firmly she turned her thoughts toward the gitar duet and ran through the tricky passages, slowly at first and then finally at time. One of the chords modulated into tones that were so close to the agonized cry of the previous night that she repeated the phrase.

"Don't leave me alone" and then found another chord that fit, "The cry in the night/Of anguish heart-striking/Of soul-killing fright." That's what Sebell had said: that Brekke would not want to live if Canth and F'nor died. "Live for my living/Or else I must die/Don't leave me alone./A world heard that cry."

By the time Menolly had arranged the chords in the plaint to her satisfaction, Beauty, Rocky and Diver were softly crooning along with her. So she worked on the verse.

"Well, you approve?" she asked her fair. "Perhaps I ought to jot it down on something . . ."

"No need," said a quiet voice behind her, and she whirled on the stool to see Sebell seated at the sandtable, scribing quickly. "I think I've got most of it." He looked up, saw the startled expression on her face and gave her a brief smile. "Close your mouth and come check my notation."

"But . . . but . . ."

"What did I tell you, Menolly, about apologizing for the wrong things?"

"I was just tuning . . ."

"Oh, the song needs polishing, but that refrain is poignant enough to set a Hold to tears." He beckoned again to her, a crisp gesture that brought her to his side. "You might want to change the sequence, give the peril first, the solution next . . . though I don't know. With that melody . . . do you always use minors?" He slid a glass across the sand so the scribbling couldn't be erased. "We'll see what the Harper thinks. Now what's wrong?"

"Leave it? You can't be serious."

"I can be and usually am, young Menolly," he said, rising from the stool to reach for his gitar. "Now, let's see if I put it down correctly."

Menolly sat, immersed in acute embarrassment to hear Sebell playing a tune of her making. But she had to listen. When her fire lizards began to croon softly along with Sebell's deft playing, she was about ready to concede—privately—that it wasn't a bad tune after all.

"That's very well done, Sebell! Didn't know you had it in you," said the Masterharper, applauding vigorously from the doorway. "I'd rather dreaded transferring that incident to music . . ."

"This song, Master Robinton, is Menolly's." Sebell had risen at the Harper's entrance, and now he bowed deferentially to Menolly. "Come, girl, it's why the Harpers searched a continent for you."

"Menolly, my dear child, no blushes for that song." Robinton seized her hands and clasped them warmly. "Think of the chore you just saved me. I came in halfway through the verse, Sebell, if you would please . . ." and the Harper gestured to Sebell to begin again. With one long arm, Robinton snaked a stool out from under the flat-bottomed sandtable, and still holding Menolly by the hand, he composed himself to listen as Sebell's clever fingers plucked the haunting phrases from the augmenting chords. "Now, Menolly, think only of the music as Sebell plays, not that it is *your* music. Learn to think objectively, not subjectively. Listen as a harper."

He held her hand so tightly in his that she could not pull away without giving offense. The clasp of his fingers was more than reassuring: it was therapeutic. Her embarrassment ebbed as the music and Sebell's warm baritone voice flowed into the room. When the fire lizards hummed loud, Robinton squeezed her hand and smiled down at her.

"Yes, a little work on the phrases. One or two words could be altered, I think, to heighten the effect, but the whole can stand. Can you scribe. . . . Ah, Sebell, well done. Well done," said the Masterharper as Sebell tapped the protecting glass. "I'll want it transferred to some of those neat paper sheets Bendarek supplies us with, so Menolly can go over it at her leisure. Not too much leisure," and the Masterharper held up a warning hand, "because that fire lizard echo swept round Pern, and we must explain it. A good song, Menolly, a very good song. Don't doubt yourself so fiercely. Your instinct for melodic line is very good, very good indeed. Perhaps I should send more of my apprentices to a sea hold for a time if this is the sort of talent the waves provoke. And see, your fair is still humming the line . . ."

Menolly drew out of her confusion long enough to realize that the fire lizards' hum had nothing to do with her song: their attention was not on the humans but . . .

"The eggs! They're hatching!"

"Hatching!" "Hatching!" Both master and journeyman crowded each other to get through the door to the hearth and the fire-warming pots. "Menolly! Come here!"

"I'm getting the meat!"

"They're hatching!" the Harper shouted. "They're hatching. Grab that pot, Sebell, it's wobbling!"

As Menolly dashed into the room, the two men were kneeling at the hearth, watching anxiously as the earthen pots rocked slightly.

"They can't hatch IN the pots," she said with a certain amount of asperity in her voice. She took the pot from the protecting encirclement of Sebell's curved fingers and carefully upended it on the hearth, her fingers cushioning the egg until the sand spilled away from it. She turned to Robinton, but he had already followed her example. Both eggs lay in the light of the fire, rocking slightly, the striations of hatching marking the shells.

The fire lizards lined up on the mantel and the hearth, humming deep in their throats. The pulsing sound seemed to punctuate the now violent movements of the eggs as the hatchlings fluttered against the shells for exit.

"Master Robinton?" called Silvina from the outer room. "Master Robinton?"

"Silvina! They're hatching!" The Harper's jubilant bellow startled Menolly and set the fire lizards to squawking and flapping their wings in surprise.

Other harpers, curious about the noise, began to crowd in behind Silvina, who stood at the door to the Harper's sleeping quarters. If there were too many people in the room, Menolly thought . . .

"No! Stay out! Keep them out!" she cried before she realized she'd said anything.

"Yes. Stay back now," Silvina was saying. "You can't all see. You've got the meat, Menolly? Ah, so you have. Is it enough?"

"It should be."

"What do we do now?" asked the Harper, his voice rough with suppressed excitement as he crouched above the egg.

"When the fire lizard emerges, feed it," Menolly said, somewhat surprised, for the Harper must have been a guest at numerous dragon hatchings. "Just stuff its mouth with food."

"When *will* they hatch?" asked Sebell, washing his fingers in his palms with excited frustration.

The fire lizards' hum was getting more intense: their eyes whirling with participation in the event. Suddenly a second little golden queen erupted into the room, her eyes spinning. She let out a squeal which Beauty answered, lifting her wings higher, but in greeting, not challenge.

"Silvina!" Menolly pointed to the queen.

"Master Robinton, look!" said the headwoman and, as they all watched, the newly arrived queen took her place on the mantel beside Beauty, her throat vibrating as fast as the others.

"That's Merga, Lord Groghe's queen," said the Harper, and then he glanced over his shoulder at the door. "I hope it isn't an awkward time for him. This sort of summons could be inconvenient . . ."

Above the fire lizards' vibrant sounds, they all heard the Harper's name bellowed.

"Someone go and escort Lord Groghe," ordered the Harper, his eyes never leaving the hearth and the two eggs.

"Robinton!" It would seem that his order was unnecessary for the bellower was rapidly approaching. "Robin. . . . What? They are? D'you know what? That Merga of mine's in another taking. Forced me to come *here!* Here now, what's all this? Where *is* Robinton?"

Menolly tore her eyes from the two eggs, though she was certain she saw a widening crack in the one on the left, to see the entrance of the Fort Lord Holder. As his voice indicated, he was a big man, almost as tall as the Harper but much broader in the torso, with thick thighs and bulging calves. He walked lightly for all his mass although he was breathing heavily from having come to the Hall at a fair pace.

"There you are! What's this all about?"

"The eggs are about to hatch, Lord Groghe."

"Eggs?" The brows of the Holder's florid face were contracted into a puzzled scowl. "Oh, your eggs. They're hatching? And Merga's reacting?"

"I trust not at any inconvenience to you, Lord Groghe."

"Well, not so's I wouldn't come when she insisted. How'd the creature know?"

"Ask Menolly."

"Menolly?" And suddenly Menolly found herself the object of his intense, frowning scrutiny. "You're Menolly?" The brows went up in surprise. "Little bit of a thing, aren't you? Not at all what I expected. Don't blush. I don't bite. My fire lizard might. Wouldn't worry you, though, would it? These are all yours? Why, my queen's beside yours, friendly as can be. They're not dangerous at all."

"Menolly!" The Harper's exclamation brought her attention back to the hearth.

His egg had given a convulsive rock, all but spinning itself off the hearthstone. Gasping, he'd put out both hands to prevent its falling. The shell cracked wide open, and a little bronze fire lizard rolled into his hands, creeling with hunger, its body glistening.

"Feed it! Feed it!" Menolly cried.

Robinton, unable to take his eyes off the fire lizard, fumbled for the piled meat and shoved food into the fire lizard's open mouth. The little bronze, shaking its wings out for balance, snatched ferociously at the meat, gobbling so fast that Menolly held her breath for fear the creature would choke in its greed.

"Not too much. Make it wait! Talk to it. Soothe it," Menolly urged. Just then the other egg split.

"It's a queen!" shouted Sebell, rocking back on his heels in the excess of his surprise. Only Lord Groghe's quick hand on his back kept him from falling over.

"Feed her!" the Lord Holder barked.

"But I'm not to have the queen!" For one split second, Sebell started to turn and offer the queen to the Harper.

"Too late!" Menolly shouted, diving forward to intercept the gesture. She jammed meat on Sebell's seeking hand and then pushed it back to the frantically creeling queen. "You're supposed to have a fire lizard. It doesn't matter which!"

The Harper was oblivious to the interchange. He was intent on his bronze, stroking it, feeding it, crooning to it. The little queen had gobbled Sebell's initial offering, her tail wrapping so firmly about his wrist that he could not have disentangled himself had he managed to sustain his moment of sacrifice.

Menolly turned to assist the Harper, but Lord Groghe was kneeling beside him, encouraging him. When the two hatchlings were bulging with food, Menolly removed the meat bowls.

"They'll burst with another mouthful," she told the reproachful Harpers. "Now, hold them against you. Stroke them. They should fall asleep. There now." As the men complied with her urgings, the new fire lizards, sated for the present, wearily closed their eyes, their little heads dropping to the protecting forearms. She'd forgotten what a scant handful a newly hatched fire lizard was. Her friends had grown so much since hatching. Lord Groghe's Merga was as tall in the shoulder as Beauty, but not so deeply chested. The two were now exchanging compliments, stroking heads and touching curved wings.

"Its incredible," the Harper said, his words no more than an articulated whisper, his eyes brilliant with joy. "It is absolutely the most incredible experience I have ever had."

"Know what you mean," Lord Groghe replied in an embarrassed mumble, ducking his head, but Menolly could see that the burly Holder's face was flushed. "Can't forget it myself."

Carefully Master Robinton rose from his knees, his eyes on the sleeping fire lizard, his free hand poised in case an incautious movement unsettled the little bronze. "It explains so very much that I could never have understood about dragonriders. Yes, it opens a whole new area of understanding." He sat down on the edge of his bed. "Now I can sense, dimly, what Lytol, what Brekke must have suffered. And I know why young Jaxom must have Ruth." He smiled at Lord Groghe's grunt at that statement. "Yes, I have stood so long peering through a small opening into another Hold of understanding. Now I can see without obstruction." His chin had dropped to his chest as he spoke in soft reflective tones, more to himself than those close enough to catch the whispered words. He shook himself slightly and looked up, his smile again radiant. "What a gift you have made me, Menolly. What a magnificent gift!"

Beauty came to perch on Menolly's shoulder, her humming now diminished to a soft murmur of sound. Lord Groghe's queen, Merga, flew to his shoulder, wrapping her tail about his thick neck, just as Beauty did.

"I don't know how it happened, Master Robinton," Sebell said, rising from the hearth with exaggerated care. His manner was both defensive and apologetic. "The pots were in the wrong order. I don't understand. You should have had the queen."

"My dear Sebell, I couldn't care in the slightest. This bronze fellow is everything I could ever want. And frankly, I believe that it might be more advantageous for you to have the queen, going out and above the land as you'll have to do. Yes, I think chance has worked more for than against us. And I am quite content, oh, indeed I am, with my bronze man here. What a lovely, lovely creature!" He had eased himself back against the bolster, the fire lizard snuggled in the crook of his arm, his other hand protectingly cradling the open side. "Such a lovely big fellow!" His head fell back, his eyes heavy, all but asleep himself.

"Now that's a real miracle," said Silvina in a very soft voice. "Asleep without wine or fellis juice? Out! Out!" She shook her hands at those crowding the door, but her gesture to Lord Groghe to precede her from the room was a touch more courteous. The Lord Holder nodded agreement and made a great show of tiptoeing quietly across the room. His exit cleared the doorway of onlookers.

Silvina picked up the half-filled bowls by the fire and put one near the Harper's hand. Menolly beckoned to the rest of her fair and they flitted out the window.

"Got them well-trained, haven't you?" Lord Groghe said once Silvina had closed the door to the Harper's chamber. "Want to have a long chat with you about 'em. Robinton says they'll fetch and carry for *you*. D'you believe, as he does, that what one fire lizard knows, th'others do, too?"

Too disconcerted to reply, Menolly glanced frantically at Silvina and saw her nod encouragingly. "It would seem logical, Lord Groghe. Ah . . . it would certainly account for . . . for what happened the other night. In fact, there's no other way to account for that, is there? Unless you can speak to dragons."

"Unless you can speak to dragons?" Lord Groghe laughed ponderously, poking Menolly's shoulder with his finger in good humor. "Speak to dragons? Hahaha."

Menolly felt herself grinning because his laughter was a bit contagious, and she didn't know what else to do. She hadn't meant to be funny. Then Silvina shushed them imperiously, pointing urgently at the Harper's closed door.

"Sorry, Silvina," Lord Groghe said, contritely. "Most amazing thing! Woke me up out of a sound sleep, scared out of my wits. Never happened to me before, I can tell you." He nodded his head emphatically, and Merga chirped. "Wasn't your fault, pet," he said, stroking her tiny head with a thick forefinger. "Only doing the same as the others. That's what I want you to teach me, girl." The forefinger now pointed at Menolly. "You will, won't you? Robinton says you have yours trained a treat."

"It would be my privilege, sir."

"Well spoken." Lord Groghe turned his heavy torso in Silvina's direction, favoring the headwoman with a fierce stare. "Well-spoken child. Not what I expected. Can't trust other people's opinions. Never did. Never will. I'll arrange something with Robinton later. Not too much later. But later. Good day to you all." With that the Lord Holder of Fort strode from the room, nodding and smiling to the harpers still gathered in the corridor.

Menolly saw Sebell and Silvina exchanging worried glances, and she moved across the room to stand before them.

"What did Lord Groghe mean, Silvina? I'm not what he expected?"

"I was afraid you'd catch that," Silvina said, her eyes narrow with a contained anger. She patted Menolly's shoulder absently. "There's been loose talk, which has done them no good and you no harm. I've a few knees to set knocking, so I have."

Menolly was thoroughly and unexpectedly consumed with anger. Beauty chittered, her eyes beginning to whirl redly.

"Those cot girls stay up at the Hold during Threadfall, don't they?"

Silvina gave Menolly a long, quelling look. "I said I'll handle the matter, Menolly. You," and Silvina pointed at her, "will occupy yourself with *harper* business." She was clearly as furious as Menolly, and flicked imaginary dust from her skirt with unnecessary force. "You're to stay here, both of you, and be sure nothing disturbs the Harper. Nothing, you understand!" She pinned apprentice and journeyman with a stern glare. "He's asleep, and he's to stay asleep as long as that little creature lets him. That way he might get caught up on himself for a change before he's worn to death." She picked up the tray. "I'll send your suppers up with Camo. And their suppers as well."

She closed the door firmly behind her. Menolly looked at the closed door for a long moment, still feeling the anger in her guts. She'd not really done the girls any kind of harm, so why would they try to prejudice the Lord Holder against her? Or perhaps it was all Dunca's connivance? Menolly knew that the little cotholder hated her for the humiliation caused by the fire lizards. Now that Menolly was at the Hall, why should Dunca persist? She glanced back to Sebell, who was regarding her even as he cradled his sleeping queen.

"Leave it, Menolly," he said in a quiet but emphatic tone. He gestured her to the sandtable. "Harper business is better business for you now. Master Robinton said you were to copy the song onto sheets." Moving carefully so as not to disturb his little queen, he got supplies from the shelves and put them on the center board. "So, copy!"

"I don't understand what they thought they'd accomplish, prejudicing Lord Groghe against me. What would he do?"

Sebell said nothing as he hooked a stool under him, and sat down. He pointed at the music.

"It's only right for me to know. The insult is mine to settle."

"Sit down, Menolly. And copy. That's far more important to the Harper and the Hall than any petty machinations of envious girls."

"They *could* do me a mischief, couldn't they? If they'd got Lord Groghe to believe what they said. I never hurt those girls."

"True enough but that is not harper business. The song is. Copy it! And one more word from you on any other subject and I'll—"

"If you're not quiet, you'll wake your fire lizard," Menolly said, but she sat down at the table and started copying. She could recognize obstinacy when she saw it, and it would do her no good to set Sebell against her. "What are you going to name her?" she asked.

"Name her?" Sebell was startled, and Menolly was dismayed to realize how much of his joy in his queen had been diminished by her silly concern over gossip. "Why, I can have the privilege of naming her, can't I? She's mine. I think . . ." and his eyes glowed with affection for the hatchling, "I think I'll call her Kimi."

"That's a lovely name," replied Menolly and then bent to her copying with a good heart.

Chapter 8

Gather! Gather! It's a gather day!
No work for us, and Thread's away.
Stalls are building, square's swept clear,
Gather all from far and near.
Bring your marks and bring your wares,
Bring your family for there's
Food and drink and fun and song.
The Hold flag flies: so gather along!

"What's wrong with the Hold?" Menolly asked Piemur the next morning as she, the boy and Camo were feeding the fire lizards. Piemur kept craning his neck past the roofs of the Harper Hall to see the fire heights of Fort Hold.

"Nothing's wrong. I want to see if the gather flag's up."

"Gather flag?" Menolly recalled that Sebell had mentioned a gather.

"Sure! It's spring, and sunny. It's a restday. Thread's not due, so there ought to be a gather!" Piemur regarded her a long moment, then his face screwed up into an incredulous expression. "You mean, you don't have gathers?"

"Half Circle *is* isolated," Menolly replied defensively. "And with Thread falling . . ."

"Yeah, I forgot that. No wonder you're such a smashing musician," he said, shaking his head as if this were no real compensation. "Nothing to do but practice! Still," he added somewhat skeptical, "you must have had gathers *before* Thread started?"

"Of course we did. Traders came through the marshes three and four times a Turn." Piemur was unimpressed. Menolly realized that she herself had only the vaguest memories of such events. Threadfall had started when she was barely eight Turns old.

"We have gathers as often as it's sunny on a restday," Piemur said, chattering away, "and there isn't any Thread due. Of course, our being a Hold with several small crafthalls, as well as the main Harper Craft Hall, does make for great gathers. You don't happen," and he cocked his head slyly, "to have any marks on you?"

"Marks?"

Piemur was thoroughly disgusted with her obtuseness. "Marks! Marks! What you get in exchange for what you're selling at a gather?" He reached into his pocket and pulled out four small white pieces of highly polished wood, on which the numerals 32 had been incised on one side and on the other, the mark of the Smithcraft. "Only thirty-seconds, but with four I got an eighth, and Smithcraft at that."

Menolly had never actually seen marks before. All trading transactions had been carried out by her father, the Sea Holder. She was astonished that so young a boy as Piemur had possession of marks and said so.

"Oh, I sang, you know, even before I got apprenticed. I'd always get a mark of some amount or other. My foster mother kept them for me until I came here." Piemur wrinkled his nose in disgust. "But you don't get paid for singing at gathers if you're a harper, and you have to do your own turn anyway. I haven't *anything* to give the marksmen here. I keep *trying*, but Master Jerint won't put his seal on my pipes, so I have to figure out other ways of turning the odd. . . . Hey, look, Menolly," and he grabbed her arm, "there goes the flag! There'll be a gather!" He went flying across the court as fast as he could to the apprentice dormitory.

On the top of the Fort Hold fire heights, Menolly now saw the bright yellow pennant, and flapping below it on the mast, the red and black barred streamer that apparently signaled a gather. She heard Piemur's cries echoing in the apprentice dormitory and the sounds of sleepers stirring in complaint.

As if Piemur's sighting of the pennant had been a signal, the drudges, herded by Abuna and Silvina, entered the kitchen. The flag and pennant on the Hold mast were duly noted and the meal preparations were conducted in a cheerful humor.

Menolly dispersed her fair to their sunning and bathing and, finding Silvina in the kitchen with Abuna, offered to take breakfast to the Harper and his bronze, whom he'd named Zair.

"I told you, Abuna, that with Menolly to help, two more fire lizards would be no problem," Silvina said, pushing the kitchen woman onto some other task as she smiled warmly at Menolly. "Not that the Harper will be here much with his, nor Sebell either," she called to Abuna who went off grumbling to herself. "Long as she's lived in the Harper Hall, you'd think she'd be used to change-about."

Menolly wanted to ask Silvina about the girls and their gossiping, but Silvina was avoiding her eye. Just then they both heard Menolly's name being called in a frantic voice. Sebell came crashing down the kitchen steps, holding up his trousers with one bare arm, wincing at the clutch of his fire lizard queen on the other. Kimi was creeling wildly with hunger.

"Menolly! There you are! I've been searching everywhere. What's the matter with her? Ouch!" Sebell was wide-eyed with anxiety.

"She's only hungry."

"*Only* hungry?"

"Here, come with me," and Menolly took Sebell by the arm, picked up the tray she had prepared for the Masterharper and pulled the journeyman out of the kitchen, to spare him Abuna's black scowl, and into the relative peace of the dining hall. "Now, feed her!"

"I can't. My pants!" Sebell nodded to his trousers, which, beltless, threatened to slip off his hips.

Stifling a giggle, Menolly unbuckled her own worn belt and secured Sebell's pants for him. He grabbed a handful of meat and held it out for Kimi. The ungrateful wretch hissed and lunged at the meat, digging her claws into his forearm.

Well, Menolly couldn't give him her tunic, too. She spotted a scrap of towelling by the service hatch. Deftly she disengaged the queen's legs from Sebell's forearm and wrapped the cloth about his scratched and bleeding arm, then managed to redeposit Kimi before the queen was aware of being shifted.

"Oh, thank you, thank you, thank you!" sighed Sebell, sinking to the nearest bench. "And you had nine of these creatures to feed every day?" He gave her a look of renewed respect. "I don't know how you did it! I really don't!"

Menolly pointed to his klah as she took up a handful of meat. Kimi didn't care whose hand held the meat, so Sebell gratefully gulped some klah.

"Menolly!" Another voice roared from the top of the stairs.

"Sir?" Menolly dashed to the foot of the steps.

"He's making the most outlandish noises," the Harper yelled. "Is he hurt or just hungry? His eyes are flaming red."

"Here you are," said Silvina, appearing from the kitchen with a second tray of food for human and fire lizard. "I thought we'd be hearing from him once Sebell appeared."

Menolly could not keep from laughing with Silvina. She took the steps two at a time without spilling so much as a drop of the klah or tumbling a glob of meat from the piled bowl.

The Harper had taken time to dress, and he'd thought to wrap his arm against the needle-sharp claws of his little bronze, but he looked not a whit less harried or distressed than Sebell.

"You're sure it's only hunger?" asked Master Robinton. But his fire lizard's creeling abated with the first mouthful of meat.

Robinton gestured Menolly toward his quarters, but the fire lizard, believing the food was being withdrawn, let out an indignant shriek and swatted at Menolly's hand.

"Here, here, eat, you greedy thing," said the Harper with great affection in his voice. "Just don't wake everyone. It's restday."

"Too late," remarked Domick, in an acid tone of voice, his sleeping rug pulled around him as he stood in the doorway of his room. "Between you howling like an injured dragon, Sebell sounding like a flight of 'em, and these pesky beasts with tones that could bend metal, no one's going to enjoy a restday."

"The gather flag is flying," the Harper said in a conciliatory way. He continued to feed Zair as he and Menolly proceeded to his room.

"A gather? That's all I need." Domick slammed his door.

"I trust there won't be a repetition of this," said Master Morshal as the Harper and Menolly came abreast of his room. He wore a loose robe, but he obviously had been drawn from his bed by the creeling and shouts. His sour gaze was directed fully on Menolly, as if she were the sole cause of the commotion.

"Probably," the Harper replied cheerfully, "until I figure out this precious creature's habits. He only hatched yesterday, Morshal. Do give him a few days' grace."

Morshal spluttered something, glared balefully and accusingly at Menolly, and then shut his door, pointedly without slamming it. Menolly all too clearly heard other doors closing along the corridor, and she was very grateful to be in the Harper's company.

"Don't let old Morshal upset you, Menolly," said Master Robinton in a quiet voice.

Menolly looked up quickly, grateful for his reassurance. He smiled again as he nodded for her to enter his room and gestured for her to set the tray down on the center of the sandtable.

"Fortunately," he went on, slouching in a chair, all the

167

while supplying meat bits for Zair, "you don't have to sit classes with Morshal."

"I don't?"

Robinton chuckled at the note of relief in her voice and then laughed again as Zair missed a morsel, creeled anxiously until the Harper had retrieved it from the floor and deposited it neatly in the open mouth.

"No, you don't. Morshal teaches only at the apprentice level." The Master Harper sighed. "He really is adept at drilling basic theory into rebellious apprentice minds. But Petiron already taught you more than Morshal knows. Relieved, Menolly?"

"Oh, yes. Master Morshal doesn't seem to like me."

"Master Morshal has always considered it a waste of time and effort to teach any girls. What good would it do them?"

Menolly blinked, surprised to hear her father's opinion echoed in the Harper Hall. Then she realized that Master Robinton had been speaking in deft mimicry of Master Morshal's testy manner. Warm fingers caught her chin, and she was made to look up at the Harper. The lines of fatigue and worry were plainly visible, despite his good night's rest.

"Morshal's dislike of the feminine sex is a standing joke in this Hall, Menolly. Give him the courtesy due his rank and age, and ignore his biased thinking. As I said, you don't have to sit classes with him. Not that Domick will be any easier to study with. He's a hard taskmaster, but Domick will take over your tuition where Petiron left off in musical form and composition until I can. Unfortunately," and the Harper's smile of regret was sincere, "I am badly pressed for time with all that's happening, much though I would prefer to undertake the task myself. Still, Domick's understanding of the truly classical form is superior, and he's keen to monopolize any instrumentalist capable of playing his intricate music. Don't miss your lessons with Master Shonagar, for you must be able to sing your songs effectively, but," and he lifted a warning finger, "don't fall for Brudegan's importunings about fire lizard choruses. That can be scheduled for a later time when we've settled you properly in your craft.

"I'd like you to concentrate on your instruments . . . as far and as fast as that hand of yours permits. How is it healing, by the way?" And he reached for her left hand. "Hmmm, you've done too much by the look of those splits. Does it hurt? I won't have you crippling yourself in your zeal, Menolly, understand that!"

Menolly, sensing his kind concern, swallowed against the lump in her throat and managed a tentative smile.

"It is never easy, sweet child, to have a real gift: something else is withheld to compensate."

Menolly was startled at the sadness, that melancholy in his eyes and face, and he went on, almost to himself, "If you won't surrender the mark, you'll never be more than half alive. Speaking of marks . . ." and his expression altered completely. He leaned forward, across the sand-table, rummaging in the compartments of the central bridge built above the actual sand level. "Ah, here," and he pressed something into her hand. "There's a gather today, and you deserve some relaxation. I suspect diversions were few and infrequent in your Sea Hold. Find something pretty to wear at the stalls . . . a belt perhaps . . . and buy some of the bubbly pies. Piemur will lead you to them, the scamp.

"But tomorrow," and Master Robinton waggled a finger at her, "back to work for you. Sebell says you make a good copyist. Did you have a chance to polish the Brekke song yesterday evening? I think you'll agree the melodic line falters in the fourth phrase . . ." and he hummed it. "Then I want you to rewrite the ballad observing all the traditional musical forms. Think of it as an exercise in musical theory. Mind you, I'm of the opinion that the strength of your work will lie in a looser, less formalized style. There are, however, purists in the Craft who must be mollified while you're an apprentice."

Zair, his belly so swollen that the individual lumps of meat could be discerned against his skin, gave a sudden burp and collapsed into sleep in the crook of the Harper's arm.

"I say, Menolly, how long will he do nothing but eat and sleep?" The Harper sounded disappointed.

"The first sevenday, and maybe a few days longer," Menolly answered, still trying to assimilate his astonishing instructions and philosophy. "He'll develop a personality in a very short time."

"That's a relief." The Harper heaved an exaggerated sigh. "I'd been worrying that perhaps his brains had got addled, going *between* so much in the egg. Not that I'd care for him any the less," and he smiled tenderly down at the sprawled form. "How did you ever manage to fill *nine* rapacious bellies?" Now his smile was all for her. "And what a relief to have you here to help us. In this I am your apprentice." His eyes held hers a moment longer, still twinkling with amusement although his face settled into a serious expression. "In all other matters, you are to consider yourself *my* apprentice, you know.

"Now, you may take the tray back to the kitchen, and you are dismissed to the gather. Unless, of course," he added with that winning smile, "something untoward happens to this fellow."

She brought the tray and empty dishes to the kitchen, where Abuna, with more than her usual courtesy, suggested that Menolly had better get some breakfast before it was all gone. They'd be clearing the tables soon, and if the lazybones hadn't eaten, too bad. Not but what they couldn't stuff themselves at the gather's stalls.

That reminded Menolly of the mark that the Harper had put in her hand. At first she thought it was the dim light of the passage, but when she got into the entrance hall, she could plainly see that the two was underscored: it wasn't a half-mark, which would have been scored above. She clenched the precious piece in her fist, amazed. The Master Harper had given her a whole two-mark piece to spend on herself. Two whole marks! Why, she could buy anything!

No, he'd said that she was to buy something pretty to wear. A belt. The Harper's keen eye had noted the absence of hers. And it was a worn belt, anyhow. But a new one, instead of one handed down . . . a belt she could choose for herself! How very kind of Master Robinton. And he'd said she was to buy bubbly pies. She looked about the scattering of boys at the apprentice tables for Piemur's curly head of hair. He was, as usual, deep in conversation with several boys, and probably planning mischief to judge by the closeness of all the heads. There were no masters at the circular table and just a few journeymen at the oval ones, clustered about Sebell, admiring Kimi, asleep on his arm.

"She couldn't give 'em away if she wanted to," Piemur was saying in a strident tone as Menolly approached his group. Someone must have jabbed him in the ribs because he glanced over his shoulder and, while he looked in no way abashed, it was obvious from the expression of the others that Menolly had been the "she" he'd meant. "Can you?" he asked bluntly.

"Can I what?"

"Give anyone else one of your fire lizards?"

"No."

"I told you!" Piemur pointed an accusing finger at Ranly. "So Sebell couldn't have given Robinton the queen. Could he, Menolly?"

"But the Masterharper should have had the queen," said Ranly, rebellious and unconvinced.

"Sebell did offer the queen to Master Robinton when she hatched," Menolly said quickly, "but it was too late. Impression had occurred, and that can't be altered."

"Well, just how did Sebell get his hands on the queen egg?" Now Ranly's eyes hotly accused her of complicity.

"Completely by accident," she said, mastering her irritation at such an outrageous suggestion. "First, there really isn't any positive way of knowing which is the queen egg in a fire lizard clutch. Second, it isn't anyone's business but Master Robinton's and Sebell's." She'd just lay this divisive rumor into an early grave and repay a little of her great debt to both men. "Third, I picked the two biggest eggs in the clutch for Master Robinton," and the boys nodded with approval, "but they could both have been bronzes." Then she laughed. "It all happened so fast when the eggs started to hatch, no one bothered to see which pot was whose. Master Robinton and Sebell just grabbed because both pots were rocking fit to fall. The little bronze hatched first, right into Master Robinton's hands, and that was that, right then. He caught it just before it could fall from the hearthstone." The boys snatched in breath for that near catastrophe. "And then there was Sebell with a queen in his hands. Then, he *tried* to give her to the Harper, but Zair had Impressed and so had little Kimi. There's no way to change that. And I don't want to hear another word from any of you as to who got what and who shouldn't have. There's enough gossip flying about this Hall." She wished she could forget her worries about what those girls had told the Lord Holder.

"I kept trying to tell them," said Piemur, throwing his hands out, his eyes bright with injured innocence because Menolly was now glaring at him. Then he clutched dramatically at his throat because his voice had squeaked on the last word. "I've gone hoarse talking . . ."

"Can't have the golden throat hoarse, can we?" said Ranly sarcastically.

Piemur was testing klah pots on the table to see if there were any that was still warm. Finding one he poured two mugs, offering one to Menolly. He gurgled as he downed half a mug, rubbed his hand across his mouth and then told her that she'd better eat quickly because they'd be clearing any minute.

"Now, let's get *back* to the mark problem. This will be only the second gather of the Turn, so I figure that they'll be sending an older journeyman from the Smithcraft Hall, to keep an eye on the younger fellows and supervise the bargaining. And that journeyman is just likely to be my father's friend, Pergamol; and if it's Pergamol, then I can guarantee that you'll get top marks for your work. And . . ." he held up a silencing hand as Ranly opened his mouth to comment, "if it isn't Pergamol, it'll be someone who knows him."

"And if it's just a young journeyman who's on to you, Piemur?" Ranly asked in a caustic tone.

"Then I blubber!" Piemur dismissed this problem with

all the disdain of the practiced dissembler. "I'm just a li'l feller, and I never have much and I . . ." Great tears welled up in his eyes, and his face was a mask of trusting and anxious innocence.

"If I may disturb this tactical meeting," said a different voice, and all the boys looked guiltily around to see Sebell, fire lizard cradled in his arm, "for a few words with Menolly . . ."

She rose and followed the journeyman to the window. He pressed her rolled-up belt in her hand, as he thanked her for saving his dignity that morning.

"Now, can I keep Kimi with me all the time?" he asked, lightly stroking the fire lizard's folded wings. Even in her sleep she responded to his touch with a sigh.

"The more she's with you the stronger the bond will grow. If not on you, near you."

"Is she too young to be taught to sit on my shoulder like your Beauty does? I've got to have both hands for a while today."

"When she wakes, put her on your shoulder." Menolly grinned. "And get used to having your neck throttled."

"How often does she eat?"

"She'll let you know." Menolly laughed at Sebell's consternation. "At least you don't have to go catch it. Keep a few meatrolls in your belt pouch, although I'm sure Camo will always be ready to chop-chop for you anytime." Sebell chuckled, too. "One thing you'll need to do daily is oil her skin."

"Does it have to stink like the stuff you use?" Sebell was dismayed.

Menolly suppressed a giggle. "Master Oldive had that oil on hand. He said he makes it for the ladies of the Hold to use on their faces . . ."

"Oh, no."

"But I'm sure he'd make you something more suitable for your . . ." She paused, not certain just how much she could tease Sebell.

"My male dignity and rank?" Sebell grinned at her. "I'll just have a word with him now," and he strolled off with a lilt in his step.

Menolly was very pleased that she'd suppressed the boys' misapprehension over the fire lizards' hatching. Sebell was so nice. And, it wasn't as if Master Robinton had been upset at Impressing the bronze. He genuinely hadn't cared a whit once Zair had Impressed and was his very own. And if Master Robinton was content, the rest of the Hall shouldn't quarrel!

Then she worried about the girls' gossip: if the apprentices could take a simple switch like the Hatching and derive deep insult from it, what had the girls done with her reputation at the Hold?

"Look, Menolly," Piemur said, popping up beside her, "I gotta couple of things to do now, but after dinner, you want me to take you round the gather? Seeing as how you haven't been to one . . . here, that is."

She readily agreed, curious to see just how his plans would affect his bargaining. He darted out of the Hall then, the others boys hard on his heels.

A few journeymen still lounged at the oval table, drinking klah, but most of the apprentices had dispersed. At the round table, Master Morshal now glowered darkly at her as he ate in solitary dignity. Menolly left the dining hall for the sanctuary of her room.

Her fire lizards were curled up on the deep window ledge, their wings glinting brilliantly in the sun but their jeweled eyes closed behind their several lids. Beauty stirred, raised her head, parted the outer lid, squeaked softly and, when Menolly stroked her reassuringly, sighed and resumed her interrupted nap.

From the vantage point of the second level, Menolly could see the square beyond the Harper Hall and the broad roadway. There was already considerable activity: burdenbeasts moving up the river road, their slow long stride one of indolence, rather than labor under heavy weight. Stalls were being assembled, forming a loose square about an open space. Tables and benches were already in place, facing the dance square. For dancing there would surely be, with a hundred or more harpers to do the playing. There'd be more dancing than she'd even seen. And probably different dances from the ones popular in her Sea Hold. Oh, this would be a grand gather. Her first here, and her first since Thread started falling.

Menolly caught sight of the girls emerging from the cot, brightly clad, with filmy scarves to protect their hair from the light wind. Oh, what she'd like to do to their hair! Pona's hair, with its long neat plaits to be pulled out by the roots. . . . Menolly stopped her thoughts, a little appalled at the intensity of her dislike. After all, the girls had failed in their aim—to prejudice Lord Groghe against her. Why was she bothering her head about them? She'd better things to occupy herself with. She was an apprentice harper, not a sometime student. She was Masterharper Robinton's apprentice. Of course, since he was Master of the Harper Hall, everyone within was *his* apprentice.

But she was an apprentice. And she intended to remain one. More than ever now that the girls had made an effort to jeopardize her tenure. She was going to stay, to spite them, and her parents. She was going to make her place here because this was where she belonged, as Master Robinton had said. Here was where she could perfect her music. Here she could make her own place for herself, not slip into a spot left by someone else, anyone else. Just as she'd made the cave her own, she would make her own place here in the Harper Hall. And no one, particularly a sneaky little twitterhead whose only claim to importance was being someone's granddaughter, was going to dislodge her! Or a conniving coward like cotholder Dunca!

Menolly wondered if Silvina had done anything about settling the rumors. Really, it just wasn't important, Menolly told herself sternly. Particularly when Lord Groghe seemed to approve of her and had actually suggested that she help him train his queen, Merga.

Menolly laughed to herself. Just wait till those sissies heard about that! She, apprentice trainer of fire lizards, the only successful one on Pern. The teacher just one step ahead of the student. She giggled now, covering her mouth with her hands because she knew she was acting the wherry. But she'd been silly not to see before that she had several tunes to play in this Harper Hall: the tunes she made, her fire lizards—yes, and how to gut fish and trim sail whenever some harper needed to know. And why did Sebell need to know? She sighed gustily.

Too bad about those girls, though. She wished Audiva didn't have to stay with them; she was above the general sort at the cot, and it would have been nice to have a girl friend. Not that she didn't have a good friend in Piemur. When Piemur grew up and lost his brilliant voice, would he have to leave the Craft Hall? No, because they must surely be training him to play one of those "other" tunes. She didn't quite see him stepping into Master Shonagar's slippers . . .

She rose from the window ledge, reminded of the task that Master Robinton had set her as his apprentice. She tuned her gitar and began to rehearse the Brekke song, softly lest the Harper was busy in his rooms. Did he honestly think that song, a twiddle to while the time away until Sebell returned, was good enough to be perfected?

Of their own volition, her fingers were plucking out the melody. She found herself caught up once more in the poignancy of Brekke's anguished command! *Don't leave me alone!* She played the song through, agreeing with the Harper that the fourth phrase needed polishing . . . ah, yes, if she dropped to the fifth, it would intensify the phrase and compliment the chord.

The tocsin rang for mealtime finally, and shouts and laughter broke her concentration. She was almost angry with the disruption. But with a renewed awareness of her surroundings, she realized how her hand ached. Her back and neck muscles were stiff from crouching over the gitar. She'd no idea she'd been practicing that long, but the song was set in her hand and her fingers now. She would have it finished in next to no time once she had more ink and those paper sheets.

She changed into the clothes she wanted to wear to the gather: not as rich as the girls would be wearing, but new. The close-woven trousers and the contrasting colored tunic with the sleeveless hide jumper displaying the apprentice badge meant more to her than fine cloth and filmy scarves. As she pulled on her slippers, she noticed that the constant scuffing on the stone floors was wearing soles and toes out. At least here, she needn't fear to approach Silvina, and perhaps her feet were healed enough for proper boots, which would last longer.

Chapter 9

The fickle wind's my foe,
With tide his keen ally.
They're jealous of my sea's love
And rouse her with their lie.

Oh sweet sea, oh dear sea,
Heed not their stormy wile
But bear me safely to my Hold
And from their watery trial.
                    Eastern Sea Hold Song

There was an excitement in the air of the dining hall, the boys chattering more loudly than ever, a conversational buzz that dropped off only slightly when they were seated and the heavy platters of steaming meat slices were brought around. She sat with Ranly, Piemur and Timiny, who all urged her to eat heartily for they'd be lucky to get stale bread for supper.

"Silvina counts on our stuffing ourselves on our own marks at the gather," Piemur told Menolly as he crammed meat into his mouth. He groaned as she heaped tubers on his plate. "I hate 'em."

"You're lucky to have 'em. They were treats where I come from."

"Then you have mine." He was generosity itself, but she made him eat his own.

No one spent time over the meal, and the diners were

178

dismissed as soon as Brudegan had called out the list of names.

"Well, I'm not on a turn today," said Piemur with the air of a last minute reprieve.

"Turn?"

"Yeah, being Harper Hall and all, this Hold expects continuous music, but no one does more than one set, either singing or dance music. No great problem. You know, Menolly, you'd better tell your fire lizards to stay away," Piemur said as they all made their way across the courtyard to the archway. The other boys nodded in agreement. "No telling what ragtag is going to appear at a gather." He sounded darkly foreboding.

"Who'd hurt a fire lizard?" Menolly asked, surprised.

"Not hurt 'em. Just want 'em."

Menolly looked up and saw her friends sunning on the window ledges. As if her notice was sufficient, Beauty and Rocky came streaking down to her, chirping inquiringly.

"Couldn't I just take Beauty? No one sees her when she hides in my hair."

Piemur shook his head slowly from side to side. The other boys mimicked him with earnest expressions of concern.

"*We*," and he meant Harpers, "know about you and having nine. There're some dimwits coming today who wouldn't understand. And you're wearing an apprentice badge: apprentices don't own nothing or count for anything. They're the lowest of the low and have to obey any journeyman, or master, or even a senior apprentice in any other craft. Shells, you know how Beauty acts when someone tries to rank you? You can't have Beauty taking a swipe at an honorable journeyman or craftmaster, now can you? Or someone from the Hold?" He jerked his thumb toward the cliffside as he dropped his voice to keep the mere possibility of such discourtesy from exalted ears.

"That would get Master Robinton in trouble?" Considering the gossip work already done at the Hold, Menolly would as soon remain anonymous to them.

"It could!" Ranly and Timiny nodded in solemn accord.

"How do *you* manage to stay out of trouble, Piemur?" Menolly asked.

"'Cause I watch my step at a gather. One thing to cut up in the Hall when it's all Harpers, but . . ."

"Hey, Piemur." They all turned and saw Brolly and another apprentice whom Menolly did not know running toward them. Brolly had a brightly painted tambourine and the other a handsomely polished tenor pipe.

"Thought we might have missed you, Piemur," the boy gasped. "Here's my pipe, and Master Jerint stamped it and Brolly's tambourine. Will you take 'em to the marksman now?"

"Sure. And it's my father's friend, Pergamol, like I told you it would be."

Piemur took charge of the instruments, and with a quirk of a smile at Menolly, led the way toward the loosely arranged stalls on the perimeter of the gather's square.

For the first time Menolly realized how many people lived in this Hold area. She would have liked to watch a bit on the sidelines, to get used to such a throng of people, but grabbing her hand, Piemur led her right into their midst.

She nearly piled into Piemur when he came to a sudden complete stop in the space between two booths. He glanced warningly over his shoulder, and Menolly noticed that he had the instruments behind his back as he composed his face into an expression of wistful ingenuousness. A tanner journeyman was bargaining with the well-dressed marksman in the stall, his Smithcraft badge gleaming with a gold thread in the design.

"See, it is Pergamol," Piemur said out of the side of his mouth. "Now you lot go on, across there to the knife stand until I'm finished. Men don't like a lot of hangers about when they're agreeing the mark. No, Menolly, you can stay!" Piemur snatched her back by the jerkin as she obediently started to follow the others.

Although Menolly could see Pergamol's lips moving,

she heard nothing of his speech and only an occasional murmur from the bargaining journeyman. The Smithcraft marksman continually stroked the finely tanned wherhide as he dickered, almost as if he hoped to find some flaw in the hide so he could argue a further reduction. The hide was a lovely blue, like a summer sky when the air is clear and the sun setting.

"Probably dyed to order," Piemur whispered to her. "Selling it direct neither has to pay turnover fee. With us, once Jerint has stamped the instrument, the marksman doesn't *have* to say it was apprentice-made. So we get a better price not selling at the Harper booth, where they have to say who made it."

Now Menolly could appreciate Piemur's strategy.

The bargain was handsealed, and marks slipped across the counter. The blue hide was carefully folded and put away in a travel bag. Piemur waited until the journeyman had chatted, as courtesy required, and then he skipped to the front of the stall before anyone else could intervene.

"Back so soon, young rascal. Well, let's have a look at what you've brought. Hmm . . . stamped as you said . . ." Pergamol examined more than the stamp on the tambourine, Menolly noticed, and the Smithcrafter's eyes slid to hers as he pinged the stretched hide of the tambourine with his finger, and raised his eyebrows at the sweet-sounding tinkle of the tiny cymbals under the rim. "So how much were you looking to receive for it?"

"Four marks!" said Piemur with the attitude that he was being eminently reasonable.

"Four marks?" Pergamol feigned astonishment, and the interchange of bargaining began in earnest.

Menolly was delighted, and more than a little impressed by Piemur's shrewdness when the final figure of three and a half marks was handclasped. Piemur had pointed out that for a journeyman-made tambourine, four marks was not unreasonable: Pergamol did not have to say who made it, and he saved a thirty-second on turnover. Pergamol replied that he had the carriage of the tambourine. Piemur discounted that since Pergamol might very well sell the item here at the gather, since he could price it under the Harpercraft stall. Pergamol replied that he had to make more than a few splinters profit for his journey, his effort and the rent of the stall from the Lord Holder. Piemur suggested that he consider the fine polish on the wood, listen again to the sweet jingle of the best quality metal, thinly hammered, just the sort of instrument for a lady to use . . . and a hide tanned evenly, no rough patches or stains. Menolly realized that, for all the extreme seriousness with which the two dickered, it was a game played according to certain rules, which Piemur must have learned at his foster mother's knee. The bargaining for the pipe went more smartly since Pergamol had noticed a pair of small holders waiting discreetly beyond the stall. But the bargaining was done and hand-sealed, Piemur shaking his head at Pergamol's stinginess and sighing mightily as he pocketed the marks. Looking so dejected that Menolly was concerned, the boy motioned for her to follow him to the spot where the others waited. Halfway there, Piemur let out a sigh of relief and his face broke into the broadest of his happy grins, his step took on a jauntier bounce and his shoulders straightened.

"Told you I could get a fair deal out of Pergamol!"

"You did?" Menolly was confused.

"Sure did. Three and a half for the tambourine? And three for the pipe? That's top mark!" The boys crowded round him, and Piemur recounted his success with many winks and chuckles. For his efforts, he got a quarter of a mark from each of the boys, telling Menolly that that was an improvement, for them, on the full half-mark the Harpercraft charged for selling.

"C'mon, Menolly, let's gad about," Piemur said, grabbing her by the arm and tugging her back into the stream of slowly moving people. "I can smell the pies from here," he said when he had eluded the others. "All we have to do is follow our noses . . ."

"Pies?" Master Robinton had mentioned bubbling pies.

"I don't mind treating you, since today is your first gather . . . here . . ." he added hastily, looking to see if

182

he'd offended her, "but I'm not buying for those bottom-less pits."

"We just finished dinner—"

"Bargaining's hungry work." He licked his lips in anticipation. "And I feel like something sweet, bubbling hot with berry juice. Just you wait. We'll duck through here."

He maneuvered her through the crowd, going across the moving traffic in an oblique line until they reached a wide break in the square. There they could see down to the river and the meadow where the traders' beasts were grazing, hobbled. People were moving up all the roads, arriving from the outlying plain and mountain holds. Their dress tunics and shirts made bright accents to the fresh green of the spring fields. The sun shone brilliantly over all. It was a glorious day, thought Menolly, a marvelous day for a gather. Piemur grabbed her hand, pulling her faster.

"They can't have sold all the pies," she said, laughing.

"No, but they'll get cold, and I like 'em hot, bubbling!"

And so the confections were, carried from an oven in the baker's hold on a thick, long-handled tray: the berry juices spilling darkly over the sides of the delicately browned crusts that glistened with crystalized sweet.

"Ho, you're out early, are you, Piemur? Let me see your marks first."

Piemur, with a show of great reluctance, dragged out a thirty-second bit and showed it to the skeptic.

"That'll buy you six pies."

"Six? Is that all?" Piemur's face reflected utter despair. "This is all me and my dorm mates could raise." His voice went up in a piteous note.

"Don't give me that old wheeze, Piemur," said the baker with a derisive snort. "You know you eat 'em all yourself. You wouldn't treat your mates to as much as a sniff."

"Master Palim . . ."

"Master me nothing, Piemur. You know my rank same as I know yours. It's six pies for the thirty-second or stop wasting my time." The journeyman, for that was the badge on his tunic, was slipping six pies off the tray as he spoke. "Who's your long friend here? That dorm mate you're always talking about?"

"She's Menolly . . ."

"Menolly?" the baker looked up in surprise. "The girl who wrote the song about the fire lizards?" A seventh pie was set beside the others.

Menolly fumbled in her pocket for her two-mark piece.

"Have a pie for welcome, Menolly, and any time you have a spare egg that needs a warm home. . . ." He let the sentence peter out and gave her a broad wink, and a broader smile so she'd know he was joking.

"Menolly!" Piemur grabbed her wrist, staring at the two-marker, his eyes round with surprise. "Where'd you get that?"

"Master Robinton gave it to me this morning. He said I'm to buy a belt and some bubbly pies. So please, Journeyman, I'd like to pay for them."

"No way!" Piemur was flatly indignant, knocking her extended hand away. "I said it was my treat 'cause this is your first gather. And I *know* that's the first mark piece you've ever had. Don't you go wasting it on me." He had half turned from the baker and was giving Menolly a one-eyed wink.

"Piemur, I don't know what I'd've done without you these past few days," she said, trying to move him out of her way so she could give Palim the marker. "I insist."

"Not a chance, Menolly. I keep my word."

"Then put your money where your mouth is, Piemur," said Palim, "you're blocking my counter," and he indicated the hulking figure of Camo bearing down on them.

"Camo! Where've you been, Camo?" cried Piemur. "We looked all over for you before we started for the pies. Here's yours, Camo."

"Pies?" And Camo came forward, huge hands outstretched, his thick lips moist. He wore a fresh tunic, his face was shining clean, and his straggling crop of hair had been brushed flat. He had evidently homed in on the sweet aroma of the pies as easily as Piemur.

"Yes, bubbly pies, just like I promised you, Camo," Piemur passed him two pies.

"Well, now, you wasn't having me on, was you, about feeding your mates. Although how come Menolly and Camo . . ."

"Here's your money," said Piemur with some haughtiness, thrusting the thirty-second piece into Palim's hand. "I trust your pies will live up to standard."

Menolly gaped, because there were now nine small bubbly pies on the counter front.

"Three for you, Camo." Piemur handed him a third. "Now don't burn your mouth. Three for you, Menolly," and the pastry was warm enough to sting Menolly's scarred palm, "and three for me. Thank you, Palim. It's good of you to be generous. I'll make sure everyone knows your pies . . ." and despite the heat of the crust, Piemur bit deeply into the pastry, the dark purple juices dribbling down his chin, " . . . are just as good as ever," and he said that last on a sigh of contentment. Then more briskly, "C'mon, you two." He waved to the baker who stared after them before he uttered a bark of laughter. "See you later, Palim!"

"We got nine pies for the price of six!" she said when they'd got far enough away from the stall.

"Sure, and I'll get nine again when I go back, because he'll think I'm sharing with you and Camo again. That's the best deal I've pulled on him yet."

"You mean . . ."

"Pretty smart of you to flash that two-marker about. He wouldn't have been able to change it this early in the afternoon. I'll have to try that angle again, next gather. The large marker, I mean."

"Piemur!" Menolly was appalled at his duplicity.

"Hmmmm?" His expression over the rim of the pie was unperturbed. "Good, aren't they?"

"Yes, but you're outrageous. The way you bargain . . ."

"What's wrong with it? Everyone has fun. 'Specially this early in the season. Later on they get bored, and even being small and looking sorrowful doesn't help me. Ah,

Camo," and Piemur looked disgusted. "Can't you even eat clean?"

"Pies good!" Camo had stuffed all three pies into his mouth. His tunic was now stained with berry juices, his face was flecked with pastry and berry skins, and his fist had smeared a purple streak across one cheek.

"Menolly, will you look at him! He'll disgrace the Hall. You can't take your eyes off him a moment. C'mere!"

Piemur dragged Camo to the back of the line of stalls until he found a water skin dangling from a thong on a stall frame. He made Camo cup his hands and wash his face. Menolly found a scrap of cloth, not too dirty, and they managed to remove the worst of the pie stains from Camo's face and front.

"Oh, blast the shell and sear the skin!" said Piemur in a round oath as he took up his third pie. "It's cold. Camo, you're more trouble than you're worth sometimes."

"Camo trouble?" The man's face fell into deep sorrowful lines. "Camo cold?"

"No, the pie's cold. Oh, never mind. I like you, Camo, you're my friend." Piemur patted the man's arm reassuringly, and the numbwit brightened.

"Cold or not," Menolly said after she took a bite from her third, and cooled, pastry, "they're every bit as good as you said, Piemur."

"Say," and Piemur eyed her through narrowed lids, "maybe you'd better bargain the next lot out of Palim."

"I couldn't eat another . . ."

"Oh, not now. Later."

"It'll be my treat then."

"Sure thing!" He agreed with such amiability that Menolly decided that she'd taken the bait, hook and all. "First," he went on, "let's find the tanner's stall." He took her by the hand and Camo by the sleeve and hauled them down the row. "So you're really Master Robinton's apprentice? Wow! Wait'll I tell the others! I told 'em you would be."

"I don't understand you."

Piemur shot her a startled look. "He did say that you

were his apprentice when he gave you that two-marker, didn't he?"

"He'd told me I was before today, but I didn't think that was unusual. Aren't all the apprentices in the Hall his apprentices? He's the Masterharper . . ."

"You sure don't understand." Piemur's glance was one of undiluted pity for her denseness. "Every master has a few special apprentices . . . I'm Master Shonagar's. That's why I'm always running his errands. I don't know how they did it in your Sea Hold, but here, you get taken in as a general apprentice. If you turn out to be specially good at something, like me at voice, and Brolly at making instruments, the Master of that craft takes you on as a special apprentice, and you report to him for extra training and duties. And if he's pleased with you, he'll give you the odd mark to spend at a gather. So . . . if Master Robinton gave you a two-marker, he's pleased with you, and you're his special apprentice. He doesn't tap many." Piemur shook his head slowly from side to side, with a soft emphatic whistle. "There's been lots of heavy betting in the dorm as to who he'd pick since Sebell took his walk as journeyman . . . not that Sebell doesn't still look to the Masterharper even if he is a rank up . . . but Ranly was so sure he'd be tapped."

"Is that why Ranly doesn't like me?"

Piemur dismissed that with a gesture. "Ranly never had a chance, and the only one who didn't know that was Ranly! He thinks he's so good. Everyone else knew that Master Robinton was hoping to find you . . . the one who'd written those songs! Look, there's the tanner's stall. And just spy that beautiful blue belt. It's even got a fire lizard for a buckle tongue!" He'd pulled her up and lowered his voice for the last words. "And blue! You let me bargain, hear?"

Before she could agree, Piemur approached the stall, acting casually, glancing over the tabards, soft shoes and boots displayed, apparently oblivious to the belt he'd just indicated to Menolly.

"They've got some blue boot hide, Menolly," he said, to her.

Knowing the shrewdness Piemur had already displayed, Menolly followed his cue, and, glancing at the tanner for permission, touched the thick wherry leather. She could see the belt over his shoulder, and the tongue had been fashioned like a slim fire lizard.

"Now, don't tell me you have money in your trous, short stuff," the tanner journeyman said to Piemur and then peered uncertainly at Menolly's cropped hair, trousers and apprentice badge.

"Me? No, but she's buying. Her slippers are a disgrace."

The tanner did look down, and Menolly wanted to hide her scuffed footwear.

"This is Menolly," Piemur went on, blithely unaware of the embarrassment he was causing her. "She's got nine fire lizards, and she's Master Robinton's new apprentice."

Wondering what on earth was possessing Piemur, she glanced anywhere but at the curious journeyman. She caught a glimpse of bright filmy materials, and richly decorated tunics. She steadied her gaze and saw Pona, her arm through a tall lad's. He was wearing the yellow of Fort Hold and the shoulder knot of the Lord Holder's family. Behind Pona came Briala, Amania and Audiva, each of the girls escorted by a well-dressed youth, fosterlings of Lord Groghe's to judge by the different hold colors and rank knots.

"Here, Menolly, what do you think of this hide?" asked Piemur.

"And be sure she has the marks for it," said Pona, pausing. Her voice was too smooth to be insulting, and yet her manner gave her words an offensive ring. "For I'm certain she's only wasting your time and will finger your wares dirty. Whereas I want to commission you to make me some soft shoes for the summer . . ." She held up a well-filled waist pouch.

"She's got two marks," Piemur said, turning to challenge Pona, his eyes flashing with anger.

"If she does, she stole it," replied Pona, abandoning her indolent manner. "She'd nothing on her when she was still permitted to live in the cot."

"Stolen?" Menolly felt herself tensing with fury at the totally unexpected accusation.

"Stolen, nothing!" Piemur replied hotly. "Master Robinton gave it to her this morning!"

"I claim insult from you, Pona," cried Menolly, her hand on her belt knife.

"Benis, she's threatening me!" Pona cried, clinging to her escort's arm.

"Now, see here, apprentice girl. You can't insult a lady of the Holders. You just hand over that mark piece," said Benis, gesturing peremptorily to Menolly.

"Menolly, don't take insult," Audiva pushed her way past the others and grabbed her arm, restraining her. "It's what she wants."

"Pona's given me too many insults, Audiva."

"Menolly, you mustn't—"

"Get the mark, Benis," Pona said in a hiss. "Make her pay for threatening *me*!"

"Out of the way, Benis, whoever you are," said Menolly. "Pona has to answer for the insults she gives, lady holder or not." Menolly moved sideways, countering Pona's attempt to evade her.

"Benis, she can be dangerous! I told you so!" Pona's voice went up in a frightened, breathless squeak.

"You mustn't, Menolly," Audiva said, catching Menolly's sleeve. "She *wants* you to . . . Piemur, help me!"

"Don't you dare, Audiva!" Pona's voice was now edged with angry malice. "Or I'll settle you good as well."

"Come, girl, the money. Hand it over and we'll say no more about attempted insult . . ." said Benis in a patronizing tone.

"Pona's insulted Menolly!" cried Piemur indignantly. "Just because you're a—"

"Close your mouth!" Benis wasted no courtesies on Piemur. He took a stride to close the distance between himself and Menolly, his jaw set in a disagreeable grin as he disdainfully measured the three slight and defiant adversaries.

Pona gave a little squeal as Benis left her standing on

her own. Then, another as Menolly, stepping away from Benis, made a lunge at her, trying to catch her long plaited hair.

"Hey, now just a minute, you," said the tanner in a loud voice, sensing an imminent fight. He ducked under the counter of his stall, emerging into the walkway. "This is a gather, not a . . ."

Benis was quick on his feet, too, and he grabbed Menolly by the shoulder, spinning her toward him and securing her left arm, which he immediately twisted up behind her. With a cry of triumph, Pona darted forward, her hands busy with Menolly's belt pouch. Piemur sprang to Menolly's assistance, kicking Benis in the shins and grabbing Pona by the hair. The kick made Benis loosen his hold on Menolly's arm. With a strength developed by Turns of hauling and handling heavy nets, she wrenched free of his grasp, dancing out of his way.

"I settle Pona!" She shouted to Piemur, beckoning him away.

"Benis, save me!" Pona screamed, rushing to the young Holder, but Piemur was still hanging onto her plait.

Benis let fly a kick at Piemur, tripping him up and added another one to the ribs as the boy measured his length in the dust.

"Leave him alone!" Forgetting her quarrel with Pona, Menolly launched herself at Benis. Putting shoulder and body behind her fist, she drove it right into Benis's face. He staggered back, roaring in outrage and pain. One of the other fosterlings came charging forward, fist cocked to slam Menolly, but Audiva hung onto his arm.

"Viderian! Menolly's a seaholder! Help us!"

Startled, her escort bounded in to help Audiva, just as Menolly ducked under Benis's swing and tried to protect Piemur, who was struggling to get on his feet, blood streaming from his nose.

The next moment, the air was full of shrieking, clawing, fighting fire lizards. Piemur was screaming that Benis better not hit the Harper's apprentice, or there'd be real trouble; Camo was howling that his pretty ones were afraid, and he waded in, thick arms flailing, hitting indiscriminately at friend and foe. Menolly got a clout across the ear as she tried to restrain the misguided Camo.

"Shells! It's the Hall's dummy!" "Scatter!" "Get her!" "Knock him down!" "Got her, Menolly!"

The fire lizards were not hampered by Camo's inability to distinguish friend and foe. They went for Pona, Briala, Amania, Benis and the other lads. Menolly, trying to catch her breath, realized that things were completely out of hand and desperately tried to call off the fire lizards. The girls were scattering, screaming, vainly trying to cover their heads, hair and eyes. Attacked from above, so did the fosterlings.

"*Be still! Everyone!*" The bellow was stentorian enough to penetrate shriek, howl and battle cries, and stern enough to command instant obedience. "You there, hang on to Camo! Douse him with that skin of water! You, tanner, help them with Camo. Sit on him, knock his feet out from under him if necessary. Menolly, control your fire lizards! This is a gather, not a brawl!"

The Harper strode into the midst of the melee, yanking a fosterling to his feet, spinning one of the girls to the arms of the folk who had converged on the scene, giving a bloody-nosed Piemur a hand up from the dust. The Masterharper's actions were somewhat hampered by the distressed squeals of the little bronze fire lizard clinging tightly to his left arm, but there was little doubt of the Master's fury. A silence broken by the gulping sobs of Pona and Briala held attacker, attacked and witnesses alike.

"Now," said the Harper, his voice controlled although his eyes were flashing with anger, "just what has been going on here?"

"It was her!" Pona staggered a step toward Master Robinton, jabbing her finger at Menolly and struggling to control her sobs. Long scratches marred her cheeks, her head scarf was torn and her hair pulled from its plaits. "She's always causing trouble—"

"Sir, we were minding our own business," said Piemur indignantly, "which was buying a belt that you said Menolly ought to have, when Pona here—"

"That little sneak tripped me as we were passing, and then her hideous beasts attacked all of us. They've done it before. I have witnesses!"

She stopped mid-gulp, arrested by the look on the Harper's face.

"Lady Pona," he said in an all too gentle voice, "you are overwrought. Briala, take the child back to Dunca. The excitement of a gather appears to be too much for such a fragile spirit. Amania, I think you ought to help Briala." Though his voice expressed concern for their well-being, it was obvious that the Harper was disciplining the three girls who bore evidence of the unfriendly attentions of the fire lizards.

Now he turned to the Hold fosterlings. Benis, his left eye already bruising, his lip cut, his hair tousled and forehead bearing fire lizard marks, was straightening his tunic and brushing dust from his sleeve and trousers. The other youths who had been escorting the now banished girls maintained the rigid stance they had adopted as soon as they recognized the Masterharper.

"Lord Benis?"

"Masterharper?" Benis continued to adjust his garments, awarding the briefest of glances to the Harper.

"I'm glad you know my rank," said Robinton, smiling slightly.

Menolly had been soothing Beauty and Rocky who had refused to leave when she sent the others away. At his tone, she looked at the Harper, amazed that he could express so profound a reprimand with a brief phrase and a smile.

One of the other fosterlings jabbed Benis in the ribs, and the young man looked angrily about.

"I expect you have business elsewhere . . . now!" said the Masterharper.

"Business? This is a gather day . . . sir."

"For others, indeed, it is, but not, I think, for you," and the Masterharper indicated with his hand that Benis had better retire. "Or you, and you, and you," he added, indicating the other fosterlings who displayed claw marks. "Will you occupy yourselves quietly in your quarters or will I have to mention this to Lord Groghe?" He accepted the frantic shakings of their heads.

Then he turned his back on them and pleasantly indicated to those who were avidly observing his summary justice that they should now continue their interrupted pursuits. He walked to where Camo was still being restrained by three large journeymen, blubbering noisily about his pretties being hurt and struggling to free himself.

"The pretties are not hurt, Camo. Not hurt. See? Menolly has the pretties." The Harper's voice soothed the wretched man as he gestured for Menolly to come forward into Camo's line of sight.

"Pretties not hurt?"

"No, Camo. Brudegan, who else is about?" the Harper asked his journeyman. Several other harpers obediently moved against the tide of the dispersing crowd. "Camo had better go back to the hall. Here," and the Harper reached into his pouch and passed Brudegan a mark piece. "Buy him a lot of those bubbly pies on your way back. That'll help settle him."

The crowd had melted away. The Masterharper, stroking his gradually quieting fire lizard, turned back to the small group still clustered together. He gestured them to the unoccupied space between the nearest stalls.

"Now, let me hear the sequence of events, please," he said, but his voice no longer held that chilling note of displeasure.

"It wasn't Menolly's fault!" said Piemur, batting at Audiva's hands as she tried to staunch the flow from his nose with the berry-stained cloth used earlier on Camo. "We were looking at belts . . ." He turned to the tanner for confirmation.

"I don't know about belts, Master Robinton, but they weren't causing any trouble when the blonde girl, Lady Pona, started pulling rank on your apprentice. Made a nasty accusation about the girl having money she oughtn't to have."

A look of dismay crossed the Harper's face. "You didn't lose the mark in the fuss, did you, Menolly?" He scuffed around the trampled area with his boot toe. "I don't have many two-mark pieces, you know."

The tanner stifled a bark of laughter, and the Harper sighed with almost comic relief as Menolly solemnly displayed the cause of the trouble.

"That's a mercy," Master Robinton said with a smile of approval for Menolly. "Go on," he added to the tanner.

"Then this lass," and the tanner gestured toward Audiva, "took Menolly's part. So did the young seaholder. I think all would have come to nothing if Camo hadn't got upset, and the next thing I know the air's full of fire lizards. Are they all hers?" He jerked his thumb at Menolly.

"Yes," said the Harper, "a fact that ought to be borne in mind since they do seem able to recognize Menolly's . . . ammm . . ."

"Sir, I didn't call them . . ." Menolly said, finding her voice.

"I'm sure you didn't need to." He closed his hand reassuringly on her shoulder.

"Master Robinton, Pona bears a grudge against Menolly," said Audiva in a rush as if she had to make the admission before she could change her mind. "And she's got no real cause at all."

"Thank you, Audiva, I've been aware of the prejudice." The Harper made a slight bow, acknowledging the tall girl's loyalty. "The Lady Pona will not trouble you further, Menolly, nor you, Audiva," he continued, that hint of implacability tinging an otherwise pleasant tone. "Good of you, Lord Viderian, to support another seaholder, though it is a loyalty I would prefer to render unnecessary."

"My father, Master Robinton, is very much of your mind, which is why I am fostered in a landbound Hold," said Viderian with a respectful bow. He stiffened, his eyes widening at some disturbing sight. He swallowed hard, anxiety plainly written on his face.

"Ah," said the Harper, having followed the direction of Viderian's gaze. "I wondered how long it would take Lord Groghe to respond to promptings. . . ." He grinned, highly amused at some inner reflection. "Viderian, do make off with Audiva. Now! And enjoy yourselves!"

Audiva needed no urging and grabbed the young sea-holder's arm, hastening down the aisle until they were lost in the crowd.

"It's Lord Groghe!" said Piemur in a croak, pulling at Menolly's sleeve.

The Harper caught the boy by the shoulder. "You'll stay by me, young Piemur, so we may have an end of this affair now!" Then he turned to the tanner. "Which belt tempted Menolly?"

"The one with the fire lizard on the buckle," said Piemur in an undertone to the Harper and then edged himself carefully so that the Harper was between him and the oncoming Lord Holder.

"Robinton, my queen's doing it again. . . . Ah, Menolly, just the person!" said Lord Groghe, his florid face lighting with a smile. "Merga's been . . . humph! She's stopped!" The Holder regarded his queen accusingly. "She's been fussing! Right up until I reached the square . . ."

"That's rather easily explained," said Robinton in an off-handed manner.

"Is it? Both of 'em are at it now."

Menolly had been aware of it first, because Beauty was chirping and squeaking at Merga through Lord Groghe's conversation. She felt color rising in her cheeks. The discourse finished as quickly as it had begun. The two little queens flipped their wings closed on their backs and became totally disinterested in each other.

"What was that all about?" Lord Groghe demanded.

"I suspect they were catching up on the news," said Robinton, with a chuckle, for that was what it had sounded like: a spate of urgent gossip. "Which reminds me, Lord Groghe; I heard that the wineman has a keg of good, aged Benden wine."

"He does?" Lord Groghe's interest was diverted. "How did he get his hands on it?"

"I think we ought to check."

"Humph! Yes! Now!"

"Wouldn't do to waste good Benden wine on people

unable to appreciate it, would it?" Robinton took Lord Groghe's arm.

"Not at all." But the Holder could not be completely diverted and turned to frown at Menolly. She steeled herself before she realized that his frown was not menacing. "Want a chance to talk to this girl. Didn't seem the time or place to do so t'other day with the Hatching and all."

"Of course, Lord Groghe, when Menolly's finished her bargaining . . ."

"Bargaining? Humph. Well, can't interrupt a bargain at a gather . . . humph!" Lord Groghe pushed out his lower lip as he looked from Menolly to the hovering tanner. "Don't be all day about it, girl. Th'afternoon's a good time to talk. Don't have many chances to sit and talk."

"Finish your dicker for that belt, Menolly," the Harper told her, one arm gently propelling the Lord Holder away from the apprentices, "and then join us at the wineman's stall. And you," the Masterharper's forefinger pointed down at Piemur, "wash your face, keep your mouth closed, and stay out of trouble. At least until I've had some Benden wine to fortify me." Lord Groghe humphed at the delay. "If it *is* Benden wine. . . . This way, my Lord Holder." The two men walked off together, in step, each steadying the fire lizards they carried.

A soft whistle at her elbow broke the trance holding Menolly as she stared after the two most influential men in the Hold. Piemur was dramatically dragging a hand across his brow to signalize a close escape.

"What do you bet, Menolly, that the subject of your cracking Benis in the face never comes up? And where'd you learn to punch like that?"

"When I saw that big bully kicking you, I was so flaming mad, I . . . I . . ."

"May I add my congratulations to Piemur's?" asked a quiet voice. The two whirled to see Sebell, leaning against the side of the tanner's stall. The eyes of his young queen were still whirling with the red of anger.

"Oh, no," said Menolly with a groan, "not you, too! What *am* I going to do with them?" She was utterly dis-

196

couraged and dejected. It had been bad enough to have the fire lizards diving and swooping at plain noise; outrageous of them to have flown at Master Domick because he'd only spoken angrily to her. And now this very public fracas with the son of the Fort Lord Holder.

"It wasn't *your* fault, Menolly," said Piemur stoutly.

"It never is, but it *is!*"

"How long have you been here, Sebell?" Piemur asked, ignoring Menolly's wail.

"On the heels of Lord Groghe," said the journeyman, grinning. "But I caught a glimpse of young Benis making tracks out of the Hold proper, so it wasn't hard to figure out where he got the scratches," he went on, glancing at the perched fire lizards and absently stroking Kimi. "I have only one burning question: Who had the audacity to give Benis a colored eye?"

"A rare sight that was," said the tanner who'd been keeping back but now stepped up. "The girl landed as sweet a punch in that young snot's eye as ever I've seen, and I've been to many a gather that boasted a good brawl. Now, young harper girl, which belt had you in mind before the fracas started? I thought you was after boot leather." He eyed Piemur sharply.

"Menolly wants the blue one with the fire lizard buckle."

"It'd be much too expensive," Menolly said hastily.

The tanner ducked back under his counter and picked the coveted belt from its hook.

"This the one?"

Menolly looked at it wistfully. Sebell took it from the tanner's hands, examined it, gave it a tug to see if there were flaws or if the hide was too thin to wear well.

"Good workmanship in that belt, Journeyman," the tanner said. "Proper for the girl to have it, with her owning the fire lizards."

"How much were you asking for it?" asked Piemur, settling down to the business of bargaining.

The tanner looked down at Piemur, stroked the belt, which Sebell had handed back to him, then glanced at Menolly.

"It's yours, girl. And I'll not take a mark from you. Worth it to me to see you plant one on that young rowdy's face. Here, wear it in good health and long life."

Piemur gaped, mouth wide, eyes popping.

"Oh, I couldn't," and Menolly extended the two-mark piece. The tanner promptly closed her fist over the marker and laid the belt on her wrist.

"Yes, you could and you will, apprentice harper! And that's the end of the matter. I've struck the bargain." He pumped her hand in the traditional courtesy.

"Ah, Tanner Ligand," Sebell stepped up, leaning on the counter and beckoning the tanner to bend close to him. "While I didn't see much of the affair . . ." Sebell began to rub his forefinger on one side of his nose, "it's not exactly the sort of incident . . ."

"I take your meaning, Harper Sebell," the tanner replied, nodding his head in acceptance of the adroit suggestion. His grin was rueful. "Not that the truth doesn't make fine telling. Still, those fire lizards of yours are young, aren't they, girl, excitable-like, not used to a gather, I expect. . . . Oh, I'll say what's proper. Don't you worry, harpers." He patted Menolly's hand, still outstretched with the marker. "Now cheer up, you've a face like a wet Turn. You've done more good than harm this gather day. And when you've the need for slippers to match the belt, just you send me the work. I won't do you in the mark," and he flashed a look at the skeptical Piemur. "Not that I don't like a good tight bargain now and then . . ."

Piemur made a gargling sound in his throat and would have disputed the statement.

"Let's clean you up, Piemur, as Master Robinton suggested," said Sebell, warning the boy by the tilt of his head to be silent.

"I've a water-carrier at the back of the stall you're welcome to use," said Ligand, "And here's a cleaner cloth than the one Menolly has!" He held out a white square to her and dismissed her profuse thanks with a smile and a wave to be off.

No sooner had Sebell and Menolly pulled Piemur to the back of the tanner's stall than people began to step up to his counter.

"Hah!" said Piemur, looking over his shoulder. "He's sly, that Ligand, *giving* you the belt. He'll get three times as much business because you—"

"Close your mouth," suggested Sebell, as he rubbed firmly at the bloody streaks on Piemur's face. "Hold him, Menolly."

"Hey . . . I . . ." but Piemur's complaints were effectively muffled by the damp cloth Sebell used in earnest.

"The less mentioned about this matter, Piemur, the better. And what I said to Ligand holds for you as well. Here and in the Hall. There'll be enough rumor and wrangle without you adding your bits."

"Do you think . . . mumble . . . mumble . . . I'd do anything . . . leave me alone . . . to hurt Menolly?"

Sebell suspended the cleaning operation and regarded the boy's flashing eyes and the indignant set of his jaw. "No, I guess you wouldn't. If only not to lose your chance at feeding the fire lizards . . ."

"Now, that's not fair . . ."

"Sebell, what am I going to do about them?" Menolly asked, finally getting out the fears she'd been suppressing.

"They were only protecting . . ." Piemur began, but Sebell silenced him with a hand over his mouth and a stern look.

"Today they apparently had cause, as Piemur said. The other evening they reacted to what was going on at Benden Weyr with F'nor and Canth, through Brekke's fire lizard. Again, cause." Sebell glanced back toward the tanner's stall and noticed that some of the throng were surreptitiously regarding the three harpers. He motioned to Menolly and Piemur to walk out of sight, down behind the stalls, away from the curious. "All of this," and Sebell's hand took in the towering face of the Hold cliff behind them, the Harper Hall across the paved square now lined with stalls, "is as new to you as to them. Enough to cause alarm and apprehension. They're young and so are you, for all you've managed to accomplish. It's again a question of discipline," he said, but his smile was reassuring.

"I had no discipline this afternoon," she said, repenting of her attack on Pona. She might well have jeopardized everything, crying insult from Pona.

"What d'you mean? You had a fantastic right punch!" cried Piemur, demonstrating with a grunt. "And you'd every right to cry insult on Pona, after all she's done to you . . ." Piemur hastily covered his mouth, his eyes widening as he realized he was being indiscreet.

"You cried insult on Pona?" asked Sebell, frowning in surprise. "I thought that Silvina and I told you to leave the matter."

"She called me a thief. She tried to get Benis to take my two-marker from me."

"The two-marker that Master Robinton himself had given Menolly to buy that belt," said Piemur, staunchly confirming the affair.

"If Pona has added insult to the injury she's already tried to do you," said Sebell slowly, "then, of course, you had to take action, Menolly." He smiled slightly, his eyes still considering her face. "In fact, it's good to know that you will take action on your own behalf. But, the fire lizards' part . . ."

"I didn't call them, Sebell. But, when Benis tripped Piemur and then kicked him, I was scared. He just lay there . . ."

"Sure, smartest thing to do in a kicking fight," Piemur replied, unperturbed.

"I cannot, however, condone apprentices fighting with each other or with holders . . . especially holders of any rank. . . ."

"Benis is the biggest bully in the Hold, Sebell, and you know we've all had trouble with him."

"Enough, youngster," said Sebell more sharply than Menolly had yet heard him speak. As quiet and self-effacing as the journeyman usually was, when he spoke in that authoritative tone of voice, it would take a stalwart person to disobey him. "That was not, however, what I meant by discipline, Menolly. I meant the ability to stick with a project, like that song you wrote yesterday. . . . Was it really only yesterday?" he added. He smiled tenderly down at Kimi who was now asleep in a ball, snuggled between his body and elbow.

"You wrote a *new* song?" Piemur brightened. "You didn't tell me. When'll we get to hear it?"

"When will you get to hear it?" Menolly heard her voice cracking on the last few words.

"What's the matter, Menolly?" Sebell took her arm and gave her a little shake but she could only stare at them.

"It's just that . . . it's so different . . ." She stammered unable to express the upheaval in her mind, the reversal of all that she had been expected to do. "D'you know . . . d'you know what used to happen to me when I wrote a song?" She tried to stop the words that were threatening to burst from her, but she couldn't, not with Piemur's face contorted with distress for her. And Sebell quietly encouraging her to speak with the sympathy so plain on his face. "I used to get *beaten* by my father for tuning, for twiddles as he called them. When I cut my hand . . ." she held it up, looking at the red scar and then turning it to them, ". . . gutting packtails, they let it heal all wrong so I wouldn't be able to play. They wouldn't even allow me to sing in the Hall, for fear Harper Elgion would figure out that it was me who'd taught the children after Petiron died. They were *ashamed* of me! They were afraid I'd disgrace them. That's why I ran away. I'd rather have died of Threadscore than live in Half-Circle another night. . . ."

Tears of bitter and keenly felt injustice streamed down Menolly's cheeks. She was aware of Piemur urgently begging her not to cry, that it was all right, she was safe now, and he loved every one of her songs, even the ones he hadn't heard. And he'd tell her father a thing or two if he ever met him. She was conscious that Sebell had put his right arm about her shoulders and was stroking her with awkward consolation. But it was Beauty's anxious chirping in her ear that reminded her that she'd better get her emotions under control. Master Robinson and Lord Groghe wouldn't be pleased by a second alarm incited by her lack of self-discipline. Particularly if it dragged them away from good Benden wine.

She dashed the tears from her eyes, and gulping down one last sob, looked defiantly into the startled faces of Sebell and Piemur.

"And I wanted you to teach me how to gut fish!" Sebell let out a long sigh. "I wondered why you were so hesitant. I'll find someone else, now I understand why you hate it."

"Oh, I *want* to teach you, Sebell. I want to do everything I can, if it's gutting fish or teaching you to sail. I may be only a girl, but I'm going to be the best harper in the entire Hall . . ."

"Easy, Menolly," said Sebell, laughing at her excess. "I believe you."

"I do, too!" said Piemur in a low, intense tone of reassurance. "I never knew you'd had *that* kind of hold life. Didn't anyone *ever* listen to your songs?"

"Petiron did, but after he died . . ."

"I can see now why it's been so hard for you, Menolly, to appreciate how important your songs are. After what you've been through," and Sebell gently squeezed her left hand, "it would be hard to believe in yourself. Promise me, Menolly, to believe from now on? Your songs are very important to the Harper, to the Hall and to me. Master Domick's music *is* brilliant, but yours appeals to everyone, holder and crafter, landsman and seaman. Your songs deal with subjects, like the fire lizard and Brekke's call to F'nor and Canth, that will help change the sort of set attitudes that nearly killed you in your home hold.

"There's something wrong in not appreciating one's own special abilities, my girl. Find your own limitations, yes, but don't limit *yourself* with false modesty."

"That's what I've always liked about Menolly: she's got her head on right," said Piemur with all the sententiousness of an ancient uncle.

Menolly looked at her friend and then began to laugh, as much at Piemur as at herself. Her outburst had at long last lifted a weight of intolerable depression. She straightened her shoulders and smiled at her friends, flinging out her arms to signal her release.

They all heard the happy warbling of the fire lizards. Beauty crooned with pleasure, rubbing her head against Menolly's cheek, and Kimi gave a drowsy chirp that made the trio of harpers laugh.

"You are feeling better now, aren't you, Menolly?" said Piemur. "So we'd better follow orders, because it doesn't do to keep a Lord Holder waiting, much less Master Robinton. You've got your belt and I'm washed up, so we'd better get to the wineman's stall."

Menolly hesitated just a moment.

"Well?" asked Sebell, raising his eyebrows to encourage her to answer.

"What if he finds out I'm the one who hit Benis?"

"Not from Benis he won't," replied Piemur with a snort. "Besides, he's got fifteen sons. And only one fire lizard. He wants to talk to *you* about her. Not even the Masterharper knows as much about fire lizards as you do. Come *on!*"

Chapter 10

Then my feet took off and my legs went, too,
And my body was obliged to follow.
Me with my hands and my mouth full of cress
And my throat too dry to swallow.
                    Menolly's "Running Song"

To Menolly's intense relief, all Lord Groghe did want to talk about was the fire lizards—his in particular and in general. The four of them, Robinton, Sebell, Lord Groghe and herself, sat at a table apart from the others, on one side of the square, each of them with a fire lizard. Menolly was torn between amusement and awe that she, the newest of apprentices, should be in such exalted company. Lord Groghe, for all his clipped speech and an amazing range of descriptive grimaces, was very easy to talk to, once she got over her initial nervousness about the fracas with Benis. She heard, in detail, about the Hatching of Merga, smiled when Lord Groghe guffawed reminiscently over his early anxieties about her.

"Could've used someone with your knowledge, girl."

"You forget, sir, that my friends broke shell at about the same time Merga did. I wouldn't have been much help to you then."

"You can be now, though. How do I go about teaching Merga to fetch and carry for me? Heard about your pipes."

"She's just one. It took all nine of mine to bring me the

pipes. They're heavy." Menolly considered the problem, seeing the disappointment on Lord Groghe's features. "For just Merga alone, it would have to be something light, like a message, and you'd have to *want* it very badly. It was . . . well, my feet still hurt and it was such a long walk to the cot. . . ."

His eyes, which were a disconcertingly light brown, fixed on hers. "Got to want it badly, huh? Humph. Don't know as I want anything *badly!*" He gave a snort of laughter at her expression. "You want things *badly* when you're young, girl. When you're my age, you've learned how to *plan.*" He winked at her. "Take the point, though, since Merga's a bundle of emotion, aren't you, pet?" He stroked her head with a remarkably tender touch for a big, heavy-fingered man. "Emotion, that's what they respond best to. Want's sort of an emotion, isn't it? If you want something bad enough . . . Humph." He laughed again, this time with an oblique look at the Harper. "Emotion, then, Harper, not knowledge, is what these little beasties communicate. Emotion, like Brekke's fear t'other night. Hatching's emotional, too. And today . . ." he turned his light eyes back to Menolly.

"Today . . . that was all my fault, sir," Menolly said, grabbing at a remark of Piemur's for excuse. "My friend, Piemur, the little fellow," and Menolly measured Piemur's height from the ground with her free hand, "stumbled in the crowd. I was afraid he'd be trampled . . ."

"Was that what that was all about, Robinton?" asked Lord Groghe. "You never did explain," but Lord Groghe seemed more interested in the lack of wine in his cup. Robinton politely topped the cup from the wineskin on the table.

"It never occurred to me, Lord Groghe," said Menolly with genuine contrition, "that I'd be alarming you or the Masterharper or Sebell."

"The young of every kind tend to be easily alarmed," remarked the Harper, but Menolly could see the corners of his mouth twitching with amusement. "The problem will disappear with maturity."

"And increases now with so many fire lizards about

her," added Lord Groghe with a grunt. "How much more d'you think they'll grow, girl, if yours are the same age as Merga?" He was frowning at Beauty and glancing back to Merga.

"Mirrim's three fire lizards at Benden Weyr were from the first clutch, weren't they? They're not more than a fingertip longer," said Menolly, eagerly seizing on the new topic. "They'd be older by several sevendays, I think." She glanced at the Masterharper who nodded in confirmation. "When I first saw F'nor's queen, Grall, I thought it was my Beauty." Beauty squeaked indignantly, her eyes whirling a little faster. "Only for a moment," Menolly told her in apology and stroked Beauty's head, "and only because I didn't know the Weyrs had also discovered the fire lizards."

"Any notion how old they must be to mate?" asked Lord Groghe, scowling in hopes of a favorable answer.

"Sir, I don't know. T'gellan, Monarth's rider, is going to keep a watch on the cave where my fire lizards hatched, to see if their queen will come back to clutch there again."

"Cave? Thought fire lizards laid their eggs in sand on the beaches?"

Master Robinton indicated that she was to speak freely to the Lord Holder, so Menolly told him how she'd seen the fire lizard queen mating near the Dragon Stones, how she'd happened to be back that way, looking for spiderclaws ("Good eating, those," Lord Groghe agreed and gestured for her to get on with the tale) . . . and helped the little fire lizard queen lift the eggs from the sea-threatened strand into the cave.

"You wrote that song, didn't you?" Lord Groghe's frown was surprised and approving. "The one about the fire lizard keeping the sea back with her wings! Liked that one! Write more like it! Easy to sing. Why didn't you tell me a girl wrote it, Robinton?" His scowl was now accusatory.

"I didn't know it was Menolly at the time we circulated the song."

"Humph. Forgot about that. Go on, girl. Did it happen just as you wrote the song?"

"Yes, sir."

"How come you were there in the cave when they hatched?"

"I was hunting spiderclaws and went further down coast than I should have. Threadfall was due. I was caught out, and the only shelter I could think of was the cave where I'd put the fire lizard eggs. I arrived . . . with my sack of spiderclaws . . . just as the eggs began to break. That's how I Impressed so many. I couldn't very well let them fly out into Thread. And they were so hungry, just out of the shell . . ."

Lord Groghe grunted, sniffed and mumbled to the effect that he'd had enough trouble keeping one fed, his compliments for handling nine! As if mention of food had penetrated their sleep, Kimi and Zair roused, creeling.

"I mean no discourtesy, Lord Groghe," said Master Robinton, rising as hastily as Sebell.

"Nonsense. Don't go. They eat anything, anywhere." Lord Groghe swung his heavy torso about. "You there, what's your name . . ." and he waved impatiently at the wineman's apprentice, who came running. "Bring a tray of those meatrolls from the stalls. A big tray. Heaped. Enough to feed two hungry fire lizards and a couple of harpers. Never known a harper who wasn't hungry. Are you hungry, harper girl?"

"No, sir; thank you, sir."

"Making a liar out of me, harper girl? Bring back some bubbly pies, too," the Lord Holder roared after the departing apprentice. "Hope he heard me. So you're the daughter to Yanus of Half-Circle Sea Hold."

Menolly nodded acknowledgement of the relationship.

"Never been to Half-Circle. They brag about that cavern of theirs. *Does* it hold the fishing fleet?"

"Yes, sir, it does. The biggest can sail in without unstepping the masts, except, of course when the tides run exceptionally high. There's a rock shelf for repairs and careening, a section for building, as well as a very dry inside cave for storing wood."

"Hold above the docking cavern?" Lord Groghe seemed dubious about the wisdom of that.

"Oh, no, sir. Half-Circle Sea Hold really is a half circle." She cocked her thumb and curved her forefinger. "This," and she angled her right hand to show the direction of the curve, after squinting to see where the sun was, "my thumb is the docking cavern, and this," and she pointed to the length of her forefinger, "is the Hold . . . the longer part of the half circle, and then this much," and she touched the webbing, "is sandy beach. They can draw dinghies up on it or gut fish, sew nets and mend sail there in fair weather."

"*They?*" asked Lord Groghe, his thick eyebrows rising in surprise.

"Yes, sir, *they*. I'm a harper now."

"Well said, Menolly," replied Lord Groghe, slapping his thigh with a crack that made Merga squeal in alarm. "Girl or not, Robinton, you've a good one here. I approve. I approve."

"Thank you, Lord Groghe, I was confident you would," said the Masterharper with a slight smile, which he shared with Sebell before he nodded reassuringly at Menolly.

Beauty chirped a question, which Lord Groghe's Merga answered in a sort of "that's that" tone.

"Cross-crafting works, Robinton. Think I'll have to spot a few more of my sons about. Seaholds, too."

The notion of Benis in Half-Circle Sea Hold appealed to Menolly, though she didn't know if that was whom Lord Groghe had in mind.

The slap of running feet and hoarse breathing interrupted the conversation as the apprentice lad, juggling two trays, all but slid the contents into the laps of those he served.

As the new fire lizards were fed, Menolly saw that more and more people were filing into the central square, taking seats at tables and benches. At one end was a wooden platform. Now a group of harpers took their places and began to tune up. Immediately sets were formed for a call-dance. A tall journeyman harper gave his tambourine a warning shake and then called out the dance figures in a loud voice that carried above the music while his tambourine emphasized the step rhythm.

Those watching on the sidelines clapped in time to the music, shouting good-natured encouragements to the dancers. To Menolly's surprise, Lord Groghe added a hearty smacking beat of his hands, stamping his feet and cheerfully grinning about at everyone.

Once the music started, the square filled up, and still more benches were angled into any free space. Menolly saw colors of all the major crafts on journeymen and apprentices from the halls of the Fort Hold complex. Groups of men stood about, drinking wine and watching the dancing, their heavy boots and clean, though earth-stained, trousers marking them as small holders in from neighboring farms for the restday and a bit of trading at the gather. Their womenfolk had congregated along one side of the square, chattering, tending smaller children, watching the dancing. When the sets changed, some of the holders dragged their giggling but willing women out to make up new groups as the musicians began another foot-tapping, hand-clapping tune.

The third was a couple's dance, a wild gyration of swinging arms and skipping legs, an exercise that rendered every participant breathless and thirsty to judge by the calls on the wineman's lads when the dance ended.

A change of harpers occurred now, the dance-players giving up the platform to Brudegan and three of the older apprentices who ranged themselves slightly behind Brudegan. At his signal they sang the song that Elgion had sung the night of his arrival at Half-Circle Sea Hold: it was one Menolly had never had a chance to learn. She leaned forward, eager to catch every word and chord. On her shoulder, Beauty sat up, one forepaw lightly clasping Menolly's ear for balance. The little queen gave a trill, glanced inquiringly at Menolly.

"Let her sing," said Master Robinton. Then he leaned forward, "But, if you can keep the others where they are on the roofs, I think that might be wise."

Menolly sent a firm command to her friends just as Merga rose to her haunches on Lord Groghe's shoulder and added her voice to Beauty's.

As the fire lizards' descant rose above the harpers'

voices, Menolly was conscious of being the focus of startled attention. Lord Groghe was beaming with pride, a smug smile on his face, the fingers of one hand drumming the beat on the table while he waved the other as if he were directing the extemporaneous chorus.

Wild applause followed the song, and cries of " 'The Fire Lizard Song'!" "Sing the Queen's song!" "Does she know it?" "Fire lizard!"

From the platform, Brudegan beckoned imperiously to Menolly.

"Go on, girl, what's holding you back?" Lord Groghe flicked his fingers at her to obey the summons. "Want to hear you sing it. You wrote it. Ought to sing it. Shake yourself up, girl. Never heard of a harper not wanting to sing."

Menolly appealed to Master Robinton, but the Harper had a wicked twinkle in his eyes, despite the bland expression on his face.

"You heard Lord Groghe, Menolly. And it's time you did a turn as a harper!" She heard the emphasis on the last word. He rose, holding out his hand to her as if he knew very well how nervous she was. She'd no choice now, for to refuse would be to shame him, slight the Hall, and annoy Lord Groghe.

"I'll accompany you, Menolly, if I may. You do remember the new wording?" Robinton asked as he handed her up to the platform.

She mumbled a hasty affirmative and then wondered if she did. She hadn't actually sung the new words, or the tune, for that matter, since she'd composed it so very long ago in the little hall in Half-Circle Hold. But there was Brudegan, grinning a welcome, and gesturing to two gitar players to hand over their instruments to her and the Masterharper.

Menolly turned and saw all the faces, all the people massed on each side of the square. A hush fell, and into that attentive silence, the Harper struck the first chords of her fire lizard song. Master Shonagar's oft-repeated advice flashed through her mind: "Stand straight, take your

breath into your guts, shoulders back, open your mouth
. . . and sing!"

> *"The little queen all golden*
> *Flew hissing at the sea.*
> *To stop each wave*
> *Her clutch to save*
> *She ventured bravely."*

The applause that greeted the final verse of the song
was so deafening that Beauty rose on wing, squealing with
surprised alarm. Then the crowd laughed and gradually
the noise subsided.

"Sing something from your Sea Hold," said the Master
Harper in her ear as he played a few idle chords. "Something these landsmen might not have heard. You start:
we'll follow."

The crowd was noisy, and Menolly wondered how
she'd be heard, but as soon as she struck the first notes,
the gather quieted. She used the chorus for introduction,
giving the Masterharper the chording, and smiling, even
as she sang, to find herself so well accompanied.

> *"Oh wide sea, oh sweet sea,*
> *Forever be my lover.*
> *Fare me on your gentle wave*
> *Your wide bed over."*

Over the applause when she finished, she heard the
Masterharper saying right in her ear, "They've never
heard that one before. Good choice." He bowed, gestured
for her to take a bow and then motioned to the harpers
waiting just beyond the platform to start the second
dance group.

Smiling and waving to various people, he led Menolly
from the platform and back to the table where Lord
Groghe was still enthusiastically clapping. Sebell grinned
approvingly and rose to pass back to the Masterharper the
very irritated little Zair.

Menolly would have preferred to sit down and recover from the surprise of her first public appearance as a harper and the warmth of the reception, but Talmor came up.

"You've done your duty by crafthall now, Menolly, let's dance!" He spied Beauty on her shoulder. "But could she sit this one out? No telling how she'd misconstrue my man-handling you in a dance!"

The harpers had already struck a fast prance tune.

"Will she stay with me?" asked Sebell, offering his arm and a padded sleeve. "Zair didn't mind too much . . ."

Menolly coaxed Beauty, who chattered with annoyance but allowed herself to be transferred to Sebell's shoulder. Talmor, one arm about Menolly's waist, swung her expertly and quickly into the whirling dancers.

After that, it seemed to Menolly that she'd no more than time to take a quick sip of wine to moisten her parched throat and reassure Beauty, before she was claimed by another partner. Viderian took her for the next set dance, with Talmor partnering Audiva in the same group. Then Brudegan caught her hand for a dance and, to her complete surprise, Domick after him. She acceded to Piemur's boast that he could dance as well as any journeyman and master and wasn't he her best friend, despite a lack of hands in height and Turns in age.

Quartets of singers spelled the dance players until Menolly was certain that every single harper must have performed. Both of the songs that Petiron had sent to the Harper were so frequently requested that Menolly writhed a bit with embarrassment until Sebell caught her eye, cocking an eyebrow and grinning at her discomfort.

As full dark settled over Fort Hold, the crowd began to thin, for those with a distance to travel had to start their journeys home. Stalls were taken down and folded away, the grazing herdbeasts and runners were captured and saddled to bear their owners down the roads from the Hold. The wineman, since he kept a hold in the Fort cliff, continued to serve those unwilling to end a gather.

Pecking Menolly urgently on the cheek, Beauty reminded her that the fire lizards had politely waited for their supper long enough. Abashed at her thoughtlessness,

Menolly rushed back to the Harper Hall. On the kitchen steps, Camo sat disconsolately, his thick arms cradling an enormous bowl of scraps, his eyes on the archway. The instant he caught sight of her and the fire lizards wheeling and diving as escort, he rose, calling to her.

"Pretties hungry? Pretties very hungry! Camo waiting. Camo hungry, too."

From nowhere, Piemur appeared.

"See, Camo, I *told* you she'd be back. I told you she'd want us to feed her fire lizards!"

Piemur stopped her breathless apologies as he handed out gobs of meat to his usual trio.

"Told you gathers were fun, didn't I, Menolly? Told you it was about time you had some, too. And you sang just great! You should always sing 'The Fire Lizard Song'! They loved it! And how come *we* don't know that sea song? It's got a great rhythm."

"That's an old song—"

"I never heard it."

Menolly laughed because Piemur sounded as testy as an old uncle instead of a half-grown boy.

"Hope you know some more new ones like that because I'm so bored with all the stuff I've heard since I was a babe . . . Hey, you had the last piece, Lazy. It's Mimic's turn . . . there! Behave yourself."

The hungry fire lizards made short work of Camo's bowl. Then Ranly leaned out of the dining room window, urging them to come and eat before the food was cleared away. There weren't many in the dining hall: Piemur had been right that they got scanty rations on a gather day, but the cheese, bread and sweetings were all Menolly could eat.

When the Apprentice Master marshalled the younger ones to the dormitory, Menolly quietly ascended the steps to her own room. The lilting strains of still another dance tune drifted on the night air. She'd done her first turn as a harper, and done well. She felt like a harper for the first time, as if she really did belong here in the Hall. Lulled by the music and distant laughter, she fell asleep, the warm bodies of the fire lizards nestling against her.

The next morning, looking from her window to the place where the gather had been held, she saw few traces of litter, only the dew-glistening trampled earth of the dancing square. Holders trudged toward the fields, herdsmen were guiding their beasts to the meadows, and apprentices dashed up and down the holdway on their errands. Down the ramp from Fort Hold paced a troop of leggy runners, fresh after a day's rest, fretting against the slow pace to which their riders held them until they were past the ambling herdbeasts. They disappeared in a cloud of dust down the long road to the east.

Menolly heard the noise from the apprentices' dormitory, and a soft, all but inaudible, creeling closer by. She threw on her clothes and dashed down the steps.

"Knew you wouldn't miss, Menolly," said Silvina, meeting her on the steps from the kitchen. She carried a tray, which she thrust ahead. "Do take this up to the Harper, like a pet, would you? Camo's just about finished wielding that chopper of his for your fair."

Menolly's polite tap at the Masterharper's door brought an instant response. He had a fur clutched around him and an insistently creeling fire lizard clawing at his bare arm.

"How'd you know?" he asked, delighted and relieved to see her. "Thank goodness you did. I really can't appear in the kitchen wrapped in a sleeping fur. There, there! I'm stuffing your face, you bottomless pit. How long does this insatiable appetite continue, Menolly?"

She held the tray for him so he could feed Zair as they crossed the room. She slid the tray onto the middle of the sandtable and, anticipating the Harper's own requirements, offered Zair his next few pieces of meat while Master Robinton gratefully gulped down steaming klah. He grabbed a piece of bread, dipped it into the sweeting, had another sip of klah and then, his mouth full, waved at Menolly to leave.

"You've got your own to feed, too. Don't forget to work on your song. I'll require a finished copy later this morning."

She nodded and left him, wondering if she ought to

check and see if Sebell was managing with Kimi. He was, seated at one of the journeymen's tables, with more than enough willing assistants.

Her fire lizards waited patiently at the kitchen steps with Piemur and Camo. Once her friends had been fed, she was enjoying a second cup of klah when Domick came striding across the court toward her.

"Menolly," and he was frowning with irritation, "I know Robinton wants you to finish that song for him, but will it take *all* morning? I wanted you to go through that quartet music with Sebell, Talmor and myself. Morshal has the girls for theory on firstday so Talmor's free. I'll never get that quartet ready for performance unless we have a few more good rehearsals."

"I'll start the copy right now, only . . ."

"Only what?"

"I don't have any copying tools."

"Is that all? Finish your klah quickly. I'll show you Arnor's den. Just as well I'm taking you," Domick said, guiding her toward the door in the opposite corner of the court. "Robinton wants the song done on those sheets of pulped wood, and Arnor won't hand *them* out to apprentices."

Master Arnor, the Hall's archivist, occupied the large room behind the Main Hall. It was brilliantly lit with glow baskets in each corner, in the center of the room, and smaller ones depending above the tilted worktables where apprentices and journeymen bent to tasks of copying faded record hides and newer songs. Master Arnor was a fusser: he wanted to know why Menolly was to have sheets; apprentices had to learn how to copy properly on old hide before they could be entrusted with the precious sheets; what was all the hurry about? And why hadn't Master Robinton told him himself if it was all this important? And a girl? Yes, yes, he'd heard of Menolly. He'd seen her in the dining hall, same as he saw all the other nuisancy apprentices and holder girls and, oh, well, all right, here was tool and ink, but she wasn't to waste it now, or he'd have to make more and that was a lengthy process and apprentices never paid close attention to the simmering and if the solution boiled, it would be ruined and fade too soon and oh, he didn't know what the world was coming to!

A journeyman had been unobtrusively assembling the various items, and he handed them to Menolly, giving her an amused wink for his master's querulousness. His smile also conveyed to Menolly the tip that the next time she should come directly to him rather than approach his cranky master.

Domick got her away from the old archivist after the barest of courtesies. As they walked back to the Hall entrance, he again directed her not to be all morning at the copying or he'd never get the new quartet sufficiently rehearsed before the Festival. As he opened the door to the Main Hall, she heard the Masterharper's voice and sped up the stairs.

As she worked in her room, her concentration was penetrated now and then by voices raised in discussion in the Hall below. Absently she identified the various masters: Domick, Morshal, Jerint, the Masterharper and, to her surprise, Silvina, and others whose voices she couldn't recognize as readily. As the conversations apparently had to do with posting journeymen to various positions about the country, she paid scant heed.

She was, in fact, just finishing the third and looser interpretation of the song when a brisk tapping at the door startled her so much she almost smeared the sheet. At her answer, Domick strode in.

"Haven't you finished yet?"

She nodded to the sheets, spread out to dry. Scowling with exasperation, he strode across the room and picked up the nearest sheet. Before she could warn him about damp ink, she noticed that he took the sheet carefully by the edges.

"Hmmm. Yes. You copy neatly enough to please even old Arnor. Yes, now . . ." he was scanning the other sheets. "Traditional forms all duly observed. . . . Not a bad tune, at all." He gave her an approving nod. "Bit bare of chord, but the subject doesn't need musical embellishment. Come, come, finish that sheet, too." He pointed to the one before her. "Oh, you have! Fair enough." He blew gently across the sheet to dry the last line of still glistening ink. "Yes, that'll do. I'll just be off with these. Take your gitar across to my quarters, Menolly, and study the music on the rack. You're to play second gitar. Pay special attention to the dynamic qualities of the second variation."

With that he left her. Her right hand ached from the cramped position of copying, and she massaged it, then shook her fingers vigorously from the wrist to relieve the strain.

"Now," she heard the Masterharper's voice from the room below, "the point is that all but one of the formalities has been observed. Admittedly, there's not been much time spent in the Hall, but an apprenticeship served elsewhere under a competent journeyman has always been admissible. Does anyone wish to register any reservations about the competence of that journeyman?" There was a short pause. "So that's settled. Ah, yes, thank you, Domick. Now, Master Arnor . . ." and Menolly lost the sound of his voice as he evidently moved away from the window.

She was uncomfortably aware that she was not only an inadvertent eavesdropper on Craft matters not her business, but disobedient to Master Domick's orders. Not that she didn't wish to follow them. She picked up her gitar. Playing with Talmor, Sebell and Domick was a pure delight. Had Master Domick meant to intimate that she'd be part of that quartet in a performance? Well, if yesterday was any sample of being a harper, yes, she probably would be performing in that quartet, new as she was to the Harper Hall. That was part of being a harper, after all.

When Menolly entered Domick's quarters, Talmor and Sebell, Kimi disposed on his shoulder and not looking too pleased to be shifted from the crook of his arm, were already discussing the music. They greeted her cheerfully and asked if she'd enjoyed her first go in a gather at Fort Hold. They both laughed at her enthusiastic replies.

"Everyone's the better for a good gather," said Talmor.

"Except Morshal," said Sebell, and, glancing sideways at Talmor as if they shared some secret, rubbed the side of his nose.

"Let us play, Journeyman Sebell," Menolly thought that Talmor sounded reproving.

"By all means, Journeyman Talmor," said Sebell, not the least bit perturbed. "If you will join us, Apprentice Menolly." The brown man gestured elaborately for Menolly to take the stool beside him.

As Menolly checked the tuning of her gitar, Talmor turned the sheets of music on the rack. "Where does he want us to start?"

"Master Domick told *me* to study the dynamics of the second variation," said Menolly with helpful deference.

"That's right, that's where," said Talmor, snapping his fingers before he flipped the correct sheets to the front. "At the beat then . . . sweet shells, he's changing the time in every third measure . . . what does he expect of us?"

"Are the dynamics difficult?" asked Menolly, feeling apprehensive.

"Not difficult, just Domick all over," said Talmor with the sigh of the long-suffering. But he tapped the appropriate beat on the wood of his gitar and gave a more emphatic fifth beat for them to start.

They'd had a chance to go through the second variation once before Domick entered the room. Nodding courteously to them, he took his place.

"Let's start at the beginning of the second variation, now that you've had a chance to play through it."

They worked steadily, going straight through the music once. The second time they paused frequently to perfect the more difficult passages and balance the parts. The dinner bell punctuated the brisk notes of the finale. Talmor and Sebell put down their instruments with small sighs of relief, but Menolly refingered the final three chords softly before she laid her instrument down.

"Does your hand hurt?" asked Domick with unexpected solicitude.

"No, I was just wondering if the string was true."

"If you heard a sour sound, it was my stomach," said Talmor.

"Too much gathering?" asked Sebell with little sympathy.

"No, not enough breakfast, thank you!" replied Talmor with the brusqueness of someone being teased. He rose and left the room, followed closely by the silently laughing Sebell.

"Master Shonagar has you this afternoon, Menolly?" asked Domick, motioning for Menolly to come with him.

"Yes, sir."

"Well, then you'd have to continue that voice instruction anyway," he said in a cryptic fashion. Menolly decided he must be wishing to have her practice with him more steadily, but Master Robinton had been specific: her mornings were scheduled to Master Domick; afternoons she was to go to Master Shonagar.

When they entered the dining hall, the room was already well filled. Domick turned to the right toward the masters' table. Menolly caught one glimpse of Master Morshal, already seated, his face set in the sourest lines she had yet seen on the bad-tempered old man, so she looked quickly away.

"Pona's gone!" Piemur pounced on her from the left, his face wreathed with smug satisfaction. "So I can sit with you, near the girls, now. Audiva said I could 'cause it was Pona who got snotty. Audiva says will you please sit with her."

"Pona's gone?" Menolly, both surprised and nervous, permitted Piemur to pull her toward the hearthside table. There were two empty places, one on either side of Audiva, who smiled hesitantly as she saw Menolly approaching. She beckoned to the seat on her right, away from the other girls.

"See, Pona is gone! She got taken away a-dragonback," Piemur added, his pleasure in her departure somewhat allayed by the prestigious manner of her going.

"Because of yesterday?" The thin knot of worry in her middle grew larger and colder. Pona in the cot, contained by the discipline of the Harper Hall, was bad enough; but, in her grandfather's Hold, pouring out acid vengeance, she was much more dangerous for Harper apprentice, Menolly.

"Naw, not just yesterday," Piemur said firmly. "So don't you go feeling guilty about it. But yesterday was the final crack, the way I heard it, bearing false witness against you. And Dunca's been raked over by Silvina! That pleased her no end; she's just been itching to take Dunca down."

Timiny was straddling three seats across from Audiva, and gesturing urgently to Menolly and Piemur to take them.

"You sit with Timiny, Piemur. I'm going to sit next to Audiva. Looks like she's being put on by Briala with that empty seat and all."

As she stepped to the place, she caught Briala's startled, antagonistic glance. The dark girl nudged her neighbor, Amania, who also turned to glare at Menolly. But Menolly smiled at Audiva and, as she stood by the tall craftgirl, she felt Audiva's hand fumble for hers and the grateful pressure of her fingers. Stealing a sideways glance, she noticed that Audiva's eyes looked red and her cheeks showed the puffiness of recent and prolonged weeping.

The signal to be seated was given, and the meal began. If Menolly felt too self-conscious and Audiva too upset to talk, Piemur suffered no inhibitions and babbled on about how he'd made his marks count.

"I got nine more bubbly pies, Menolly," he told her gaily, " 'cause the baker thought they were for you, me and Camo. I did share with Timiny, didn't I, Tim? And then I won a wager on the runners. Anyone with half an eye could tell the one with the sore hoof would run faster . . . so he wouldn't have to run so long."

"So, how many marks did you come back with?"

"Ha!" Piemur's eyes flashed with his triumph. "More'n I went to the gather with, and I'm not saying how much that is."

"You're not keeping it in the dorm, are you?" asked Timiny, worried.

"Hawl I gave it to Silvina to keep safe for me. I'm no fool. *And* I told the entire dorm where my marks are, so they know it's no good putting on me to find out where I've hid 'em. I may be small, but my glow's not dim!"

Briala, who was pretending to ignore them all, made a disagreeable sound. Piemur was about to take umbrage when Menolly kicked his shin to warn him to be silent.

"You know what, Menolly," and now Piemur leaned across the table, exuding mystery as he glanced from her to Audiva and Timiny, "they're posting journeymen."

"Are they?" asked Menolly, mystified.

"You ought to know. Couldn't you hear anything in your room? I saw the windows of the Main Hall open, and you're right over 'em."

"I was busy," Menolly said sternly to Piemur. "And I was brought up not to listen to other people's private conversations."

Piemur rolled his eyes in exasperation for such niceties. "You'll never survive in a Harper Hall then, Menolly! You've *got* to be one jump ahead of the masters . . . and the Lord Holders . . . A harper's supposed to learn as much as he can . . ."

"Learn, yes; overhear, no," replied Menolly.

"And you're an apprentice," added Audiva.

"An apprentice *learns* to be a harper by overhearing his master, doesn't he?" demanded Piemur. "Besides, I gotta think ahead. I gotta be good at something besides singing. My voice won't last forever. Do you realize that only one out of hundreds," and he waved his arms in such an expansive gesture that Timiny had to duck, "of boy sopranos have any voice when they hit the change? So, if I'm not lucky, but if I'm good at digging things out, maybe I'll get posted like Sebell and have a fire lizard to take important messages from hold to hall . . ." Then Piemur froze, and cautiously turned to look at Menolly, his eyes wide with consternation.

She laughed; she couldn't help it. Timiny, who had

obviously heard Piemur's long-range plan before, gulped so fiercely that his neck cartilage bobbed up and down his throat like a net floating in a fast current.

"I really do like the fire lizards, Menolly, I really do," said Piemur, trying to undo the indiscretion and reinstate himself in Menolly's good graces.

She couldn't resist a pretense of disdain, and ignored him, but his expression was so genuinely panic-stricken that she relented sooner than she intended.

"Piemur, you've been my best and first friend in the Hall. And I really do think my fire lizards like you. Mimic, Rocky and Lazy let you feed them. I may not be able to help, but if I *do* ever have any say in the matter, you'll get an egg from one of Beauty's clutches."

Piemur's exaggerated sigh of relief attracted attention from the other girls, who were still pretending that that end of the table didn't exist. Platters of stewed meats and vegetables were now being served, and Menolly took advantage of the general noise to ask Audiva how things were with her.

"All right, once the furor died down. I rank the rest of them, even if rank is *not* supposed to be a consideration while we're at the Harper Hall."

"You're also the best musician of the lot," said Menolly, trying to cheer Audiva. She sounded very depressed, and she must have been crying a lot to have such puffy cheeks.

"Do you really think I can play?" asked Audiva, surprised and pleased.

"From what I heard that morning, yes. The others are hopeless. If there's no reason you *have* to stay at Dunca's when you have free time, maybe you'd like to come to my room. We could practice together if that would help."

"Me? Practice with you? Oh, Menolly, could I please? I really do want to learn, but all the others want to do is talk about the fosterlings at the Hold, and their clothes, and who their fathers are likely to choose as husbands for them, and *I* want to learn how to play well."

Menolly extended her hand, palm up, and Audiva gratefully seized it, her eyes sparkling, all traces of her unhappiness erased.

"Just wait till I tell you what happened in the cot," she said in a confidential tone that reached only Menolly's ears. She saw Piemur cocking his head to try and hear, and waved him away. "It was a treat! A rare treat! What Silvina said to Dunca!" Audiva giggled.

"But won't there be trouble about Pona being sent back? She is the granddaughter of the Lord Holder of Boll."

Audiva's face clouded briefly. "The Harper has the right to say who stays in his own Hall," replied Audiva quickly. "He has equal rank with a Lord Holder, who can dismiss any fosterling he chooses. Besides, you're a holder's daughter."

"Holder's, not Lord Holder's. Only I'm an apprentice now." Menolly touched her shoulder badge, which meant more to her than being her father's daughter.

"You're the Masterharper's apprentice," said Piemur who indeed had sharp ears if he'd heard their whispers. "And that makes you special." He glanced toward Briala, who had also been trying to overhear what Menolly and Audiva were saying. "And you'd better remember that, Briala," he said, making a fierce grimace at the dark girl.

"You may think you're special, Menolly," said Briala in a haughty voice, "but you're only an apprentice, after all's said and sifted. And Pona's her grandfather's favorite. When she tells him all that's been going on here, you may not be *that* anymore!" And she snapped her fingers in a derisive gesture.

"Close your mouth, Briala! You talk nothing but nonsense," said Audiva, but Menolly caught the note of uncertainty in her voice.

"Nonsense? Just wait'll you hear what Benis plans for that Viderian of yours!"

They were all distracted by a sudden groan from Piemur.

"Shells, Pona *has* gone! That means that I'm stuck with singing her part! What a ruddy bore!" His dismay was comic, but it turned the talk to a discussion of the upcoming Spring Festival.

Piemur told Menolly that if she thought a gather was

fun, she should just wait for the Festival. Everyone in the Hold cliff doubled up so that the entire western half of Pern could be under shelter there for the two days of the Festival. Dragonmen came from all over, and harpers and craftmasters and holders, large and small. That's when any new craftmasters were made, and new apprentices tapped, and it was great fun, even if he would have to sing Pona's role, and there'd be dancing all night long instead of just until sundown.

The gong sounded, and the chores were assigned: most of the sections were to clean up the gather area and rake the fields where the beasts had been tethered. Piemur made a huge grimace since his section drew the field duty. Briala smiled maliciously at his chagrin, and he would have answered in kind, but Menolly toed his shins sharply again. He rolled his eyes at her but, when she cocked her head meaningfully and tapped her shoulder, he subsided, realizing that he would have to stay in her good record to get his fire lizard.

She reported, as ordered, to Master Oldive who checked her feet and pronounced them sound enough. He suggested that she see Silvina about boots. Her hand showed improvement, but she was to be careful not to overstretch the scar tissue. Slowly but surely was the trick, and she wasn't to neglect the healing salve.

As she crossed the courtyard for her lesson with Master Shonagar, the fire lizards appeared in the air. Beauty landed on her shoulder, broadcasting images of a lovely swim in the lake and how warm the sun had been on the flat rock. Merga had evidently been with them, for Beauty projected a second golden queen on the rocks. They were all in good spirits.

Master Shonagar had not moved. One thick fist upheld the heavy head on the supporting arm, his other arm was cocked, hand on thigh. At first Menolly thought he was asleep.

"So, you return to me? After *singing* at the gather?"

"Wasn't I supposed to sing?" Menolly halted so abruptly in her astonishment at the reprimand in his voice that Beauty cheeped in alarm.

"You are never to sing without my express permission." The massive fist connected with the tabletop.

"But the Masterharper himself . . ."

"Is Master Robinton your voice instructor? Or am I?" The bellowed question rocked her back on her heels.

"You are, sir. I only thought . . ."

"You thought? I do the thinking while you are my student . . . and you will remain my student for some time, young woman, until your voice is properly trained for your duties as a harper! Do I make myself clear?"

"Yes, sir. I'm very sorry, sir. I didn't know I was disobeying . . ."

"Well," and his tone abruptly modified to one of such benevolence that Menolly again stared in disbelief, "I hadn't actually mentioned that I didn't consider you ready to sing in public yet. So I accept your apology."

Menolly gulped, grateful for the reprieve.

"You didn't, all things considered, perform too badly yesterday," he went on.

"You heard me?"

"Of course I heard you!" The fist landed again on the table, though with less force than the previous thump. "I hear every singing voice in this Hall. Your phrasing was atrocious. I think we'd better go over that song now so that you can correct your interpretation." He heaved a sigh of profound resignation. "You will undoubtedly be obliged to sing it again in public; that's obvious, since you wrote it, and it is undeniably popular. So you might just as well learn to sing it *well!* Now, we shall start with breathing exercises. And we can't," another crash on the sandtable, "do that when you're halfway across the hall and trembling all over. I won't eat you, girl," he added in the gentlest of the voices he had yet used in her presence. A slight smile parted his lips. "But I will," and his tone took on a sterner note, "teach you to make the most of your voice."

Although the lesson began with a totally unexpected scolding, Menolly left Master Shonagar's presence with a feeling of considerable accomplishment. They had gone over "The Fire Lizard Song," phrase by phrase, occasionally accompanied by Beauty's trilling. By the end of the session, Menolly stood in further awe of Master Shonagar's musical acumen. He had drawn from her melody every possible nuance and shading of tone, heightening its total impact.

"Tomorrow," Master Shonagar said as he dismissed her, "bring me a copy of that latest thing you wrote. The one about Brekke. At least you have wit enough to write music *you* can sing, that lies in the best part of your voice. Tell me, do you do that on purpose? No, no, that was an invidious question. Unworthy of me. Inapplicable to you. Away with you now, I'm excessively wearied!"

His fist came up to support his head, and he was snoring before Menolly could express her gratitude for his stimulating lesson.

Beauty flew to her perch on Menolly's shoulder, chittering happily, and Menolly, beginning to feel as weary as Master Shonagar claimed to be, absently checked to see where her other friends were. As usual, they were sunning on the rooftops, where they'd undoubtedly remain until feeding time.

Menolly entered the Hall, wondering if she should ask Silvina about boots, but she could hear a lot of bustle and noise from the kitchen and decided to bide her time. She made her way to her room, saw the door ajar, and was surprised to find Audiva waiting for her.

"I took you at your word, Menolly, but, honestly, if I had to stay one more moment in that poisonous atmosphere . . ."

"I meant it."

"You look tired. Master Shonagar's lessons are exhausting. We have only one in the week, and you have to go every day? Was he in one of his banging moods?" Audiva giggled, and her eyes sparkled with merriment.

Menolly laughed, too. "I sang yesterday at the gather *without* his express permission."

"Oh! Great stars." Audiva was torn between giggles and concern. "But why would he complain? You sang so beautifully. Viderian said it was the best he'd heard that sea song done. You've made another good friend in Viderian, if that's any consolation. That fist in Benis's face. He's wished so often that he could bang that arrogant booby."

"Audiva, could Lord Sangel of Boll make Master Robinton . . . "

"You didn't pay heed to that spiteful wherry, Briala? Oh, Menolly . . ."

"But can an apprentice . . ."

"An apprentice, an *ordinary* apprentice, yes," Audiva said, with a reluctant sigh for the truth, "because apprentices have no rank. Journeymen do. But you are Master Robinton's *own* special apprentice, just as Piemur said, and it'd take more than a Lord Holder to shift Master Robinton when he's made up his mind. Besides, you weren't at fault. Pona was. Bearing false witness. Now, you listen to me, Menolly, don't you dare let that bunch of sly slippers worry you! They're just jealous. That was Pona's problem, too. Besides," and Audiva's face brightened as she thought of the telling argument, "Lord Groghe needs you here to help him train Merga. There's your new song. Oh, Menolly, Talmor was playing it, and it's the most beautiful thing I've ever heard. 'Live for my living/or else I must die.' " Audiva had a throaty contralto voice that throbbed poignantly on the deep note. "I wanted to weep, and while I know I'm just a silly girl—"

"You're not just silly. You stood up for me against Pona . . ."

Audiva bit her lip guiltily, her expression contrite. "I *didn't* tell you about Master Domick's first message . . ." She paused, full of self-reproach. "I knew about it. I heard him tell Dunca. We all did. And I knew they were trying to make trouble for you because you had the fire lizards . . ."

"But you told Master Domick that I hadn't been told."

"Fair's fair."

"Well, then, if fair's fair, you did stand up with me against Pona *and* all those fosterlings when it really mattered. Let's forget everything else . . . and just be friends.

I've never had a girl friend before," Menolly added shyly.

"You haven't?" Audiva was shocked. "Weren't you fostered out?"

"No, being the youngest and Half-Circle being so isolated and with Thread falling, and that's what the Harper usually does, and Petiron never . . ."

"Just as well old Petiron kept you by him, the way things turned out, isn't it?" Audiva grinned. "But *we're* friends now, aren't we?"

And they sealed the bargain with a handshake.

"Are they really practicing my song?" asked Menolly, a little apprehensive.

"Yes, and hating every minute of it because you wrote it." Audiva was delighted. "I'd be obliged if you'd teach me some simpler chords than the ones you've written. I cannot get my hands . . ."

"They are simple."

"For you, maybe, but not for me!" Audiva groaned over her inadequacy.

"Here," and Menolly thrust her gitar at Audiva. "You can start with a simple E chord . . . go on, strum it. . . . Now, modulate to an A Minor . . ."

Menolly soon realized that she didn't have as much patience as she ought to with Audiva, especially since Audiva was her best friend now, and she certainly did try to follow Menolly's instructions; but both girls were relieved when Beauty's creeling interrupted the practice. Audiva declared that she'd have to fly to change before supper. She wouldn't have the time after, or she'd be late to rehearsal. She gave Menolly a quick and grateful embrace, and dashed down the steps ahead of her.

Camo and Piemur were waiting for Menolly at the kitchen level. It seemed incredible to Menolly as she fed her hungry friends that she'd only been at Harper Hall a sevenday. So much had happened. And yet the fire lizards had settled in as if they'd never lived anywhere else. She had established a routine in her sessions with Domick and the journeymen in the mornings, with Shonagar in the afternoon. Above all, she had the right, the exquisitely sweet right—no, an *injunction* from the

Masterharper—to write the songs that had once been totally forbidden her.

Seven days ago, standing in this very courtyard, she'd been scared to tears. What had T'gellan said? Yes, he'd given her the sevenday to get adjusted. And he'd been right in that, though she'd doubted him at the time. He'd also said that she didn't have anything to fear from harpers. True enough, but she had experienced envy and to some extent overcome it: she'd made staunch friends and good impressions on those in Hall and Hold who mattered to her future. She'd made not one, but several places for herself in the Craft Hall: with her songs, her fire lizards and, unexpectedly, her knowledge of seacraft.

Only one small worry nagged at her: what if the vengeful Pona could prejudice her grandfather, Lord Sangel, against a lowly apprentice in the Craft Hall? Not all Lord Holders were tolerant men like Lord Groghe. Not all of them had fire lizards. Menolly had had too much stripped from her before in her home Hold to calm that anxiety.

Chapter 11

O Tongue, give sound to joy and sing
Of hope and promise on dragonwing!

Domick caught her before she left the dining hall the next morning.

"That sea song you sang at the gather? Would it take you long to note it down? I never heard it before." Menolly wasn't sure from his frown if he blamed her for that oversight or not. "Master Robinton wants sea songs inland and land songs on the seaside . . ." Domick looked annoyed, until he saw Menolly's expression. "Oh, I agree with him in principle, but she wants things done *now*. With the journeymen to be posted today, he wants as many copies to go with them as possible. Save trips later . . ."

"I could make several copies as easily as one," she said.

Domick blinked as if he'd forgotten. "Of course, you could. And a mighty neat hand you've got. Even old Arnor had to admit that!" For some obscure reason this amused Domick. He continued in a much better humor. "All right then, to save a lot of useless talk and wasted time, would you please copy that sea song? And do a couple of "The Fire Lizard Song." I'm not certain how many Arnor has completed, and you got a taste of his attitude yesterday . . ." Menolly grinned. "You remember who to go to if you need more materials? Dermently's his name."

With that he left Menolly, but he whistled absently as he strode toward the now closed door of the main hall.

Sea songs inland and land songs on the seaside, thought Menolly as she climbed the steps to her room. She wondered just how Yanus, her father, would approve of land songs at Half-Circle Sea Hold. Well and good, and wouldn't it be the best of all jokes if the land songs introduced at Half-Circle by Harper Elgion were ones she herself had written or copied out? Disgrace the Hold, indeed!

Now she wondered if she should write her mother, Mavi, or her sister, and just casually mention that she was apprentice to the Masterharper of Pern. That all her twiddles and tunings had considerably more merit than anyone at Half-Circle had the wit to appreciate. Except, of course, Harper Elgion. And Alemi, her brother.

No, she wouldn't write her mother or her father, and certainly not her sister. But she might write Alemi. He'd been the only one who cared. And he'd keep the knowledge to himself.

But right now she had things to do. She organized her materials, her ink and tools, and carefully set about copying down the sea song. She worked quickly, though she had to sand out several small errors. Nevertheless, she had six fair copies by the time the dinner bell rang.

Domick was in the hallway, in earnest conversation with Jerint who appeared annoyed about something. Domick caught sight of her, excusing himself from Jerint but with just that hint of reprieve that suggested Menolly's appearance was a welcome excuse.

"Six . . ." he leafed through her sheets, "and every one a fair copy. My thanks, Menolly. Can you do. . . . No, you must work with Shonagar this afternoon . . ."

"I'd need more paper, Master Domick, but I'll have time to do two or three more copies before supper, if you need them . . ."

Domick glanced at the slowly filling dining room. He took her hand. "If you could squeeze in maybe three copies of your fire lizard song, I'd be in your debt. Come with me. Arnor should have retreated from his domain,

and we can get as much paper as we want from De×
mently. At least, today."

They were out the door with no more delay, headin,
toward the Archive room.

"I don't mean to make a habit of this with you, Me
nolly, because it's more important that you create that
that you copy. Any apprentice can copy. But, with s
many journeymen going off. . . . That's why Jerint i
looking peeved. And wait till Arnor hears . . ."

"Journeymen going off?"

"You didn't think they stayed here forever and
moldered . . ."

Actually Menolly had experienced a swift pang o
regret because Talmor and Sebell were journeymen, and
Sebell said he "journeyed."

"Don't worry about our quartet," replied Domick with
sudden perception. "It's one thing to send away someone
who's really needed here and quite another for a master
to refuse to let a qualified journeyman go out of the Hall
because *he'll* be put to the bother of training a new
assistant. The whole point of the Harper Hall is to extend knowledge." Domick's arms swept wide to include
all Pern. "Not to confine it," and his right fist made a
tight ball. "That's what's been wrong with Pern, why we
haven't really matured; everything's been kept in shallow
little minds that forget important things, that resist new
knowledge, and experience . . ." He grinned at her,
"That is why, I, Domick, Composition Master, *know*
that your songs are as important to the Craft Hall, and
Pern, as my music. They are a fresh voice, fresh new ways
of looking at things and people, with tunes no one can
keep from humming."

"Would you ever leave the Hall?" asked Menolly,
greatly daring. She was storing up his words to think
about later.

"Me?" Domick was startled, and then frowned. "I
might, but it would serve little purpose. Might be good
for me, at that." Then he shook his head again, rejecting
the idea. "Perhaps, when there's a big occasion at one of
the larger Holds or another Craft Hall . . . Or a Hatch-

ing . . . But there really isn't a Hold or Craft that needs a man of my abilities." Domick spoke without conceit and also with modesty. It was a fact.

"Do masters always stay in the Hall?"

"Shells, no. There are any number assigned to the larger Holds and Crafthalls. You'll see. Ah, Dermently, just a moment . . ." and Domick signaled the journeyman who was about to leave by another door at the far end of the Archive's well-lit hall.

Menolly just had time to get to her room with an arm-load of supplies and off to the dining hall before everyone sat down. It was true that Master Jerint and Master Arnor wore expressions of sullen discontent. She wondered who was leaving. But she had no time to speculate. There was dinner, and then her lesson.

No sooner was she released by Master Shonagar than she returned to her copying, this time of "The Fire Lizard Song." At first she felt awkward copying her own music, then she began to relish the notion. Her songs, going inland so that people would get some understanding of seaside creatures that had once been thought to be pure invention. That lovely old sea song, one she'd heard at Half-Circle since her first conscious appreciation of music, was a fine one to teach inland people how the seaman regards the broad ocean.

Domick's attitude toward her music had been reassuring, too. It was a relief to her to know that there was no awkwardness between them. He thought her songs were serving a purpose, and that suited and pleased her.

It was, Menolly thought, one thing to work hard day in and day out to bring in food enough to feed oneself, one's family and one's Hold; it was quite another thing, and vastly more satisfying, to provide comfort for other lonely minds and tuneless hearts. Yes, Master Robinton and T'gellan had been right: she did belong in the Harper Hall.

Before she realized how time had flown, it was evening. She carefully put away her instruments, the ink and the unused sheets, delivered the music to Master Domick's room, and went to the kitchen level to feed her friends.

Beauty and the bronzes were crowded round her when, though scarcely sated, they suddenly looked skyward. Beauty crooned softly in her throat. Rocky and Diver answered, as if agreeing with her, then all three again demanded food.

"What was all that about?" asked Piemur.

Menolly shrugged.

"Will you look at that?" Piemur cried, excitedly, pointing skyward as three, then four, dragons appeared in the sky, slowly circling down to the wide fields. "And your fire lizards knew! D'you realize that, Menolly? Your fire lizards knew there were dragons coming."

"Why would dragons be coming?" Menolly asked, and that lump of fear grew a few sizes larger. "It isn't time for Threadfall again, is it?" She doubted that Lord Sangel would send dragonriders to discipline a mere apprentice.

"I told you," and Piemur sounded exasperated with her obtuseness. "The masters were closeted yesterday and today, reassigning journeymen. So," and he shrugged as if that explained the presence of dragonriders, "the dragons transport them to the new holds. Two blues, a green, and . . . hey . . . a bronze!" He was impressed. "I wonder who rates the bronze!"

Now the Fort Hold watch dragon bugled a welcome and was answered by the circling beasts. Beauty and the other fire lizards added their trill of greeting.

"Oh, no," Piemur groaned. "They're landing in the field, and we just got it cleaned up!"

"Dragons are not runner beasts," said Menolly in a tart voice. "And don't stuff Lazy, Rocky and Mimic so fast. They'll choke. You'll see the dragonriders soon enough, I expect, if they're coming here for the journeymen."

Piemur was not the only apprentice with sharp eyes. Soon the courtyard was spotted with groups of curious lads. The dragonriders strode out of the shadows of the arch, and Menolly distinguished the colors of Istan, Igen, Telgar and Benden Weyrs on the dragonriders' tunics. And none of them a watch-dragonrider wearing the colors of Boll. Then she recognized the Benden dragonrider as T'gellan.

"Menolly! I've got 'em for you," he shouted across the courtyard, waving an oddly shaped mass above his head. He spoke to his companions, who continued onward to the steps of the Hall where Domick, Talmor and Sebell waited to greet the dragonmen. T'gellan then strode at an oblique angle toward Menolly. As he neared her, she realized that he carried a pair of boots by their laces: boots tanned blue with cuffs of blue-hued wild wherry down.

"Here you are, Menolly! Felena was in a state, worrying that those light slippers would wear out before you got these. I see the toes are going, aren't they? Keeping you on 'em here, are they? But you're looking good. Say, your fire lizards are growing, aren't they?" He beamed approvingly at Menolly, then at Camo and Piemur, whose eyes were enormous at this proximity to a real bronze dragonrider. "Glad you've got some help."

"This is Piemur and that's Camo, and they've both been marvelous help."

"Will this lad be ready for a fire lizard then?" asked T'gellan with a sly wink at Menolly.

"Why do you think he's helping me?" asked Menolly, unable to resist teasing Piemur.

"Aw, Menolly." Unexpectedly Piemur was blushing, eyes downcast and so thoroughly out of countenance that Menolly relented.

"Truly, T'gellan, Piemur's been a staunch and true friend since the first day I got here. I couldn't manage without him and Camo."

"Camo feed pretties. Camo very good feeding pretties!"

T'gellan gave her a startled look, but he slapped the drudge affectionately on the back. "Good man, Camo. You keep on helping Menolly with her pretties."

"More food for pretties?" Camo perked up.

"No, no more now, Camo. Pretties aren't hungry now," Menolly said hurriedly.

"Have you finished with Camo yet, Menolly?" Abuna appeared at the kitchen door. "Oh!" She was startled to see the company her half-witted drudge was keeping.

"Camo help Abuna now. Pretties fed, Camo. You help

235

Abuna!" Menolly gave Camo the customary turn and push toward the kitchen.

"Now, Menolly, you sit there, on the steps," said T'gellan, pointing, "and try these boots on. Felena gave me explicit instructions that I was to see if they fit. Because if they don't . . ." T'gellan left the threat hanging.

"They ought to: the Weyr tanner took my measure . . ." said Menolly as she discarded the worn slippers and put on the right boot. "I don't see how he could miss, even if my feet were still a bit swollen. Oh, it fits! It fits just fine. And so soft inside. Why," and she put her hand in the left boot, "he's lined it with soft hide. . . ."

"You'll need the double protection, Menolly," said T'gellan, and then his face took on a look of pure mischief, "particularly if you do any more running . . ."

"I'm not running anywhere anymore," she said firmly. And hastily forgot about Lord Sangel and Pona. "Please thank Felena, and give my love to Mirrim, and thank Manora and everyone . . ."

"Hey, hey, I just got here. I'm not going anywhere yet. I'll see you before I go, but I'd better join the others now."

"And a dragonrider . . . a bronze dragonrider brings you blue harper boots . . ." Piemur's eyes were enormous with astonishment as they both watched T'gellan's lanky figure striding toward the Hall entrance.

"I don't suppose they wanted to waste leather they'd already cut to fit me when they thought I'd be staying on in the Weyr," Menolly said, nonetheless deeply touched by the gift. She wiggled her toes against the smooth soft hide. She wouldn't need to bother Silvina for new footwear now. And harper blue! Why, she was harper-garbed from head to toe now.

The supper bell rang, and the curious knots of boys and journeymen blended into a throng, converging at various speeds on the steps. Along the walls opposite the dining hall as she and Piemur entered, Menolly saw backsacks and instrument cases.

"I told you," Piemur nudged her in the ribs. "Journeymen are being assigned tonight. There'll be gaps at the oval tables tomorrow."

Menolly nodded, thinking that there would be some frantic masters, too, with fewer journeymen to help.

T'gellan was at the round table, but Menolly noticed that the other dragonriders were standing on the journeymen's side of the dining hall. She made her way to her seat beside Audiva, still that space left between Audiva and Briala. Piemur stood opposite Audiva and Menolly.

Special meat and fish rolls accompanied the customary soup and there were sharp cheeses, bread and, afterward, wedges of beachberry pies. Piemur grumbled because the pies should be hot, and Menolly countered that he ought to be grateful for the treat so soon after a gather!

Talk was spirited throughout the hall, although the seven girls continued their silent treatment of Audiva and Menolly. There was a current of excitement in the air, much of it from the journeymen's tables.

"They're only told in advance that they're being assigned, you know," Piemur told Menolly and Audiva. "Not where. Eight of them going, if I counted the packs right. The Masterharper really means to spread the word."

"Word?" Timiny was baffled.

"Don't you listen to anything, Timiny?" Piemur was disgusted. "Bet you not one of those journeymen is going back to his own hold or crafthall, like they used to do. Master Harper's set on shuffling everyone around. Crosscrafting with a vengeance. They all got copies of your songs, Menolly?"

Suddenly the moment everyone had been anticipating happened. The gong shimmered, and before the metallic tones had died away, the hall was still. Every eye was on the Masterharper who had risen from the table.

"Now, my friends, without further ado and to permit those holding their breaths to breathe, I will announce the postings." He paused, grinning, as he glanced around the hall. Then he looked across the apprentices' tables to the journeymen.

"Journeyman Farnol, Gar is your assignment, in Ista.

Journeyman Sefran, please do what you can to improve understanding and extend enlightenment in Telgar at Balen Hold. Journeyman Campiol, you are also Telgar-bound, to the Minercrafthall under Facenden. See what you can do to improve the quality of metal for our pipes and brasses. Journeyman Dermently, I'd like you to assist Wansor, the Starsmith at Telgar Smithcrafthall." There was a murmur of surprise from Dermently's companions. "You have the finest hand with drafting, and while I am sorry to rob Master Arnor of his most accurate copyist, your efforts are essential if Wansor's studies are to progress and be properly recorded.

"There's a small seahold on Igen River mouth that requires a man of your tolerance and good nature, Journeyman Strud. I also want you to keep an eye on the beaches for possible fire lizard mounds. You are, however, to report them to your Holder, not to me." The regret in the Masterharper's voice caused a ripple of amusement to run through his audience. "Journeyman Deece is also Igen bound, to the Hold. Harper Bantur needs a young assistant. He's a dab hand at bringing on a good harper to understand the complexity of a Masterharper's job. And you've the new songs to give him as well. Journeyman Petillo, it's no sinecure, but I need your patience and tact at Bitra to bolster Harper Fransman.

"Journeyman Rammany, Lord Asgenar at Lemos has asked for someone from Master Jerint's hands. You'll work principally with Woodsmith Benelek, and I don't think you'll find that too onerous a task with such wood as Benelek dries for us. However, be sure you're on hand to choose the next consignment of wood for our use, and Master Jerint will bless you.

"Will all the journeymen please come to the Great Hall for a farewell cup of wine? Benden wine, of course. But first, I've one more very pleasant and unusual announcement.

"To be a harper requires many talents, as you all ought to realize by now," and he frowned at the very youngest of the apprentices who giggled nervously. "Not all of these skills need to be learned within these walls. Indeed, many of our most valuable lessons are more forcefully learned at some distance from this hallowed Hall," and he frowned at the journeymen, who grinned back at him. "However, when the fundamentals of our craft have been well and truly learned, I insist that we hold no one back from the rank they are entitled to by knowledge and ability, and in this case, rare talent. Sebell, Talmor, since neither of you will resign in the other's favor . . ."

A silence emphasized by Piemur's tiny gasp of astonishment fell over the dining hall as Sebell and Talmor rose from their table and walked up the aisle by the hearth. They stopped. Startled, Menolly looked up at Sebell's shy grin and Talmor's broad smile.

She couldn't grasp the significance of their presence, though she heard Audiva's cry of joy and saw the stunned amazement on the faces of Briala and Timiny. She glanced wildly about her, saw Master Robinton grinning, nodding, gesturing for her to rise. But it wasn't until Piemur kicked her on the shins that she shed her paralysis.

"You're supposed to walk the tables, Menolly," Piemur said in an audible hiss. "Get up and walk. You're a journeyman now. You've made journeyman."

"Menolly's a journeyman! Menolly's a journeyman!" echoed the other apprentices, clapping their hands in rhythm to their chant. "Menolly's made journeyman. Walk Menolly, walk. Walk, Menolly, walk!"

Sebell and Talmor took her by the elbows and lifted her to her feet.

"Never saw an apprentice so loath to take a walk," muttered Talmor under his breath to Sebell.

"We could carry her," Sebell said, in a whisper, "because, between you and me, I don't think her legs are going to walk her."

"I can walk," said Menolly, shaking off their helping hands. "I've even got harper boots. I can walk anywhere!"

The last vestige of anxiety lifted from Menolly's mind. As a journeyman in blue, she had rank and status enough to fear no one and nothing. No further need to run or hide. She'd a place to fill and a craft that was unique to her. She'd come a long, long way in a sevenday. The pulse of her words suggested a tune. She'd think of that later. Now, holding her head high, while the fire lizards swept in from the windows, trilling their happy reaction, she walked between Talmor and Sebell to the oval tables of her new station in the Harper Craft Hall of Pern.

ABOUT THE AUTHOR

ANNE MCCAFFREY has this to say about herself.

"Born on April first, I did nothing else of particular significance until I wrote my first novel during Latin class. I think things would have worked out better if I'd written it in Latin, but I didn't. Then, I wrote *Flame, Chief of Herd and Track*, an impossible western. I gave up writing in favor of the theater and, among other things, was involved in the first musical tent circuses in summer stock, directed operas and operettas and studied voice for nine years. I also got married and had three children, two boys and a girl. All of us write, and so do my older brother and three of my nieces.

"Now I live and work in Ireland with my two younger children who are still in school. I can sew for anyone except myself, embroider, knit an Arran sweater in ten days, cook well (I've edited a cookbook), play some bridge and particularly enjoy taking care of my heavy-weight, dapple-gray gelding, Mr. Ed. He answers as readily to 'Horseface' because he knows he's beautiful, and he bullies all of us, including the cat, Mr. Magoofey.

"My hair is silver, my eyes are green and I freckle: the rest is subject to change without notice."

Anne McCaffrey is the author of *Dragonsong, Dragonflight* and *Dragonquest* and is a winner of the Hugo and Nebula Awards.

*Turn the page for an exciting
Special Preview of another book.*

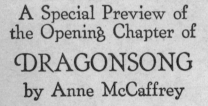

A Special Preview of
the Opening Chapter of

DRAGONSONG

by Anne McCaffrey

Chapter 1

Drummer, beat, and piper, blow
Harper, strike, and soldier, go
Free the flame and sear the grasses
Till the dawning Red Star passes.

Almost as if the elements, too, mourned the death of the gentle old Harper, a southeaster blew for three days, locking even the burial barge in the safety of the Dock Cavern.

The storm gave Sea Holder Yanus too much time to brood over his dilemma. It gave him time to speak to every man who could keep rhythm and pitch, and they all give him the same answer. They couldn't properly honor the old Harper with his deathsong, but Menolly could.

To which answer Yanus would grunt and stamp off. It rankled in his mind that he couldn't give voice to his dissatisfaction with that answer, and his frustration. Menolly was only a girl: too tall and lanky to be a proper girl at that. It galled him to have to admit that, unfortunately, she was the only person in the entire Half-Circle Sea Hold who could play any instrument as well as the old Harper. Her voice was true, her fingers clever on string, stick or pipe, and she knew the Deathsong. For all Yanus could be certain, the aggravating child had been practicing that song ever since old Petiron started burning with his fatal fever.

"She will have to do the honor, Yanus," his wife, Mavi, told him the evening the storm began to slacken. "The important thing is that Petiron is properly sung to rest. One does not have to record who did the singing."

"The old man knew he was dying. Why didn't he instruct one of the men?"

"Because," replied Mavi with a touch of sharpness in her voice, "you would never spare him a man when there was fishing."

"There was young Tranilty . . ."

"Whom you sent fostering to Ista Sea Hold."

"Couldn't that young lad of Forolt's . . ."

"His voice is changing. Come, Yanus, it'll have to be Menolly."

Yanus grumbled bitterly against the inevitable as he climbed into the sleeping furs.

"That's what everyone else has told you, haven't they? So why make so much of a necessity?"

Yanus settled himself, resigned.

"The fishing will be good tomorrow," his wife said, yawning. She preferred him fishing to stomping around the Hold, sullen and critical with enforced inactivity. She knew he was the finest Sea Holder Half-Circle had ever had: the Hold was prospering, with plenty for bartering set by in the storage caves; they hadn't lost a ship or a man in several Turns either, which said much for his weather-wisdom. But Yanus, at home on a heaving deck in foul weather, was very much adrift when taxed with the unexpected on land.

Mavi was keenly aware that Yanus was displeased with his youngest child. Mavi found the girl exasperating, too. Menolly worked hard and was very clever with her fingers: too clever by half when it came to playing any instrument in the Harper Craft. Perhaps, Mavi thought, she had not been wise to permit the girl to linger in the old Harper's constant company once she had learned all the proper Teaching Songs. But it had been one less worry to let Menolly nurse the old Harper, and Petiron had wished it. No one begrudged a Harper's requests. Ah, well, thought Mavi, dismissing the past, there'd be a new Harper soon, and Menolly could be put to tasks proper to a young girl.

The next morning, the storm had cleared off: the skies were cloudless, the sea, calm. The burial barge had been outfitted in the Dock Cavern, Petiron's body wrapped in harper-blue on the tilter board. The entire Fleet and most of the Seahold followed in the wake of the oar-driven barge, out into the faster moving current above Nerat Deep.

Menolly, on the barge prow, sang the elegy: her clear strong voice carrying back to the Half-Circle Fleet; the men chanting the descant as they rowed the barge.

On the final chord, Petiron went to his rest. Menolly bowed her head, and let drum and stick slide from her fingers into the sea. How could she ever use them again when they had beaten Petiron's last song? She'd held back her tears since the Harper had died because she knew she had to be able to sing his elegy and you couldn't sing with a throat closed from crying. Now the tears ran down her cheeks, mingled with sea spray: her sobs punctuated by the soft chant of the steersman, setting about.

Petiron had been her friend, her ally and mentor. She had sung from the heart as he'd taught her: from the heart and the gut. Had he heard her song where he had gone?

She raised her eyes to the palisades of the coast: to the white-sanded harbor between the two arms of Half-Circle Hold. The sky had wept itself out in the past three days: a fitting tribute. And the air was cold. She shivered in her thick wherhide jacket. She would have some protection from the wind if she stepped down into the cockpit with the oarsmen. But she couldn't move. Honor was always accompanied by responsibility, and it was fitting for her to remain where she was until the burial barge touched the stones of Dock Cavern.

Half-Circle Hold would be lonelier than ever for her now. Petiron had tried so hard to live long enough for his replacement to arrive. He'd told Menolly he wouldn't last the winter. He'd dispatched a message to Masterharper Robinton to send a new Harper as soon as possible. He'd also told Menolly that he'd sent two of her songs to the Masterharper.

"Women can't be harpers," she'd said to Petiron, astonished and awed.

"One in ten hundred have perfect pitch," Petiron had said in one of his evasive replies. "One in ten thousand can build an acceptable melody with meaningful words. Were you only a lad, there'd be no problem at all."

"Well, we're stuck with me being a girl."

"You'd make a fine big strong lad, you would," Petiron had replied exasperatingly.

"And what's wrong with being a fine big strong

girl?" Menolly had been half-teasing, half-annoyed.

"Nothing, surely. Nothing." And Petiron had patted her hands, smiling up at her.

She'd been helping him eat his dinner, his hands so crippled even the lightest wooden spoon left terrible ridges in the swollen fingers.

"And Masterharper Robinton's a fair man. No one on Pern can say he isn't. And he'll listen to me. He knows his duty, and I am, after all, a senior member of the Crafthall, being taught up in the Craft before him himself. And I'll require him to listen to you."

"Have you really sent him those songs you made me wax down on slates?"

"I have. Sure I have done that much for you, dear child."

He'd been so emphatic that Menolly had to believe that he'd done what he'd said. Poor old Petiron. In the last months, he'd not remembered the time of Turn much less what he'd done the day before.

He was timeless now, Menolly told herself, her wet cheeks stinging with cold, and she'd never forget him.

The shadow of the two arms of Half-Circle's cliffs fell across her face. The barge was entering the home harbor. She lifted her head. High above, she saw the diminutive outline of a dragon in the sky. How lovely! And how had Benden Weyr known? No, the dragonrider was only doing a routine sweep. With Thread falling at unexpected times, dragons were often flying above Half-Circle, isolated as it was by the bogs at the top of Nerat Bay. No matter, the dragon was awing above Half-Circle Hold at this appropriate moment and that was, to Menolly, the final tribute to Petiron the Harper.

The men lifted the heavy oars out of the water, and the barge glided slowly to its mooring at the far end of the Dock. Fort and Tillek might boast of being the oldest Sea-Holds, but only Half-Circle had a cavern big enough to dock the entire fishing fleet and keep it safe from Threadfall and weather.

Dock Cavern had moorings for thirty boats; storage space for all the nets, traps and lines; airing racks for sail; and a shallow ledge where hulls could be scraped free of seagrowths and repaired. At the very end of the immense Cavern was a shelf of rock where the Hold's builders worked when there was sufficient timber for a new hull. Beyond was the small inner cave where priceless wood was stored, dried on high racks or warped into frames.

The burial barge lightly touched its pier.

"Menolly?" The first oarsman held out a hand to her.

Startled by the unexpected courtesy to a girl her age, she was about to jump down when she saw in his eyes the respect due her at this moment. And his hand, closing on hers, gave silent approval for her singing of the Harper's elegy. The other men stood, too, waiting for her to disembark first. She straightened her shoulders, although her throat felt tight enough for more tears, and she stepped proudly down to the solid stone.

As she turned to walk back to the landside of the Cavern, she saw that the other boats were discharging their passengers quickly and quietly. Her father's boat, the biggest of the Half-Circle fleet, had already tacked back into the harbor. Yanus's voice carried across the water, above the incidental sounds of creaking boats and muted voices.

"Quickly now, men. We've a good breeze rising and the fish'll be biting after three days of storm."

The oarsmen, hurried past her, to board their assigned fishing boats. It seemed unfair to Menolly that Petiron, after a long life's dedication to Half-Circle Hold, was dismissed so quickly from everyone's mind. And yet . . . life did go on. There were fish to be caught against winter's hungry months. Fair days during the cold months of the Turn were not to be squandered.

She quickened her pace. She'd far to go around the rim of the Dock Cavern and she was cold. Menolly also wanted to get into the Hold before her mother noticed that she didn't have the drum. Waste wasn't tolerated by Mavi any more than idleness by Yanus.

While this was an occasion, it had been a sad one and the women and children and also the men too old to sea-fish observed a decorous pace out of the Cavern, making smaller groups as they headed towards their own Holds in the southern arc of Half-Circle's sheltering palisade.

Menolly saw Mavi organizing the children into work groups. With no Harper to lead them in the Teaching Songs and ballads, the children would be kept occupied in clearing the storm debris from the white-sanded beaches.

There might be sun in the sky, and the dragon-rider still circling on his brown, but the wind was frigid and Menolly began to shiver violently. She wanted to feel the warmth of the fire on the great Hold's kitchen hearth and a cup of hot klah inside her.

She heard her sister Sella's voice carrying to her on the breeze.

"She's got nothing to do now, Mavi, why do I have to...."

Menolly ducked behind a group of adults, avoiding her mother's searching glance. Trust Sella to remember that Menolly no longer had the excuse of nursing the ailing Harper. Ahead of her, one of the old aunts tripped, her querulous voice raised in a cry for help. Menolly sprinted to her side, supporting her and receiving loud protestations of gratitude.

"Only for Petiron would I have dragged these old bones out on the cold sea this morning. Bless the man, rest the man," the old woman went on, clinging with unexpected strength to Menolly. "You're a good child, Menolly, so you are. It is Menolly, isn't it?" The old one peered up at her. "Now you just give me a hand up to Old Uncle and I'll tell him the whole of it, since he hasn't legs to leave his bed."

So Sella had to supervise the children and Menolly got to the fire: at least long enough to stop shivering. Then old auntie would have it that the Uncle would be grateful for some klah, too, so when Mavi entered her kitchen, her eyes searching for her youngest daughter, she found Menolly dutifully occupied serving the oldster.

"Very well then, Menolly, while you're up there, see that you set the old man comfortably. Then you can start on the glows."

Menolly had her warming cup with the Old Uncle and left him comfortable, mournfully exchanging tales of other burials with the aunt. Checking the glows had been her task ever since she had grown taller than Sella. It had meant climbing up and down the different levels to the inner and outer layers of the huge Sea Hold, but Menolly had established the quickest way to finish the job so that she'd have some free time to herself before Mavi started looking for her. She had been accustomed to spending those earned minutes practicing with the Harper. So Menolly was not surprised to find herself, eventually, outside Petiron's door.

She was surprised, however, to hear voices in his room. She was about to charge angrily through the half-open door and demand an accounting when she heard her mother's voice clearly.

"The room won't need much fixing for the new Harper, so it won't."

Menolly stepped back into the shadow of the corridor. The new Harper?

"What I want to know, Mavi, is who is to keep the children up in their learning until he comes?" That voice was Soreel's, the wife of the First Holder and therefore spokeswoman for the other Hold women to Mavi as Sea Holder's lady. "She did well enough this morning. You have to give her that, Mavi."

"Yanus will send the message ship."

"Not today, nor tomorrow he won't. I don't fault Sea Holder, Mavi, but it stands to reason that the boats must fish and the sloop's crew can't be spared. That means four, five days before the messenger gets to Igen Hold. From Igen Hold, if a dragonrider obliges by carrying the message—but we all know what the Old-timers at Igen Weyr are like so let's say, Harper drums to the Masterharper Hall at Fort is another two–three days. A man has to be selected by Masterharper Robinton and sent overland and by ship. And with

Thread falling any time it pleases, no one travels fast or far in a day. It'll be spring before we see another Harper. Are the children to be left without teaching for months?"

Soreel had punctuated her comments with brushing sounds, and there were other clatters in the room, the swishing of bed rushes being gathered up. Now Menolly could hear the murmur of two other voices supporting Soreel's arguments.

"Petiron has taught well . . ."

"He taught *her* well, too," Soreel interrupted Mavi.

"Harpering is a man's occupation . . ."

"Fair enough if Sea Holder'll spare a man for it." Soreel's voice was almost belligerant because everyone knew the answer to that. "Truth be told, I think the girl knew the Sagas better than the old man this past Turn. You know his mind was ranging back in time, Mavi."

"Yanus will do what's proper," The finality in Mavi's tone firmly ended that discussion.

Menolly heard footsteps crossing the old Harper's room, and she ducked down the hall, around the nearest bend and down into the kitchen level.

It distressed Menolly to think of anyone, even another Harper, in Petiron's room. Obviously it distressed others that there was no Harper. Usually such a problem didn't arise. Every Hold could boast one or two musically able men and every Hold took pride in encouraging these talents. Harpers liked to have other instrumentalists to share the chore of entertaining their Holds during the long winter evenings. And it was also the better part of wisdom to have a substitute available for just such an emergency as Half-Circle was experiencing. But fishing was hard on the hands:

the heavy work, the cold water, the salt and fish oils thickened joints and calloused fingers in the wrong places. Fishermen were often away many days on longer hauls. After a Turn or two at net, trap and sail line, young men lost their skill at playing anything but simple tunes. Harper Teaching Ballads required deft quick fingers and constant practice.

By putting to sea to fish so quickly after the old Harper's burial, Yanus thought to have time enough to find an alternative solution. There was no doubt that the girl could sing well, play well, and she'd not disgraced Hold or Harper that morning. It was going to take time to send for and receive a new Harper, and the youngsters must not lose all progress in the learning of the basic Teaching Ballads.

But Yanus had many strong reservations about putting such a heavy responsibility on the shoulders of a girl not fifteen Turns old. Not the least of these was Menolly's distressing tendency toward tune-making. Well enough and amusing now and again in the long winter evenings to hear her sing them, but old Petiron had been alive to keep her to rights. Yanus wasn't sure that he could trust her not to include her trivial little whistles in the lessons. How were the young to know that hers weren't proper songs for their learning? The trouble was, her melodies were the sort that stayed in the mind so a man found himself humming or whistling them without meaning to.

By the time the boats had profitably trawled the Deep and tacked for home, Yanus had found no compromise. It was no consolation to know that he wouldn't have any argument from the other holders. Had Menolly sung poorly that morning . . . but she hadn't. As Sea Holder for Half-Circle, he was obliged to bring up the young of the Hold in the traditions of Pern: knowing their duty and how to do it. He counted himself very lucky to be beholden to Benden Weyr, to have F'lar, bronze Mnementh's rider, as Weyrleader and Lessa as Ramoth's Weyrwoman. So Yanus felt deeply obliged to keep tradition at Half-Circle: and the young would learn what they needed to know, even if a girl had the teaching.

That evening, after the day's catch had been salted down, he instructed Mavi to bring her daughter to the small room off the Great Hall where he conducted Hold business and where the Records were stored. Mavi had put the Harper's instruments on the mantel for safekeeping.

Appropriately Yanus handed Menolly Petiron's gitar. She took the instrument in a properly reverential manner, which reassured Yanus that she appreciated the responsibility.

"Tomorrow you'll be excused from your regular morning duties to take the youngsters for their teaching," he told her. "But I'll have no more of those finger-twiddlings of yours."

"I sang my songs when Petiron was alive and you never minded them . . ."

Yanus frowned down at his tall daughter.

"Petiron *was* alive. He's dead now, and you'll obey me in this . . ."

Over her father's shoulders, Menolly saw her mother's frowning face, saw her warning head-shake and held back a quick reply.

"You bear in mind what I've said!" And Yanus fingered the wide belt he wore. "No tuning!"

"Yes, Yanus."

"Start tomorrow then. Unless, of course, there's

Threadfall, and then everyone will bait longlines."

Yanus dismissed the two women and began to compose a message to the Masterharper to go when he could next spare the sloop's crew. They'd sail it to Igen Hold. About time Half-Circle had some news of the rest of Pern anyway. And he could ship some of the smoked fish. The journey needn't be a wasted trip.

Once in the hallway, Mavi gripped her daughter's arm hard. "Don't disobey him, girl."

"There's no harm in my tunes, mother. You know what Petiron said . . ."

"I'll remind you that the old man's dead. And that changes everything that went on during his life. Behave yourself while you stand in a man's place. No tuning! To bed now, and mind you turn the glowbaskets. No sense wasting light no eye needs."

Follow the enchanting adventures of Menolly in DRAGONSONG. A Bantam Book, now available wherever paperbacks are sold.

OUT OF THIS WORLD!

That's the only way to describe Bantam's great series of science-fiction classics. These space-age thrillers are filled with terror, fancy and adventure and written by America's most renowned writers of science fiction. Welcome to outer space and have a good trip!

]	11392	**STAR TREK: THE NEW VOYAGES 2** by Culbreath & Marshak	$1.95
]	11945	**THE MARTIAN CHRONICLES** by Ray Bradbury	$1.95
]	02719	**STAR TREK: THE NEW VOYAGES** by Culbreath & Marshak	$1.75
]	11502	**ALAS, BABYLON** by Pat Frank	$1.95
]	12180	**A CANTICLE FOR LEIBOWITZ** by Walter Miller, Jr.	$1.95
]	08276	**HELLSTROM'S HIVE** by Frank Herbert	$1.50
]	10930	**DEMON SEED** by Dean R. Koontz	$1.75
]	12044	**DRAGONSONG** by Anne McCaffrey	$1.95
]	11599	**THE FARTHEST SHORE** by Ursula LeGuin	$1.95
]	11600	**THE TOMBS OF ATUAN** by Ursula LeGuin	$1.95
]	11609	**A WIZARD OF EARTHSEA** by Ursula LeGuin	$1.95
]	12005	**20,000 LEAGUES UNDER THE SEA** by Jules Verne	$1.50
]	11417	**STAR TREK XI** by James Blish	$1.50
]	11527	**FANTASTIC VOYAGE** by Isaac Asimov	$1.75
]	02517	**LOGAN'S RUN** by Nolan & Johnson	$1.75

Buy them at your local bookstore or use this handy coupon for ordering:

RAY BRADBURY

America's most daring explorer of the imagination

☐	11932	S IS FOR SPACE	$1.75
☐	10750	SOMETHING WICKED THIS WAY COMES	$1.75
☐	11997	THE HALLOWEEN TREE	$1.75
☐	11957	THE ILLUSTRATED MAN	$1.95
☐	11930	DANDELION WINE	$1.75
☐	11931	R IS FOR ROCKET	$1.75
☐	10249	TIMELESS STORIES FOR TODAY AND TOMORROW	$1.50
☐	11942	I SING THE BODY ELECTRIC	$1.95
☐	2834	MACHINERIES OF JOY	$1.50
☐	11582	THE WONDERFUL ICE CREAM SUIT & OTHER PLAYS	$1.50
☐	11945	THE MARTIAN CHRONICLES	$1.95
☐	2247	GOLDEN APPLES OF THE SUN	$1.25
☐	10882	LONG AFTER MIDNIGHT	$1.95
☐	10390	A MEDICINE FOR MELANCHOLY	$1.75

Buy them at your local bookstore or use this handy coupon for ordering